CITY OF LIARS
AND THIEVES

A Novel

~ Eve Karlin ~

For Ally, Jason, and Ben

Law is whatever is boldly asserted and plausibly maintained.
—Aaron Burr (1756–1836)

PROLOGUE

The news reached Cornwall today: Aaron Burr killed Alexander Hamilton in an early-morning duel. *The New-York Gazette* and the *Evening Post* are brimming with speculation and gossip. It is said that a mob of eleven hundred has threatened to set fire to Burr's Richmond Hill estate—that or hang him.

Either way, I know he will burn in hell.

As for Hamilton, the papers reported that the bullet pierced his right hip, tore through his abdomen, and shattered his spine. In and out of consciousness, he writhed in agony for nearly twenty hours before succumbing to a most unnatural death.

Is this justice?

Sixty miles north of the Weehawken dueling ground, I stand on the banks of the Hudson and listen to the waves against the rocky shore. A hawk circles high overhead. Closing my eyes, I can almost smell the spent gunpowder. I inhale deeply and imagine the fatal encounter.

It is dawn. Hamilton and Burr stand ten paces apart below the towering cliffs of the Palisades. Hamilton assumes the dueling stance: right foot in front of left, chin positioned over right shoulder, stomach drawn in. Burr, his broad shoulders set in a military manner, steps to the mark and takes aim.

Shots ring out as lead balls pierce the morning air. Crows scatter from a cedar tree; a branch splinters and falls, narrowly missing Burr. Hamilton is lifted onto his toes, lurches to the left, then collapses His britches are torn and singed; the taut skin above his right hip is burned; his flesh is flayed.

With the same eloquence that defined his career, Hamilton declares, "This is a mortal wound."

Sunlight glimmers on brass as Burr lowers his pistol. His dark eyes match the weapon's walnut finish. His full lips compress into a thin, indecipherable line. Is it regret or satisfaction?

It is the same beguiling expression I witnessed four years earlier when he stood ten paces before me in a court of law. The room was overflowing with spectators. I can still feel their prying eyes. I can see Levi Weeks, his handsome features quivering with remorse. And I can hear Burr's voice as if he were in front of me now.

"Have the witnesses spoken with candor or have they spoken from temper, hatred, and revenge?"

It is a cruel question. One I would prefer to ignore.

All I see is Burr's penetrating gaze as he turns toward me. The crowd grows still. I hear my own shallow breath. "Madame," he says, cajoling yet firm. "Pray tell us . . ."

Explain your beloved cousin's senseless death.

I do not believe in ghosts, but spirits exist. Elma's spirit haunts me.

She appears before me, youthful and frail. Her eyes are dark and moist like the depths of a well. There is a triangle of color in her cheeks, as if she has been running into the wind. It is a vivacious hue, one I rarely saw while she lived. Elma is dressed in the same green muslin gown she wore when we last parted. The fabric is too flimsy for such bitter weather, but it is her wedding night and she wants to look her best.

She is not the girl I thought I knew. She is secretive, her passion no longer masked by decorum. Her lips are plump, bruised red with kisses. The bodice of her dress is torn, and the soft contours of her bosom are exposed. Hat and shawl are missing. Wet hair hangs in tangles around her face. A single ivory comb remains.

I cannot say what thoughts or regrets flooded Elma's mind during her final struggle. I am unable to fathom the extent of her pain or the length of her suffering. The only thing I know with certainty is that there was a sound. When I close my eyes, I hear a dull splash. It is the lonely sound of injustice, and it reverberates to this day.

My Elma has been dead nearly five years. It is high time to tell the truth. Time for justice. Aaron Burr and Alexander Hamilton have sealed their own fate. I have no more need for revenge; I can answer Burr's interrogation free of hatred. Here, with utmost candor, I will share the story of an innocent girl caught in the crossfire of our nation's most powerful men. This is how she was murdered and why she haunts me. It is not only Elma's story; it's mine.

Catherine Ring
July 12, 1804

~1~

Five Years Earlier
New York City
June 1799

The sun was sinking beyond the western horizon, the distant hills fading into dusk as Elma stepped onto dry land. The journey south from Cornwall was sixty miles, and the wind off the Hudson was calm. We had been waiting at the boat slip for hours. Elias paced, Charles whined, the baby fussed, and my heartbeat rose and fell like the swells of foamy brine in the harbor. Spring had warmed to summer and, while I was grateful for the sunny day, the stagnant air visibly hovering over the foul dock carried its own set of worries. Each year as the weather grew hot and sticky, yellow fever ravaged the city, turning its victims into monsters, vomiting black bile, bleeding from their pores. There were those who believed the scourge came from dirty water.

"Rivers will run with blood and the nation will be black with crimes!" a man on the dock cried with religious fervor. As many times as I moved the family away, he followed, waving his arms and shouting as if his dire predictions were directed solely at us. Gulls cawed overhead, and he raised his righteous voice to meet theirs. "Are you prepared to see your dwellings in flames, female chastity violated, and murder openly taught?"

"Elias," I said, when I could stand no more, "it sounds like he's ranting about the plagues on Egypt."

Elias lifted his head to assess the bizarre tirade. Stout with broad shoulders, he was not conventionally handsome, but he had a square jaw and strong profile. His eyes flashed gold in the waning light.

When we first met, I had been captivated by the intensity of his gaze, which seemed to glow with inner fortitude. After seven years of marriage, I found it slightly cynical and all too knowing. It would not be long before I understood that the qualities that drew me to Elias could serve the wicked as well as the wise.

"It is politics," he said. "The devil's religion."

Frigates, sloops, and cutters dotted New York's bustling harbor. Some were squat with sloped bows. Others had tall masts, piercing the hazy summer sky like daggers. Several brandished cannons; one or two carried harpoons. Most flew colorful flags from places I could only begin to imagine. They had quaint names like *Flying Mist* and noble ones like *Enterprise*. A British schooner called *Arbuthnot* was said to have fourteen guns and a crew of sixty. Neither ship nor ranting zealot was able to distract Charles from the excitement of Elma's arrival. She had always been able to soothe him in ways I never managed, with whimsical tales of little red calves and snowy colts. As he grew, her stories became their carefully woven collaborations. He had been moping since the day we left Cornwall, his boyish exuberance ever so slightly muted.

"Where is she?" Charles asked, balancing on tiptoe to look down the pier. Passengers, sailors, and merchants jammed the waterfront. Families welcomed one another in myriad languages; others wept as they departed.

I reached for his hand, resisting the urge to hug him close and bury my nose in his downy hair. At six, Charles, every bit his father's son, was starting to assert his independence.

"There's Elma!" he cried, and I saw her standing slightly apart from the crowd on the edge of the dock.

Never were two cousins more different. Elma's petite frame and open expression made her look like a girl of sixteen, though she was now a twenty-two-year-old woman. Only five years her senior, marriage and motherhood had matured me. I arranged my fair hair under a simple lace cap, drawn at the neck, and wore proper Quaker clothing in traditional gray. Elma favored dresses that complimented her lively eyes in periwinkle, lilac, teal. Her dark mane reached the middle of her back and, although she tied it in a thick braid, strands invariably fell loose to curl around her ready smile. When we were children, I had loved Elma the way one might love a china teapot: She was as delicate as the finest porcelain, her character as intricate as the most meticulous design. As we grew, though, I realized that beneath the luster she was as durable as the sturdiest kettle. She possessed the wholesome beauty of a girl, but time had taught me that she was also brave.

"Finally," Elias said, frowning as if I controlled wind and tide.

"We're here to welcome Elma," I said. "She's come to help." Elias flinched, reminding me, as he often did, that Elma was not part of his carefully orchestrated plan.

Less than twenty years had passed since the British occupation. Wartime fires had destroyed as many as a thousand buildings. Entire streets were gutted, and lodging was hard to come by. Where others saw shortage, Elias sensed opportunity. He spent months traveling to and from New York, scouring the city for the ideal location for a dry-goods store, calculating and saving, before moving our family from our modest home on the western banks of the Hudson to a three-story gabled building on the southwest corner of Greenwich Street.

He swelled with pride as he showed me our new home. The store occupied the largest of the ground-floor rooms, and he had done an admirable job, hanging cooking utensils and hardware along the walls and enticingly displaying fabric, ribbon, and spools of thread in specially made chests. Across a narrow entrance was a sunny parlor that also served as a kitchen. It had an ample hearth flanked by a set of rocking chairs, a long pine dining table, and a pretty hutch. Our bedroom was a cozy space behind the hearth with room for one small bed, an even smaller cot for Charles, and a cradle for the baby we were expecting.

The rooms were comfortable and more than sufficient for our young family. But something troubled me. I walked back to the cramped entrance and looked up at a steep stairwell. The steps climbed to a landing with a set of doors, then turned and ascended higher still.

It was only when I questioned the building's size did Elias tell me we would be taking in boarders. Why pay rent, he reasoned, when we could collect it. While it was difficult to dispute his logic, I was even more bothered I had never slept under the same roof as a stranger. But when Elias had a plan, arguing was futile.

A deep sunset lingered as Elma stood at the dock, looking as pale as a ghost. Men pushed past, carrying steamer trunks on their shoulders and wheeling carts laden with luggage. She clutched the handle of a worn leather valise. The sight of her delicately tapered fingers clinging to her one, small possession triggered buried memories. I thought to her arrival in Cornwall so many years ago and wondered if inviting her here had been more selfish than kind.

The first heavy snow of the season was falling the night Elma appeared at my family home, in the winter of my fourteenth year. Perfectly formed crystal flakes spiraled out of the night sky and settled into a glittering mound. It was Christmas Eve. Friends did not, as a general rule, observe Christmas. We were taught to reach out to others each day, not turn to sacred books or religion only on designated holidays. But Father, whose lighthearted spirit complemented Mother's rigid demeanor, liked to celebrate with a large meal or special treat. Mother excused the lapse, saying that the Lord may always be thanked. Despite their differences, or maybe because of them, my parents clearly and openly adored each other. I never heard them argue. Except once.

There was a knock at the door. It was such an unobtrusive noise, I wondered if I had imagined it, but Mother, whose ears were as sharp as her tongue, set aside her sewing and stood. She cracked open the door and, for the first time ever, I witnessed her utterly speechless.

A waif of a girl hovered on our threshold, and a slight, middle-aged woman stood awkwardly behind her. Though I had not seen her in years, there was enough family resemblance to recognize my father's sister. Both were dark and small with narrow frames. But while my father's mouth was framed by laugh lines, my aunt's was marred by grooves like gullies running from a stream after a heavy rain.

As I stared from the parlor, my aunt set a shaky hand on the girl's slender shoulder. "This is my daughter, Gulielma," she said, forgoing all other greetings.

Mother remained silent while Father led our visitors inside. "Such a big name for such a little girl," he said.

The girl broke free from my aunt. "People call me Elma," she said. "Elma Sands."

If Elma's first name was curious, her last name was baffling. Our family name—my father's name—was Sands. I studied her carefully, unable to understand why she had inherited her mother's surname.

"And I'm not little, I'm nine," she announced, then bit her lip, reconsidering. "Well, almost." Her complexion had the translucence of an icicle, one that was already melting, and her hair was so black as to be tinged with blue. An only child, I had often wished for a playmate. Elma was small and pale, and I doubted her ability to climb a tree or swim in the river's strong currents, but her eyes were full of mirth. She would do.

Mother stepped away as if Elma had a plague.

Elma examined the fabric of her skirt, as if she might discover the reason for Mother's apparent animosity in its folds. I was also at a loss to imagine what offense she had committed.

"It's not contagious," Father said, more abrupt than I had ever heard him.

"Art thou ill?" I asked.

"Not in the least," Elma said. She was missing two front teeth, and her words, spoken with a slight lisp, were not particularly convincing.

"Where did thou come from?"

"From our Lord, like all living creatures."

At the time I thought her answer amusingly innocent. Looking back, I realize that she was avoiding the question. It was a skill she had developed early and honed.

The precocious child raised her chin, inspecting me as closely as I scrutinized her. "Why do you speak that way?" Elma's frank tone was a stark contrast to her dainty femininity.

"We're Friends."

Dark curls swayed as she shook her head. "Mama is your father's sister. That makes us cousins."

"No," I clarified. "We are Quakers and we employ plain speech."

"It doesn't sound plain to me."

Mother smiled thinly as I repeated what she had always taught me. "We say 'thee' and 'thou' to avoid class distinction."

"But how—"

"And we name the days of weeks and months numerically, rather than use the names of heathen gods," I continued, raising my voice slightly. I refused to be interrogated by a skinny interloper, and this part of Quaker practice was easier to explain.

Elma lifted her chin again, as if she might ask another question. But I had one of my own. "Where is thy father?" I asked. It seemed to be the unspoken query on everyone's tongue.

"My father is a Methodist minister in England," Elma said with a melodious sameness, as if she had imparted the information often but did not fully comprehend it.

"To bed now," Mother said, sweeping her arm to scoot me along. It was early and I stood still, confused and dismayed. Father looked as if he might object, but he closed his mouth and nodded, and I reluctantly went upstairs.

Almost instantly, their voices began to rise.

"I won't allow it," Mother said.

"David." My aunt addressed my father. "I don't want to cause trouble."

"Thou are family," Father said. "And even if thou were strangers, it would be common charity."

I did not have to see Mother's expression to know his words had made an impact.

The house grew silent, but I could not sleep. The sudden

appearance of an eight-year-old cousin was the biggest mystery that had been posed in my young life. Where had she come from? Why had we never discussed her?

Within days, I had heard enough whispered conversations to understand that Elma's father was neither traveling nor dead. Death, in fact, would have been preferable. The disgraceful truth was that my aunt had given birth out of wedlock. "Illegitimate," people murmured, passing Elma on the street. "Bastard." Even if they did not speak, their posture conveyed their disdain. Elma would take my hand, never breaking stride. Her fingers were smaller than mine, but her grasp was strong and dry, as if she were comforting me. I feel it even now.

Eventually, new scandals arose, as they always do in a small town, and the neighbors tired of Elma's biography. Still, Mother maintained her distance. Despite her delicate health, Elma always tried to be helpful, hanging wash or sweeping. But Mother behaved as if she was in the way, muttering "useless" under her breath as she took the laundry or broom and handed it to me instead. Undaunted, Elma would shrug at me and smile, and when Mother turned her back, she would help. I admired Elma's efforts, but I could see they were in vain. Mother's affection was not easily won.

Elma's vulnerability made me love her all the more, her beauty heightened by the sadness she buried beneath a brave smile. She became my sister. Growing up, I saw myself as her champion, and now that she had joined me in the city, she was my ward.

"Elma!" Charles called, racing away. It was all I could do to keep him in sight.

I hugged the baby to my chest, pushing and apologizing through a maze of carts and people. Splashing through a dirty puddle and stumbling over chicken crates, I strained to keep my eyes on Charles's bobbing head. He vanished behind a steamer trunk, and the baby began to wail. Breathless, I was debating whether to follow or try to cut him off when Elias came up, panting, behind me.

"Where'd he go?" he asked.

The baby's cries grew louder and I bounced her on my hip, soothing us both.

"He's—" I took a few steps, then stopped dead.

A ship bearing a boldly striped flag had docked and was unloading its dreadful cargo. Emaciated prisoners, most all but naked, staggered down a gangway into the noisy crowd. Flies swarmed their faces, but shackles prevented them from shooing them away. Each man, woman, and listless child looked more desperate than the next. Some of their eyes were dark and dead, while others were alive with terror.

I did not like the idea of being so close to such suffering. "Elma!" I called, but she did not see me or could not hear.

Charles stood yards shy of the gangway, paralyzed by fascination and fear.

"Come away," Elias hollered, and Charles startled as if he were at fault, his eyes filling with tears.

This was not the welcome I had in mind. In my year in the city, I had seen slaves as well as freemen, but I had never before witnessed such ravaged souls, in limbo between a floating coffin and an unknown, perhaps even worse, fate. As a rancid stench flooded the dock, I had the distinct sense that misery was contagious. I wanted to rush to Elma's side and tell her that New York was nothing like this, but I was still a newcomer myself, constantly on guard against unknown dangers.

From the schooner Elma had disembarked, sailors were shouting orders and tossing thick ropes. As the anchor chain rattled and water slapped the hull, I fought an urge to scoop the children in my arms, snatch Elma by the sleeve, and demand passage back to Cornwall.

"Caty," Elias said, "get her and let's go home."

For the briefest instant, I thought he had read my mind. But I quickly realized my mistake. Home for Elias meant the Greenwich Street boardinghouse.

"Who's that?" Charles asked, scowling at a tall boy with sandy hair and blemished cheeks, who stood an inch or so too close to Elma.

The boy was pointing into the crowd, while Elma pinched the bridge of her nose. A distraction to fight back tears—I had seen her do it hundreds of times when Mother scolded her or neighbors wagged their tongues.

"Elma!" Charles shouted, having finally pushed through the crowd.

Elma looked up and smiled broadly as she took Charles's hands, swinging him in a wide circle the way she used to do in Cornwall.

"Thou will rip his arms from the sockets," Elias said when we caught up to the pair.

Elias held propriety in as high regard as Mother did and had never warmed to Elma—whether because of her disgraceful origins or her playful nature, so at odds with his own sense of rectitude, I was never quite sure. I once again questioned the wisdom of inviting her to join us in New York City. If my behavior was irresponsible, though, I refused to care. A fresh environment was exactly the opportunity she needed to escape the confines of Cornwall and the scandal of her birth.

"More, more," Charles begged.

Elma set Charles down. "We mustn't disobey Father," she said, sounding as if she would happily ignore Elias's scolding. She draped her arms around my neck, nuzzling with reassuring weight and warmth. "Caty," she sighed. "Has it really been a year?"

I rested my head on her shoulder and inhaled a familiar whiff of lavender. "How was the journey?" My fingertip traced a teardrop. "Elma, what's wrong?"

She waved away my questions. "Who's this little one?"

I introduced the baby with exaggerated formality. "Allow me to present the newest member of our family." I straightened the baby's bonnet and wiped a bit of drool off her chin. "Her name is Patience."

Elma dropped into a deep curtsy, burst into laughter, and reached for her. "Oh, Caty." Her voice softened. "I wish I could have been here for the birth. Mama was so reluctant, it's a wonder I came at all."

I nodded, but I did not understand my aunt's behavior. Over the last year, we had exchanged half a dozen letters, but she refused to part with Elma. Finally, when I had given up hope, a letter arrived.

"Mama is unaware that I know of your invitation," Elma wrote, "but I would cherish the opportunity to visit New York City." The letter was formally signed "Gulielma Sands," as if Elma had taken much pride in writing her signature, but there was a hastily scrawled footnote. "Caty, please don't misunderstand. I love Mama and value the home your father was generous enough to provide, but a visit . . ." Her penmanship ran to the edge of the page and blurred.

If I was concerned by Elma's duplicity, I set those worries aside in favor of my own interest. From the Christmas Eve that she first arrived in Cornwall until the day Elias and I were wed, Elma and I had lived under the same roof. Though quick to speak her mind, she rarely judged the misfortune of others. Hardship had given her a perspective few shared. I confided in her about girlish infatuations and Mother's resolute ways. After our marriage, Elias and I moved just down the street, close enough to race back and forth in wind or rain, for a cup of sugar or dose of frank advice. I shared the news of my pregnancy with Elma even before I told Elias. She was by my side when Charles was born and helped me endure those long early nights. Later, she was wonderful with him, playing games and telling stories with childlike mischief.

Now I was lonely and I missed her. I understood her desire to leave a rural home where her shame was common knowledge, and I had no reason to think it went any deeper. Not bothering to wonder why she had read her mother's mail or, more importantly, why my aunt had not shared our original correspondence, I crafted a carefully worded letter.

"Though we have lived here nearly a year, the city remains new and strange." I frowned at the page, aware that words like *new* and *strange* would hardly convince my timid aunt. "Elias has purchased an entire building and is setting up a dry-goods store on the ground floor. With the remaining space, he plans to take in tenants." I gripped the pen tighter, and it sputtered and squeaked as my argument took shape.

"With a household of men to manage—" I scratched the phrase through and began again. "With a household to manage, Charles, and the new baby, Elma's help would be a great comfort to me." I set the quill down, certain my aunt would never refuse a request to help others. And I was right. After eleven long months, Elma now stood beside me.

I watched in awe as Patience, my colicky baby, nestled happily in Elma's arms and was satisfied that the Greenwich Street house would soon feel more like a home. Inviting her had been the right decision after all. Here, she would not be haunted by her past. Here, I thought, she would have a future.

—2—

That night I dreamed of a building made of weathered red bricks, wedged in the middle of a bustling city block. The upstairs windows were dark and grimy. Dormers rested on the roof like sleepy eyelids. Inside was a tavern with a stale odor and an ethereal light. It was empty except for a long bar and round tables covered with starched white linen. Shadowy murals of distorted figures decorated the walls, and a narrow staircase ran down behind the bar.

Descending, I smelled dampness and decay.

The cellar was like a crypt. All was still. The brick walls were bound with crumbling mortar. Five strides into the darkness, I was confronted by a door. When I took the knob in hand, it refused to turn. The door looked weighty and impenetrable, but when I pushed, it swung easily open. The air was thick and beads of condensation ran down the wall like tears. I stumbled down a few more stairs and saw it framed in a cobwebbed alcove: a cylinder made of coarse bricks, stacked higher than my head, as wide as a tomb.

"Elma!" I called, certain she was there. My elbow scraped the wall. Dust trickled to the ground, and I pictured a swampy meadow and stagnant water. Just as I had at the docks, I called for her, but she did not see me or could not hear.

I woke with a jolt. Tears were running down my cheeks, and my nightgown was drenched with sweat.

Disoriented, I reached for Elias, but the bed was empty and his pillow cold. I leapt to my feet and peered around the partition where the children were sleeping. I listened to Charles sigh as I went to Patience and pressed my lips against her warm forehead, assuring myself of their safety before slipping into a dress. The house was quiet, the sun low in the sky, but birds were chirping outside.

Shadows spread in a lopsided pattern across the floor as I entered the parlor. "Elma!" I cried, as if still in the throes of my dream. A wave of fear washed over me as two figures spun around. Elma clutched a broom and Elias stood beside her, their shoulders all but touching. Between them on the floor, broken glass floated in a shallow puddle.

"Elias startled me," Elma said before I had a chance to speak. "And I broke a glass. Forgive me. I'm here to help, not destroy—She shook her head and offered an unfamiliar, stilted smile.

"Charles is six," I said, trying to console her. "Lots of things break around here." The glass had been a favorite of mine, one of a set of pressed tumblers that was a wedding gift from my parents. Elma had been by my side when I first unwrapped them, and she knew how precious they were to me. I could not imagine what she had been doing with it.

Elma set the broom aside and knelt, picking up shards and using the hem of her skirt as a dustpan. Her dark hair, which had a habit of falling across her face, was held back by a bone-white comb. A silky ribbon wound through the teeth and dangled against her curls.

"What's that?" I asked, reaching for it. "Is it whalebone?"

The comb had a graceful curve and finely tapered teeth. It was no longer than my ring finger but masterfully crafted. I could not imagine owning it, let alone wearing it, and doubted whether my stick-straight hair would even hold it in place. It belonged in thick tresses, where it would not slip free.

Elma twirled the ribbon. A glimmer in her eyes mimicked the ivory's delicate sheen. The way she shied away made it clear she preferred not to share. I blamed her reticence on Elias. I was sure that, had we been alone, she would have told me the story behind such a treasure.

"It's lovely," I said, resisting the urge to touch it.

"Is there toast or eggs?" Elias asked, though it was obvious there was none.

"It's early," I said.

"That squeaky bed needs fixing," he said, shuffling through a stack of newspapers.

The city had a handful of daily papers. My favorite was the *Commercial Advertiser*, which carried ads across the front in small boxes and even smaller print: listings for flax seeds, "female complaints," Dr. Rush's Bilious Pills, "fashionable" hats from London, claret, and German linens, as well as notices about debtors and shipwrecks, dance schools and dentists. A column called "Public Health Notices" published lists of runaway slaves with details like "middling height" or "speaks indifferent English." I especially hated seeing the ads for children. "Negro boy," one read, "about ten with a homespun brown coat." I imagined a tattered coat, short in the sleeves, with missing buttons. Had it been lovingly made by the boy's mother before they were torn apart?

I peered over Elias's shoulder to see what had captured his attention. A man had been found "with marks of a violent death," under a dock on the Hudson River. It was suspected he had been murdered while patronizing a house of bad character. Wielding axes, brooms, and fists, a mob of eight hundred gathered on Murray Street and, with three cheers, threatened to demolish the seedy establishment. They dispersed only once the mayor threatened a night in Bridewell.

Elias shifted his weight so I could no longer read. "And those should be hung before the new tenant arrives," he said, nodding toward a pair of unfinished curtains that lay across my favorite sewing chair. He had a habit of beginning conversations in the middle. When we first married, I worried that I had not been listening carefully enough, but I had come to understand that it was simply his way.

"We're leaving Cornwall?" I had asked when Elias announced we would be moving to New York City. We had spent six peaceful years together and I assumed he was satisfied.

"In the new year, we shall have a fresh start," he said.

"But my parents are here—and Elma."

Resentment flared in his eyes. "My folks wanted to tether me as well, to make me stay on their barren farm, a slave to them and circumstances. I made the choice to leave then, and I am making it again now. There's no future for us here."

I squinted at him. Elias was not from Cornwall, but early in our courtship he had told me about his recently deceased parents and his pain at leaving the small Connecticut farm where he was raised. "I thought thou moved here *after* they died." I strained to recall the conversation.

"They were old," he said. "They didn't need me."

My mouth grew dry. It was more than mincing words. Elias had deceived me, for a reason I couldn't quite grasp. "I don't understand. Are they living or not?"

"They're dead now."

I was not sure I believed him. "When did they die?"

"It's in the past."

"Did thy mother die first or thy father?" I shuddered at the idea of being elderly and alone. "How did they die?"

"I refuse to dredge up the past while I am focusing on our future." His gaze was intent, as if he were truly looking ahead to a place unknown to me.

Perhaps I should have protested or proceeded more cautiously. But Elias was hardworking and, though he could be exacting, he was a dependable husband and devoted father. Still, our marriage was not the partnership I had hoped it would be, and I never forgot that flash of disdain in his eyes.

"We have a new tenant?" I asked.

"Ezra Weeks. I met him at the docks yesterday," Elias said, speaking with an enthusiasm I had not heard for months. "He is one of the city's best-known builders and is working on Alexander Hamilton's new estate."

Broken glass jangled as Elma got to her feet. Bending to keep the sharp bits in her skirt and her hemline low, she transferred the mess to the trash. A damp stain remained on the floor, like the remnants of a squirrel run over by a heavy cart that someone had tried to scrub away—a common occurrence on Greenwich Street. I shook my head to dislodge the image.

I did not want to spoil Elias's mood, but something was amiss. "Why does a successful builder need a room in a boardinghouse?" I asked.

"It's not for him."

I counted to three, reminding myself why I'd named the baby *Patience*. By repeating her name daily, I hoped to become more tolerant. Elias had taken a seat at the table and was absorbed in the newspaper. I counted to ten, waiting for him to respond, but he didn't look up.

"Who, then?" I asked.

"His brother, Levi Weeks, will be arriving any day."

"Shall I make toast?" Elma said. Her voice had a false cheeriness I had heard her use hundreds of times with Mother, as if she were eager to mitigate tension. And, while I could not explain why, she was right: There was a strain in the room that went beyond a mild marital spat.

"If he is such a successful builder, why would he put his brother in a boardinghouse?" I persisted.

The newspaper dropped from Elias's hands and his brow creased. "That's neither here nor there," he said. "They're a well-connected family, and we should be grateful for their patronage. Ezra Weeks said this was a smart location. He even advanced a bit of rent to tide us over until all the rooms are let."

I couldn't say whether I was more surprised or confused. Borrowing money went against everything we Friends believed. Then again, since our move, Elias had worked more and attended meeting less, seeming to favor profit over prayer, explaining when pressed that a business that served the community was in keeping with our faith. He had evidently made peace with his conscience, rationalizing minor transgressions to suit his needs. But there was no excuse for being on the dole.

"Thou took money from him?"

"I did not *take* anything. Ezra Weeks invested in our boarding-house," Elias said, though he was now clearly annoyed. "It is nothing sinister."

Elma set a slice of buttered toast in front of him.

"Thank thee, Elma," I said while Elias ate in silence. "Is there no other way?" I asked him.

"I've tried, Caty. It's impossible to get a loan in this city. Hamilton and his cohorts lord over the banks, and their credit window's closed to the likes of us."

"But Friends are hardworking and honest. Everyone knows that."

"Friends?" He shook his head. "Hamilton runs a Federalist bank— it only grants loans to those who vote for their party."

"Is that legal? Or fair?" I asked.

"Legal enough. No one said anything about fair."

"Maybe—" Elma's dark eyes darted from me to Elias, then back to me, and her mouth twisted as if she were literally biting her tongue. Elma was never one to hold back, and I had the sense she was trying to be a proper guest in our home.

"Elma, what is it?" I wanted her to feel completely at ease. What's more, I valued her opinion.

"Well, if the fellow works with Alexander Hamilton, perhaps he can help," she suggested.

Elias pushed his plate away.

"She's right," I said. "If the Weeks brothers know Hamilton, maybe they can put in a good word."

Elias turned to me, but he didn't object, making it clear the idea had already occurred to him. "One day perhaps, but for now it's simply better to accept their generosity and move on."

I was not sure I agreed. "How is it better?"

"It's faster."

"And that's better?"

"It is when there are bills to pay."

As the morning sun seeped through the windows, revealing cobwebs and dust, I recalled my disturbing dream.

"Elma," I said, resting my hand on her arm. "Shall we go to the water pump?" She smiled warmly, but I felt chilled, as if we were both still trapped in that damp, decaying cellar.

Cocks were crowing and chimney sweeps shouting in a rousing medley as Elma and I made our way up Greenwich Street, swinging our empty buckets. "That's Joseph Watkins's furnishings, and David Forrest's tobacco shop is just across the way," I said, pointing out the sights of her new home. There was laundry hanging in yards, mint and rosemary sprouting in kitchen gardens, and slaves splitting piles of wood.

Elma gazed forward and back. "This is the longest, straightest street I've ever seen."

"New buildings crop up overnight," I said. After nearly a year in the city, it was still hard to fathom hundreds of houses on a single road. Cornwall's main street had nine homes, all of which I could see by leaning out my bedroom window. "Greenwich Street may not be as fashionable as the Bowery, but it's a respectable address. Many Friends have settled in this part of town. The meetinghouse is just a few blocks away," I continued. "Last week, there was a visitor from Wales. He said the simplicity of the room reminded him of home."

"It is wonderful how one can find comfort in such a far-off place," Elma mused.

"Yes." I nodded. But it wasn't completely true. Worship here was not the centering force I once cherished.

The benches in our new meetinghouse lined the walls and faced inward exactly as they had in Cornwall, and the raised ones along the northern wall were reserved for church elders. At home—for I still, ultimately, thought of Cornwall as home—I knew where floorboards creaked and which benches wobbled. I knew who would share valuable insights and who would prattle on about nonsense. Waiting for a light within, I could look past familiar faces through the tall windows to the cemetery beyond. If there were buds or frost, yellow finches or gray skies, looking outward brought me peace.

New York City was starkly different. With its high windows and thick walls, the meetinghouse blocked distractions, but it did not inspire contemplation. The Bible sat on a small table in the center of the room, just as in Cornwall, but its leather was newer, almost pristine, and less approachable. Often, my mind wandered to laundry and meals. It was wrong to fault Elias for choosing business over prayer, when I was equally lax.

"Hot corn! All you that's got money, come buy your lily-white corn!" cried a girl carrying a basket in the crook of her arm. A small child, with hair shorn so short and clothing so nondescript and soiled it was impossible to say whether it was a boy or girl, followed in her wake, gnawing an ear of discarded corn.

"Everyone moves with such purpose," Elma said as we fell in with the swarm of craftsmen dressed in leather pantaloons and vendors hollering and cursing in every direction.

"The pace is faster," I agreed. "It can be overwhelming."

"Caty," Elma said, putting a hand on my arm to make me stand still. "It is so kind of you to have me." I appreciated her gratitude and was happy to take credit for her new start. She sounded as if she were about to recite a speech but was distracted by the tumult around us.

A butcher in a bloody apron led a fat cow across our path, taking orders for different cuts of meat. Another man pulled a dung cart with a bell, followed by cawing crows. People dumped refuse from backyard privies and trash into a filthy rut running down the center of the street, where pigs rummaged, grunting and shoving to get at the choice bits. Men at work on a new home had dammed the gutter to mix mortar, creating a stagnant puddle.

Elma wrinkled her nose.

"Garbage is supposed to flow down to the rivers, but it usually just gets clogged," I said. "Then it backs up into cellars, rotting storehouses and granaries. I've heard that foreigners who live in underground rooms along the waterfront have to bail out their homes after it rains; bones and feces float in and out with the tide."

She took an exaggerated step over a pile of steaming manure, her skirts around her calves, and I could not help but laugh.

"It will be good to have thy help and company," I said, as we continued on. "I worry Elias has taken on too much. He won't say so, but bills are piling up. Thank goodness we're getting a new tenant. We've only had Isaac Hatfield so far."

"What's he like?" she asked.

I had never known Elma to express much interest in men and was mildly surprised at her curiosity. Then again, perhaps I had simply never seen her in society. Our small community in Cornwall didn't hold much intrigue. "Mr. Hatfield trades with the Lenape," I said.

"And?"

"He has a warm smile."

Elma stopped walking and put her hands on her hips.

"His teeth are a bit crooked," I admitted, knowing she would not budge until I offered a complete picture. "And his clothing smells like horse feed." I lowered my voice. "No matter how much I scrub, I can't get rid of the odor."

Laughing, Elma looped her arm through mine. I could feel my steps become lighter. At home, she had helped me plant my first garden. It felt like a hint of what our futures would yield: A garden for me, another for Elma. Husbands and children, our lives blossoming together. Our move to the city had caused a slight delay, but now things were back on schedule. Elias could have his plan; I had one of my own.

We made our way east toward the heart of the city. Housewives joined craftsmen as the dusty streets turned into paved cobblestones. The drumbeat of hammers matched the rumble of wheels as carriages, wagons, and carts raced in every direction. A mangy yellow mutt ran between us, kicking up dirt. Merchants sold pears, corn, even sand to sprinkle on kitchen floors.

"Here's clams!" one called. "Clams from Rockaway! They're good to roast, good to fry, good to make a clam potpie."

"Oh! Let's get some!" Elma cried.

"Too gritty," I said, forging on.

We climbed a small slope until we came to the corner of Chambers

Street. Elma stopped first. "It's beautiful," she said, her cheeks flushed from exertion or excitement.

From where we stood, at a slight remove, it was possible to appreciate the city's bustle. The streets looked orderly and deceptively clean. Peaked roofs and chimneys spanned our view. St. Paul's weathervane glistened in the morning sun, and shady poplars swayed around Trinity Church. Beyond the Battery, the island was framed by tall wooden masts. East, west, and south, there was nothing but ships and sails. It was picturesque, so many sails fluttering under temperate winds. The day was clear, and I could see the Brooklyn ferry as it made its way across the East River.

Elma turned toward the Hudson. "It's the same river as home, but it looks different."

I inhaled the salty breeze. "Here, the rivers are more about commerce than nature." The waterway was just as grand as in Cornwall, but its character was changed. The banks were lower, the channel wider as it fed into the harbor.

"A bit like Elias," she said, reading my thoughts, and I felt myself grow warm.

After a single day in New York, Elma had articulated something that had been troubling me for months. The store and boarding-house were Elias's sole focus. The pressures of our new home seemed to weigh on him. He woke early, worked all day, and sat awake late into the night, reading newspapers or calculating costs. Our faith and values—simplicity, austerity—seemed at risk, and I worried about the example he was setting for our children. Had the city changed Elias or simply revealed his true nature?

The streets grew muddier as Elma and I approached the water pump. A young girl passed, carrying four buckets on a yoke running across her shoulders. Her neck jutted forward and her hair swung from side to side as she balanced the heavy load.

We lifted our skirts to avoid the puddles, but our shoes were soon caked with filth. Gnats buzzed in circles around our heads. Women in aprons, many with young children, stood about, gossiping, seemingly unaware of the stench. Older children chased one another along the outskirts of the crowd. A group of Negroes scrubbed clothing on washboards. One woman took advantage of the warm weather to bathe a protesting infant. She cooed to him in a rhythmic language I did not understand. A man led his horse to drink from a wooden trough. Dogs, pigs, and toddlers splashed through shallow puddles, stirring soapsuds and dirt.

Amid the ruckus, one man stood out. He had a linen kerchief with a delicate floral border tied around his nose and he carried a yardstick, which he used to poke at the sludge. He was commanding and dignified, with broad shoulders and a shock of silver hair. People granted him a wide berth: all but one shabby fellow, who trailed in his wake.

"There's barely a trickle," the scruffy man called toward the surveyor. Red-faced and thick-necked, he spoke in a garbled British accent. Tufts of whiskers climbed his bristly cheeks like caterpillars.

"There's no water?" Elma asked.

The Brit's ears perked up at the question, and he looked at Elma appraisingly. "There's that," he said, jutting his chin toward a rusty spigot dribbling brackish muck.

"Elma," I said, shaking my head to imply that she should not invite conversation with strangers.

"Foul to taste and vile to smell; two gulps and your skin will turn yellow, three and you'll die of fever." He started to laugh, and his body convulsed into a dry, scratchy cough.

I stepped away, nudging Elma to follow. "Water comes and goes here," I explained. "And it's only to scrub floors or do wash. Never drink it." Frustration made the buckets heavy in my hands. Freshwater was hard to come by in New York City. The more difficult it was to gather, the more precious each drop became. Late at night I grew thirsty, anticipating the next day's drudgery.

"But this is an island," Elma said. "Water's everywhere."

"We only know the worth of water when the well is dry," said the Brit, obviously pleased to have an audience. As if sharing a confidence, he moved closer. "Wealth pours into city ports with the saltwater, but it's the salt that poisons the wells."

"We'll have to go to the Collect," I said. The idea of trudging to the marshy basin of the cruelly named Fresh Water Pond made me regret our leisurely stroll. The walk there was pleasant enough, but the anticipation of the haul back with sloshing buckets soured my mood. "At least the weather's cooperating," I said. The only thing worse than walking home carrying heavy water buckets was balancing them in rain, snow, or ice.

"That filthy swamp," said a woman standing nearby. "I'd save your breath. Yesterday I saw a parched horse refuse drink, and when I came home and drained my buckets, I found pebbles and even some small bones—squirrel, maybe rat."

I touched Elma's shoulder. "I suppose the tea-water men are our only option."

Her face registered the same confusion I had felt during my early days in the city. "T-water men?"

"They cart barrels of water through the streets—"

"And overcharge for it," the woman said.

"The water comes from the Tea Water Pump next door to the Old Punch House on Chatham Street," I said. "They say it once brewed the city's best tea. Cartmen gather there in the morning, fill their casks, and hawk it through the streets."

"And food?" Elma's brow furrowed. "Is there a market nearby?"

"The city has four. The Bear and the Crown are near the Hudson, but the Fly Market's best."

"No more flies than the others, though, ha!" the Brit interjected again, slapping his arm as if squashing a mosquito. "It's a Dutch name." His distinguished companion was nowhere in sight, but he continued to hover. He had milky gray eyes and seemed to possess a heightened sense of awareness, as if compensating for a deficiency. "Collect's Dutch too, means 'pond.'"

"The Fly Market's across Maiden Lane," I told Elma. Soon enough, she would be making the trip on her own.

"Maiden Lane," he called after us. "I was by that way last night. There were several ladies, but none of 'em were maidens. I'd mind your purse."

Elias met us outside the front door, frowning at our empty buckets. Still in his nightshirt, Charles skipped behind his father, tossing a ball of my best yarn, the tail unraveling like a streamer.

Elma snatched the ball mid-flight. "Do you think Patience can catch?" she asked, lobbing it back to Charles.

"No!" he said, though he looked doubtful.

"Shall we see?" Elma asked. "Maybe you can teach her."

Charles grinned as if Elma had suggested a grand adventure.

"No water," Elias said, shaking his head as if I were at fault.

"That water's not fit for animals," I said. "We'll have to buy from the tea-water men." I looked down the street. "Provided they come. Honestly, I don't know how I'm to manage a boardinghouse without water."

"Did you say you were running a boardinghouse?"

I turned, disturbed to see the portly Brit with the troubling cough.

"Richard Croucher's my name." He bowed slightly, revealing his hat's tattered rim. "I'm in need of a room."

I felt the hair rise on my neck. He had followed us.

"There's a vacancy on the top floor," Elias said.

"That cramped space under the eaves?" I shook my head, troubled by the idea of sharing intimate quarters with such a man. "I'm sure this gentleman—" I had to look away to get the word out. "He'd find it uncomfortable."

Croucher smiled, or leered. His teeth were yellow and broken. "I don't require much."

A lean horse hobbled down the street, lugging an oversize barrel. "Water! Water!" called the tea-water man, looking as exhausted as his horse. "Penny a gallon."

"What? That's robbery!" Elias said, loud enough for the man to hear.

"Elias," I said. "We can't live without water."

Elias scowled as if I had asked to buy a new ribbon or fine lace. He had always been frugal, but a plain life was in keeping with our beliefs. Now, as he dug into his pockets, he seemed stingy.

With a flourish, Croucher produced a tightly knotted sack from his behind his back.

Elias glanced up and watched closely. "Tell me," he asked, "what's thy line of work?"

"Odd jobs, but I'm not one to owe." Coins jingled and Croucher's mottled fingers shook as he pried open the handkerchief, which had a delicate floral border. I recognized it at once. It belonged to the man carrying the yardstick who had been at the water pump with Croucher. I had a hunch the coins came from him as well. I was pondering the unlikely duo when Elias's eyes lit upon the money.

His hand was out before I could stop it.

"I'm a respectful sort," Croucher said, "especially to the ladies." He cocked his head and looked past me.

"Elias—" I began.

"Just a minute," he said, pocketing the money and shaking hands, a glimmer in his eyes that I hadn't seen in a long while.

I felt tears welling up as I tried to understand how Elias could choose his purse over our home. I could still hear them talking as I took the empty buckets to the barrel. As water splattered against the cracked leather pails, a musty odor rose like a warning.

—3—

A fortnight later, Levi Weeks joined the family. It was Independence Day.

Levi was young, perhaps one-and-twenty, tall, with broad shoulders made muscular from his work as a carpenter. His hair was long and fashionably tied. A casual observer would have said his eyes were black, the lashes were so thick and dark, but a second glance showed them to be dark blue. He was unambiguously handsome, except for a restless expression that I attributed to youth and good fortune.

"We've saved the best room for thee," I said when Elias introduced us.

"I'm grateful." Levi bowed. His tone was smooth, as if he fully expected, and deserved, to occupy the best room. He tapped his thigh while he spoke: a sign of anxiety or impatience, I couldn't decide.

Levi walked to the fireplace and ran his hand along the mantel, as if to examine its construction. "My apprentice, Will," he said, waving backward.

A tall boy with sandy hair waited in the entrance. He was lugging a large sack, and his shoulders floated clumsily by his oversize ears in greeting.

"I'm Catherine Ring, the landlady," I said, sympathetic to what it must be like to be a stranger and servant in a new home.

Charles pointed at Levi. "I know him!"

"Charles," I whispered, lowering his hand, "that's not polite."

"Will, take the bags up," Levi said.

Charles whirled around toward Will. "Him, too. They were at the dock."

I did not recognize Levi, but I recalled the gawky boy standing next to Elma while she fought back tears. "Will *was* at the dock when Elma arrived," I said, while Charles nodded.

"That was the day your pa met my brother," Levi said, mussing Charles's hair, "and they arranged for me to come live here."

Charles cocked his head and frowned, looking exactly like Elias. He had inherited his father's hazel eyes and his attentiveness. Youth made him even more observant—and less tactful.

"Charles," I asked. "Thou saw Levi at the docks?"

"It must have been my brother, Ezra," Levi answered, and I turned back to him. "Brothers are easily confused." He grinned, though it did not quite reach his eyes. "I'm pleased to meet you, young man," he said, shaking Charles's hand.

Charles stood straighter, his little fingers disappearing completely in Levi's grip.

"Elias speaks highly of thy brother," I said, still trying to understand why a successful businessman like Ezra Weeks would not invite kin into his home. Elias's eyes gleamed with subtle warning, but I had a right to know about the people living under my roof. Isaac Hatfield, the trader, seemed harmless enough; Croucher was curious at best; but something in Levi's ingratiating manner troubled me.

Elias walked over to the hearth and picked up a poker, waving it in the air, before bending to separate the logs. "The fire's too high."

"I'm preparing dinner," I said, nodding at the table, where plates were set out. "Elma's gone to the pump."

"The streets are packed with Independence Day revelers," Levi said. His voice sounded youthful and animated for the first time.

The front door blew open and Elma entered. Her hair was tousled and her shawl was bunched in her arms like a pile of rags. She was not carrying the water buckets. She backed up and slammed the door with her heel. Charles rushed to her side, and she stooped down. Loose curls brushed the bundle in her arms, and a tiny paw reached out to swat them away. Elma unfurled the shawl, exposing the ears, eyes, then whiskers of a pewter-gray cat whose fur was matted with mud.

"The poor thing was hiding under the back wheel of a carriage," she said, placing her index finger on the smallest of white dots above the cat's nose. "Filthy creature," Elias said "No doubt he's coated with fleas."

Elma stroked the matted fur. "He's skin and bones." She held the cat an arm's length away, and his tail flicked anxiously as he gazed back at her with steady amber eyes.

"This house doesn't need another stray," Elias said, with a pointed glance at Elma.

Elma hugged the cat to her chest. "He won't be in anyone's way."

"Cats are very useful," Levi said.

Elma startled at the sound of his voice and turned to Levi with something more than curiosity.

"Martha Washington nicknamed her big old tomcat 'Hamilton,'" Levi continued. It was as if he wanted to steer the conversation toward his illustrious connections. "Of course, Hamilton is a dapper sort." Levi walked to Elma, reached out, and scratched the cat behind its ears. It stretched and purred while Elma stood entirely still. "This fellow is definitely more of a 'Burr.'"

"Burr rhymes with purr!" Charles clapped.

A shy smile flitted across Elma's lips and Levi watched, not bothering to hide his interest. I was not surprised she had caught his attention, but I was disturbed that she was returning it so blatantly.

"Levi," Elias said. "This . . ." He refused to look Elma's way. "This is my wife's cousin."

Elma held out her hand and spoke in a stilted voice that matched her unfamiliar smile. "Pleased to meet—"

There was an explosion outside that made us jump.

"Cannon fire for the celebration," Levi explained. "Ezra says that this will be the most festive year yet."

"Can we go see?" Charles asked, bouncing up and down.

"I think I hear drums," Levi said.

Elias reached for his hat. I had the impression that he was loath to disappoint Levi. "Might as well take a look," he said, shaking his head at Elma. "Seeing as dinner's not ready."

"The water," Elma gasped. "I completely forgot!"

"Fetch the buckets," I said, cringing as I imagined our leather water buckets flattened under the wheels of a carriage. We were in no position to replace the buckets or waste their precious content. After two weeks trudging to the pump, I would have thought Elma understood that. Still, I steadied my voice. It was not fair to scold her in front of company. "We'll make do with what's here." No matter how I sealed the wooden tub where I stored water—secretly hoping for a warm bath—it always had a film of gnats and dust..

"Forgive me," Elma said, setting the cat on his feet. He scurried away and hid under the table, and Elma looked as if she would have liked to follow.

The clamor continued while we prepared dinner. Along with the cannon fire and drumming, there were shouts and singing in the street.

Steam rose from the bowl and colored Elma's cheeks as she mashed potatoes. "Levi's very handsome," she said.

It was impossible to deny Levi's good looks, but the clear effect they had on Elma made me uneasy. "He's rather . . . worldly," I said.

Elma tasted the potatoes. "He's intelligent. Is that bad?"

"No, of course not," I said, striving to articulate my precise concern. Calling Levi too sophisticated implied she was naïve.

"Caty, you're always slow to warm to new faces. If you don't stop worrying, those lines"—she reached over, smoothing the skin between my eyebrows—"will become permanent."

I couldn't disagree: I had always been slow to trust new acquaintances. My aunt's plight had made an impression on me, but Elma appeared surprisingly unscathed in that regard—she remained trusting and open. It was something that I loved about her, but it also made me worry about her judgment.

"Isaac Hatfield is very kind," I said, "and he's always trying to make conversation with thee."

"Isaac Hatfield!" Elma looked over her shoulder and lowered her voice. "He has hairy knuckles and a potbelly."

"I can't speak for his knuckles," I said, fighting back a smile, "but it's nice to have a healthy appetite."

"Oh, Caty!" She shook her head, still mashing vigorously.

Elias, Levi, and Charles returned. Elias seated himself at the head of the dining table with Levi to his right, and Charles inserted himself between the pair. When the scent of warm food filled the house, Richard Croucher and Isaac Hatfield joined the men at the table.

"Charles, go fetch Will," I said, curious to see if Elma would recognize the boy from the dock. But when Will took a seat beside Levi, she did not look up.

"My brother, Ezra, says it will be Jefferson in 1800," Levi announced suddenly, and the other men turned to face him.

Elma elbowed me. "Handsome *and* well informed," she whispered.

"Serve the potatoes," I told her. I did not appreciate her teasing. I had always imagined Elma would find a modest husband, not necessarily as morally upright as Elias or Mother, but a man with a deep and true faith. Someone who had experienced heartache and could understand her hardships; who would be sensitive enough to look past her shortcomings and see her for the sweet and forthright young woman she was; who would value virtue over birth. Levi was not the type I had in mind.

Elma placed the potatoes in front of Levi and helped him to a hearty spoonful. Her braid brushed his shoulder as she leaned over, and he smiled appreciatively.

"Those smell tasty," Hatfield said, tucking in his napkin. He seemed more focused on Elma than on the potatoes, but his mirth faded as she heaped another serving onto Levi's crowded plate.

"Ezra likes Jefferson?" Elias asked. Just weeks earlier he had referred to politics as the devil's religion. Now he sounded keenly interested.

I served from a platter of stewed beef as I listened to the men around the table. Hearing their varying perspectives had proven to be the best thing about running the boardinghouse. I could have never imagined how the business being discussed would soon unravel our lives.

"Jefferson and the Republicans are sharpening their pitchforks and their tongues and tossing a load of rubbish about Hamilton's contempt for liberty," Croucher said. Cutlery clanged as he picked each piece up and wiped it with his napkin. "And the Federalists are lobbing it back, calling Jefferson a fanatic."

"For an Englishman, you're well versed in our system," Levi said, sounding more suspicious than impressed.

"I make it a point to understand what's going on around me," Croucher said, stabbing meat with his fork.

"Word has it Jefferson plans to build a guillotine on Capitol Hill to lop off his rival's heads, and Hamilton's will be first to go," Hatfield said, chuckling and nodding at Elma as if encouraging her to join in.

She obliged. "Jefferson doesn't like Hamilton?" she asked.

"Are there more potatoes?" I said, hoping to distract her. I secretly admired Elma for participating in the conversation, but I did not understand her need to be quite so bold at a table full of men.

"Why don't they like each other?" she persisted. She addressed Levi, but Hatfield responded.

"They have different plans for the country. Hamilton is growing banking and business, while Jefferson has manicured gardens and slaves."

Levi's expression softened as he turned to Elma. "President Adams *may be* running for reelection and he *may be* the rightful head of the Federalist Party, but everyone knows that Hamilton is really in charge. He was Washington's top adviser, and many cabinet members still listen to him. Jefferson resents him. Adams does too."

"Why doesn't Hamilton run for president?" Will asked.

Croucher banged a fist into the table, rattling the dishes. "Alexander 'amilton is the bastard brat of a Scottish peddler whose mother was a common whore!"

Charles's eyes grew wide and a hush fell over the table. I could hear Hatfield chew and see Elias clench his jaw. I couldn't bring my-self to look at Elma.

"Is it fair to judge him because of his birth?" Levi asked.

Elma's eyes locked on his with unmistakable gratitude.

"'e can dress 'imself up in silk and ruffles, but 'e don't fool me," Croucher said. "'amilton's no better 'an 'is mother. ''e couldn't cool 'is iron in 'is own trough and was conned by a pair of ne'er-do-well tricksters because of it."

The more inflamed Croucher grew, the more his speech deteriorated.

"He had a love affair and was blackmailed," Levi said. "It was dis-graceful, but he explained his position."

"'is position!" Croucher broke into a fit of laughter. "Which one? Wonder 'ow 'e explained *is position* to 'is wife. What do you say, Mrs. Ring?"

"She has nothing to say!" Elias nearly shouted. While it was impos-sible not to be offended by Croucher's vulgar manner, Elias's words were infinitely more insulting. His obliviousness to the slight made it worse.

"Hamilton's mother left a husband who beat her," I said, stating the facts as I knew them.

"To be with the man she loved," Levi added. "She's a fallen woman."

"Fallen?" Croucher barked. "Did she stumble into 'er lover's bed?"

"She fell victim to temptation and sin. Human beings . . ." Levi's voice faltered. "People can be weak."

"Leaving a cruel and nasty husband is the opposite of weak," I said, feeling color rush to my face. "She was *brave*."

A vein at the base of Elias's neck throbbed as he scraped his chair away from the table—a habit he employed, like clearing his throat, to remind the household that he sat at the head.

"Thy brother Ezra knows Hamilton," Elias said. "What does he think?"

Levi sliced his meat, separating out fatty bits and pushing them to the edge of his plate. "Hamilton's a cut above the rest," he said, holding a well-trimmed piece of beef at the end of his fork before popping it in his mouth. "Of course, my brother and I also work with Burr. Burr is well born but"—he gazed down and smiled—"hard-bitten. He has no future with the Federalists so long as Hamilton is at the helm, so he's turned to Jefferson and the Republicans."

"Jefferson needs Burr to woo New Yorkers," Hatfield said.

"It's a marriage of convenience," Croucher grumbled.

Elias sat taller, or perhaps it was merely his ears that perked up. "What business does Ezra have with Burr?"

"Burr doesn't like Hamilton either?" Elma asked sweetly.

Elias cringed as Levi, ignoring his question, responded to Elma. "Burr hates him most of all. Some say it's because they're too alike: both New Yorkers with brilliant legal minds, and both wildly ambitious."

"What work is Ezra doing for Burr?" Elias asked more firmly.

"Burr plans to fix the city's water shortage. Ezra and I are providing the lumber and the labor," Levi said.

Hatfield sat back and whistled. "If Burr can pull that off, he'll be more popular than God."

It was the first I'd heard that anyone was trying to solve the water problem, and I imagined a hundred ways my life could improve.

"The water committee meets often," Levi said. "Elias, you should join us."

"Republican meeting?" Croucher asked.

"We discuss sanitation, not politics."

"Politics *is* dirty business," Croucher said, chuckling to himself.

Elias sat forward. "Will Burr be there?"

"Yes," Levi said. "Colonel Burr is very serious about public welfare."

Croucher stood. "Burr and Hamilton aren't any more interested in public good than they are in wedding vows." He dug deep in his pocket and tossed a flyer to the center of the table.

AARON BURR! The words blazed in bold type. ACCUSED OF ABANDONED DEBAUCHERY.

Oppressive summer heat had settled over the city when we woke one night to cries of "Fire!" Church bells were ringing, night watchmen were hollering, and Elias was pulling on his boots and shouting orders. Levi, Will, and Isaac Hatfield raced down the stairs, and Richard Croucher was steps behind.

"Keep the children inside," Elias screamed, "and get the buckets."

Elma, tousled with sleep, stood barefoot on the second-floor landing, gazing serenely at the mayhem. She wore a thin cambric shift, and only her black curls and the dark night prevented it from being entirely transparent.

The men were scrambling for buckets, boots, and hats, but each one stopped in his tracks as Elma descended the stairs. She paused on the last step, a breath away from Levi.

"Be careful," she whispered, so quietly that I was not sure if she spoke the words or merely mouthed them.

I rushed over and wrapped my shawl around her shoulders, but it was impossible to cover the subtle curve of her hips. "Go back to bed," I said, trying to redirect her upstairs.

"Levi!" Elias shouted, though he was only steps away. He seemed as determined to separate the pair as I was. As Levi stole one last wistful glance at Elma, Elias practically shoved him out the door.

I followed them outside. Up and down Greenwich Street, people stood in doorways or leaned out of windows, watching as brigades of men, hands laden with water buckets, marched north.

"Where is it?" I asked.

"Chambers Street," said our neighbor Elizabeth Watkins. She, like Elma and me, was dressed in a nightgown with a shawl thrown hastily over her shoulders, though with her buxom build and graying hair, she cut quite a different figure from Elma. The mother of three grown boys, Elizabeth served as the neighborhood matriarch.

"My dear, you'll catch a chill," she cried.

I looked over my shoulder, dismayed to find Elma standing there in her flimsy shift.

"Stay inside," Levi said to her. Elias turned, clearly surprised to hear him giving orders.

Charles trailed Elias in nightshirt and bare feet, carrying a bucket. "I want to help," he said.

Elias brushed him away. "Caty, there's no time for this."

Charles began to sniffle and Levi patted his shoulder, gently taking the bucket from him. "We need a man to stay behind and look after the women."

Whether or not Charles accepted Levi's explanation, he stayed put.

Men were racing up the street. "Come now, Charles." I reached for his hand, then withdrew, thinking that he might prefer to walk on his own.

Assured that we were not in imminent danger, Elma and I gathered the children in the front room. Charles narrated from the window. "Joseph Watkins is hitching his wagon," he called. "And I see the old widower. He's swinging a lantern and wearing slippers!"

"It's a wonder he doesn't start another blaze," Elma said.

"And there's Levi," Charles said. "But he's going the wrong way."

"What?" Elma leapt from her chair to join Charles at the window.

"Levi!" Charles banged on the windowpane.

"He must be going to get more men—or supplies," she said, squinting.

I felt secretly gratified that Levi, who claimed to be so interested in public welfare, would shirk his responsibilities. Bells were ringing throughout the city, so I didn't believe he was going to fetch more men. And water was the only thing to fight fire. Walking the opposite way was no help. I turned to Elma, wondering what she thought of Levi's cowardly behavior. Her face was pressed so close to the windowpane that her breath clouded the glass, but she didn't say anything.

"Rest now. It will be a long night," I said to Charles, though I was also speaking to Elma.

As the candles burned down, the street became quieter. Elma curled up with Patience, and Charles fell asleep in my bed. I kissed the top of his head, cherishing the increasingly rare opportunity to inhale his boyish scent. Perhaps I should have taken my own advice. Instead, I headed outside.

It had not rained in more than a week, and Greenwich Street was dusty and dry. I could smell smoke and see a distant flicker of flames. I can't explain what drew me to the danger. It was more than curiosity or restlessness. The air grew thick and my eyes stung. I walked steadily north with a sense of encroaching doom.

Chambers Street was in the middle of the island, where the buildings were most tightly packed. Most were made of wood. At least three were engulfed in fire, and a fourth had bright-orange flames soaring from windows and under the roof. One wall had collapsed and men swung axes at the others, trying to contain the blaze. People raced to the scene, carrying buckets and ladders; others fled with children, dishes, even bedding, in their arms. There were shouts and tears, the sound of crackling, and the hiss of flames.

"Factory fire?" someone asked. Gray soot was smeared under his nose like a mustache.

An elderly man leaning on a cane shook his head. "Private home."

"Lizzie!" a woman screamed. Barefoot, she wore a worn dress with a singed hem, her hair was unruly, but her expression was truly wild. "Lizzie, are you here? Come out, Mama won't be angry. Lizzie!"

No one, including myself, stirred. Panic swept my soul, a fear so intense it left me mute. The elderly man next to me seemed to be holding his breath. It was only when the poor woman rushed away into a cloud of black smoke that I heard him exhale.

"How did it start?" I asked. It wasn't just macabre interest. I wanted to shield my family from whatever it was that had spawned this nightmare.

"A servant girl spilled a shovelful of live coal while carrying it from one room to the next," he said.

"Nah." The lady next to him shook her head. "Heat caused a compost pile to ignite."

"See that house there?" another woman said. "The bedsheets caught fire."

Chains of men formed to the west and south, passing buckets from fire-company tanks toward the burning homes. The wind picked up, water flew in men's faces, and the air filled with the stench of burned meat. I looked for Elias, but the darkness and commotion made it impossible to distinguish one man from the next. On second glance, though, I was certain I recognized the ranting zealot from the dock, showering bucket after bucket onto the swiftly rising flames. Or maybe it was merely his prophetic words ringing louder than any siren: "*Are you prepared to see your dwellings in flames?*"

"Tank's almost empty!" shouted a man at the head of the line.

"Fire company's not worth a damn," said a man next to me.

"Form a line to the river!" the first man called. The line shifted and spread, though it did not seem possible to reach either river.

"Mrs. Ring?" Richard Croucher seemed always annoyingly underfoot, so the sight of him should not have surprised me. But it did. It was not his presence so much as his appearance. His face was smeared with ash, his shirt was soaked through, and his left hand was raw.

"What happened?" I asked, reaching for the injury.

He flinched, and a thin trickle of perspiration ran from his temple in a crooked line down his cheek. From thumb to wrist were several angry, oozing blisters.

"Got licked by flame. It'll mend." Croucher pulled the wounded hand behind his back. "This is no place for you. You should be with the children, out of 'arm's way."

The chilling cries of the woman calling for her daughter echoed in my ears. Down the street, half-dressed men and women ran from buildings, their arms weighed down by silverware, candlesticks, books.

"The children are with Elma. Maybe I can help those people," I said, starting toward them.

Croucher caught my sleeve. "Mrs. Ring." His voice, devoid of its usual bluster, was laced with concern. "Those folks are stealing."

"Thieves?" One stout woman carried pots and pans; a girl, no more than ten, dragged a sack of flour. They looked like ordinary people, not criminals.

There were screams and a whoosh as a blazing wall tumbled to the ground. Red and gold flames leapt and danced as wood buckled and collapsed. Fiery ash landed inches from our feet, and a wave of scorching heat engulfed the street, followed by the blackest smoke I had ever seen.

—4—

The smell of smoke was still in the air when Elias attended his first water meeting. After supper, he and Levi left the house in Ezra Weeks's elegant calash. Seated on the plush upholstery, Elias was clearly pleased, nodding at neighbors and laughing a bit too loudly. I may have shook my head, but, truth be told, I was relieved Elias was adjusting to city life. My days were infinitely easier when he was in good spirits. With childlike naïveté, I buried any concern that we might be punished for our complacency and pride. Caught in the whirlpool that was engulfing our lives, I set my values aside.

Elma disappeared the moment the men were out of sight. It was unlike her to leave without cleaning up. She had spent the afternoon sewing in silence, her head resting on the back of her chair as if observing the household from afar. I know now, with a crystalline pain, that we were both errant, soon to be lost entirely. But at the time I was more concerned with fussy children and dirty dishes.

I wanted to speak to Elma about Levi, though I wasn't exactly sure what to say. Could I tell her not to sway like a blade of grass while he spoke? Not to hover as if anticipating his every whim?

I called for her in the yard and up the stairs, increasingly bothered by the silent house. Charles tagged behind me, holding my apron strings and pretending to drive a horse.

"I want a story," he said, his mood as bearish as mine. "Where's Elma?"

"I'm afraid I'll have to do tonight," I said, steering him toward the bedroom.

Only half paying attention, I told a dull tale about a well-behaved boy who was kind to his little sister. Charles interrupted with endless comments: the boy had brown hair, not blond; he hated peas and deserved a later bedtime. Eventually, his objections became fewer until, finally, he closed his eyes. I went in search of Elma.

Over the past year, I had grown accustomed to our home's odd sounds, from snoring men to rattling windows. But that night the entire house was still as death. My steps slowed, and I could hear my breath as I reached the third floor. Elma's bedroom door was closed. For some reason it filled me with dread. My hand shook as I turned the knob, and when the door swung open, I gasped. Croucher stood, candle in hand, leaning over Elma's narrow bed. For a stout man, he cast a long shadow.

"I 'eard 'er babbling," he said. "Sickness came on fast."

"Sickness?" I rushed to her side. The idea that Elma was ill had not occurred to me, but as I gazed down at her I could not help but wonder how I had been so blind. Her hair was tousled, her lips caked and dry, and her teeth chattering. I set my hand on her forehead, then snapped it back. Her face was flushed with fever, yet her skin was clammy.. "She needs a doctor!"

"Those slick doctors and their slimy leeches bleed you dry. I'd ask Ring first," Croucher warned.

I wanted to tell him that I could call for a doctor with or without Elias's approval, but I knew with a pang of anger that he was right. Elias would be irritated at an extra expense, especially one for Elma.

"Elias has gone to the water meeting," I worried out loud. "Would thou fetch him for me?" I did not like asking Richard Croucher for a favor. He was the kind of man who would request something in return.

He shook his head forcefully. "I wasn't invited," he snapped.

I was suddenly calm with purpose. "A rather odd time to stand on ceremony, I should think," I said, as I started out of the room. "Very well, then." I would get our neighbor Elizabeth Watkins to stay with the children and find Elias myself.

"Where you going?" Croucher called.

I did not think I owed him an explanation, but it was easier to answer than argue. "I'm going to find Elias."

Croucher grabbed my shoulder. "No respectable lady walks alone at night."

I frowned, suspecting he was right. I had never ventured so far after dark. "Then come along," I said, continuing down the stairs. Even if it was the insidious Richard Croucher, I would be grateful for the company.

Outside, the air was thick with fog. I pulled my shawl over my head and walked faster. Filthy men emptied soiled privies into the street— they were supposed to be dumped into the rivers, but after dark who would know? Feral cats glared at us from alleyways, their eyes shining in the moonlight. Whale-oil lamps cast dim light and bats swooped in doorways, hunting their prey. The curses of the Irish cartmen ricocheted through the streets, and the bells at St. Paul's struck eleven as we turned onto Broadway.

"Not that way," Croucher said, taking my elbow and leading me in a wide arc around a door filled with laughter and light. The sound of a fiddle spilled out onto the street, along with a few tipsy dancers. "Fighting Cocks Tavern," he sheepishly explained, "but the cocks 'ere aren't fighting, if you know what I mean." Perhaps seeing shock in my face, he stood straighter and cleared his throat. "A lady like you should stay away."

Croucher's concern for my modesty was strangely sweet. He was a conundrum: gruff, crass, and childish, prone to fibbing about tracking mud up the stairs or what time he came in at night. But he was clearly lonely and eager for attention.

"Soldiers and sailors—you know the lot. Take my word: This democracy of yours is nothing special. They can rename Crown Street 'Liberty' and change King's College to 'Columbia,' but men will be men. A city of scoundrels, adulterers, and—"

Boisterous chants came from the tavern as the door flew open and a scruffy man was tossed out into the gutter. He sat in the foul trough, lowered his head, then lay down. Moments later, another man hobbled out the door and began to pilfer through his pockets.

"—scavengers," Croucher finished.

"It was kind of thee to accompany me," I said, realizing I had not thanked him.

Croucher smiled widely, almost boyishly. "If I 'ad a wife, I'd 'ope she'd be a lady like you, not all fancy or frilly but 'ardworking and decent. Levi's boy is lucky to live in a—," he paused, inhaling deeply before pronouncing the next word with obvious care, "home like yours."

"Were thee an apprentice?"

"Me? Nah." Croucher, happy to sermonize on so many topics, was mum when it came to himself. He picked up his pace and, as he did, footsteps echoed behind us. I turned to look, but no one was there.

We headed south into the mist. At the end of the island, the sidewalks were planted with shrubs and the houses were brick, with gables and balconies facing the harbor.

"Pearl Street," Croucher said, speaking once again with authority. "Not long ago the place was paved with oyster shells."

"Where is the meeting?" I asked.

Croucher pointed to a handsome brick mansion.

I let myself in through the open door. There was a rumble of deep voices and the dull sound of ice being cracked with a hammer. I smelled sausage, but the pleasant cooking odors were overpowered by the ripe stench of men, cigar smoke, and hops.

The men's faces looked dull in the haze, but I easily spotted Elias seated at a small table on the far side of the bar. He was the only one wearing a broad-brimmed hat and dark overcoat. The others, Levi included, were stylishly dressed in tapered britches, topcoats, and gauzy cravats.

A man stood on wobbly legs and raised his glass high in the air. "When you swear, swear to your country," he hollered. "When you lie, lie for love; when you steal, steal from bad company; and when you drink, drink with me!"

There was a roar of stomping feet and shouts. "Hurrah!"

I watched, horrified, as Elias drained his glass in a single gulp.

Another man flung his over his shoulder, where it smashed on the floor. As Elias reached for a decanter of treacle-colored liquor, I was reminded of the broken glass the morning after Elma arrived and the puddle I had assumed was water. While our beliefs did not expressly prohibit drink, I had never known Elias to partake. His features were rigid, his expression unreadable, as he swigged another glass.

A commotion broke out. "This city's water is no better than that of a common sewer," a man yelled, his voice quivering with age and drink. "I want to know who's going to fix it."

"Lispenard's right," a portly fellow bellowed, then belched. "The rich buy water and leave us drinking filth."

Whiskey spilled as the fellow named Lispenard slammed his hands on the table and pulled himself to his feet, grimacing. Squat and bald, his face looked sallow in the hazy light. The lapel on his coat was unfashionably wide, and his shirtsleeves were frayed at the cuffs.

"Worse than filth," he said. "It's poison. That's my land by the Collect, a swamp of pest and plague. Every glue factory and tannery in town has set up shop practically at my dining table. I can smell the rotting hides on me now."

An elegant man in a finely tailored topcoat stood. "Lispenard," he said, "surely you know that Colonel Burr has closed those places down."

Huddled in the doorway beside Richard Croucher, I felt conspicuous and stranded. I had expected him to spare me the embarrassment of announcing myself to a room full of men, but he seemed equally out of place, hanging back, shuffling his feet, removing and replacing his hat—an annoying tic.

"That's Ezra Weeks," he said, more timid than I had ever heard him.

Ezra was shorter and stockier than Levi, cut from a coarser cloth than his younger brother but more distinguished. His thick hair was more silver than gray, as if he were surrounded by a halo of good fortune.

"I saw him at the water pump the day we met," I said, half-expecting Croucher to deny it.

"I've done some work for 'im. But 'e's too good for the likes of me these days," Croucher spat. "'e and his brother both."

"The factories are closed now," Lispenard was saying, "but what's been left behind? I've seen pits of standing water, animal carcasses, and decaying hides. Everyone knows foul water's to blame for yellow fever. Killed my son last summer, days before he was to wed." He hung his head. "We buried him in his wedding jacket."

The mention of yellow fever and the thought of Elma sick in bed made my heart skip. "We are here to get Elias," I said, nudging Croucher forward.

Croucher let out a low whistle. "And that's the devil 'imself."

"Who?"

"Burr."

Marching across the hazy room, puffing a fat cigar, Burr did resemble the devil. He was a small man, five foot six at best, dark, with a receding hairline. In a rich brown coat and a white silk waistcoat, he was tastefully dressed without being showy. His heavily lidded eyes could have seemed indolent, but Burr's gaze was completely alive, taking in the bustling room with a single sweep. Smoke curled from the end of the cigar as he raised his hands, and the raucous crowd grew still.

"Mr. Lispenard, surely you know my Richmond Hill property abuts yours. We're neighbors." Burr smiled as if the statement were slightly ironic. "Pray tell, would I settle my loved ones on polluted land?"

"Your estate and my farm are worlds apart," Lispenard said. "I don't have your view or your influence."

Burr nodded sympathetically. "What man here has not worried about our city's water and the cost to remedy the problem?" he asked. "I am here tonight to announce that I am founding the Manhattan Water Company, whose sole purpose will be to provide our parched city with pure and wholesome water."

There was a rumble of approval, but one voice stood out.

"Any company's got to be approved by the legislature," Lispenard shouted. "The Federalists in Congress are not likely to support a Republican water company."

"Not during an election year," someone agreed.

Like the flame on the stub of his cigar, Burr's shrewd eyes blazed in the smoky room. "On the contrary, this is a civic-minded effort spurred by common interest. Every man here, no matter his politics, knows our city will never rival Philadelphia or even Boston if our factories are constantly threatened by fire. To that end, I have assembled a coalition of six—three Republicans and three Federalists—who will approach the legislature on our behalf." Burr took a long drag, and smoke escaped his nostrils as his gaze veered to a table at the center of the room. "Certainly my esteemed colleague, Mr. Hamilton, needs no introduction."

Alexander Hamilton was approaching middle age, and his famously red hair was mellowing into a quieter shade of copper. He had a fair complexion and vibrant blue eyes. Pearl buttons embellished his velvet jacket, and his cravat was perfectly tied. He glided to the center of the room.

"I, myself, was struck down by fever last summer," he began, pausing for his audience to absorb the magnitude of the averted tragedy. There was a rhythmic tempo to Burr's voice, like a primitive drumbeat, but Hamilton spoke with a melodic fluency. "Thus, it is with full confidence that I say the Manhattan Water Company is precisely what our city requires. Indeed, it is essential. Not simply waterworks but a systematic plan for draining swamps and installing sewers. I have personally appealed to the legislature, drafting a proposal I believe—"

Burr tapped his cigar, making sparks fly. "Several impressive ideas have been posed—floated, if you will. . . ." A few men chuckled, and Burr winked. "One in particular is very promising. It's an ambitious plan to draw water from the Bronx River."

"The Bronx is miles north of here," one man protested.

Burr grinned, seeming to savor the debate as thoroughly as he was enjoying his cigar. "With the help of Ezra Weeks and his crew, the Manhattan Water Company will build a dam at the base of the Bronx River. From there, freshwater will be channeled into the city through six miles of pipes into a newly constructed reservoir on Chambers Street." Burr pointed over his shoulder to an easel that held an illustration of an impressive façade. Like the gateway to an ancient ruin, four imposing columns seemed to indicate an entrance, but there was nothing behind them but a foreboding brick wall. A larger-than-life bronze statue of a scantily clad Greek god lounged on top of the columns, pouring an enormous vessel of sculptured water into a stream, which flowed into a reservoir. "With the aid of this new reservoir, fire companies will be able to fill their tanks," Burr announced, "and water will be pumped directly into homes."

There was a chorus of impressed murmurs, and I resisted the urge to chime in. Burr was as inspiring as his reputation suggested, and a tap of freshwater in our home could mean clean dishes, tidy laundry, even warm baths. But Lispenard was not appeased. "It's a pretty picture," he shouted, "but who's paying for it?" His disgruntled yells drew me back to reality. Elma lay sick in bed. I took a deep breath and was about to cross the floor when Hamilton stepped forward.

"You men here are the first to be offered stock in the Manhattan Water Company," he practically purred with self-satisfaction.

"In other words," Lispenard said, "you need cash."

"'Neither a borrower nor a lender be,'" a somber man muttered as he snatched his hat and stomped out the door. His companions watched him go.

Hamilton spoke above the ruckus. "The money raised will be used to build an aqueduct and reservoir, and all who invest"—his voice dropped, and the men who had looked as if they might follow their peer out the door turned back to listen—"those seated in this very room, will benefit handsomely."

The older men folded their arms and nodded. The younger ones rapped on tables and howled, "Toast! Toast!"

Burr rested his hand on Hamilton's velvet-clad shoulder and raised his glass. "To the tempestuous sea of liberty, may it never be calm. We may subscribe to different philosophies, but Republicans and Federalists can work together when our city's future is at stake."

"Or when there's money to be 'ad," Croucher grumbled under his breath.

"Hear, hear!" Levi called, lifting his glass.

I did not doubt his enthusiasm. The Manhattan Water Company would make them all rich. More importantly, it would lay a labyrinth of pipes in a city starved for water. I could easily have stood there imagining a thousand more improvements to my life, but I had already delayed far too long. Gathering my shawl and my courage, I headed to Elias's table. Croucher followed, though I had the impression he just wanted to see Elias's reaction, not lend support.

"Caty?" Elias's jaw dropped, and he squinted as if doubting the sight before him.

"Seeking truth at the bottom of a glass, eh, Ring?" Croucher said, clearly amused.

"I encouraged him to join me in a drink," Levi put in, as if to apologize.

"He's not used to spirits," I said, too quickly and overly loud. It was easier to fault Levi than Elias.

Levi seemed oblivious to my anger. "Why have you come all this way?" he asked. His gaze traveled to Croucher, asking the unspoken question: Why had I come all this way with *him*?

"Elma is running a fever." My voice trembled. It was late at night, which somehow made the situation worse. "I'm worried."

"We can take my brother's rig," Levi said, jumping to his feet while Elias staggered up.

It was a relief to have a sympathetic man in charge. I just did not understand why it wasn't Elias.

We arrived home after midnight.

"She's going to infect us all," Elias said from the doorway of Elma's room.

Damp hair coiled around Elma's pale throat. Her eyes were shut, the lids so translucent that it would have been possible to trace the blue veins with a fingertip. I also feared for the children, but I focused on Elma, praying for her speedy recovery so that no one else would fall ill.

"Stay with her," I said. "I'll go for the doctor."

"Wait and see how she fares the night." Elias yawned, already half-way down the stairs.

From the depths of sickness, Elma moaned, "I'm useless." I immediately thought of Mother and of Elma's futile attempts to earn her affection.

I stooped to moisten Elma's lips. "That's not true," I said, sure she had heard Elias's callous words.

There were footsteps on the landing, and I was heartened to think that Elias had returned. Perhaps his rude tone had stemmed from worry, mere bluster to disguise his concern. I turned, determined to show my appreciation, but it was not Elias's stout figure in the doorway. It was Levi. I had the distinct impression he had been waiting for Elias to leave.

"She may be contagious," I warned.

"I'm strong," Levi said. He gazed down at Elma and took her frail hand in his.

"Hast thou much experience with illness?" I asked.

"Yes and no. I lost both my parents when I was a boy."

"How?" I asked, startled by his candor.

Levi's eyes grazed the floor. "My mother died in childbirth. Two months later, my father passed. The doctor couldn't understand it. My father was still a young man." Levi shook his head, perhaps realizing that talk of sickness and death was making me more anxious. "Of course, it was far worse than this. The truth is . . . well, I think—" He looked wistfully at Elma. "My parents were very close. My father died of a broken heart."

In all the times he had spoken admiringly of the Weeks brothers and their financial success, Elias had never divulged their family history. And I had never considered it. "That must have been very difficult," I said, feeling myself soften slightly.

"Fortunately, I had Ezra to look after me. No one could have done a better job."

I nodded, observing the change in him. As he spoke his brother's name, Levi's caring expression turned into a rigid mask.

"Elias thinks highly of Ezra," I said.

"Most people do," Levi said flatly.

"Has he a strong temperament?" I asked, thinking of Mother and Elias.

Levi smiled tightly. "Stubborn and strong."

"Levi." Elma's voice was breathless and weak. I was surprised that she was aware of our presence at all and felt a stab of concern that had nothing to do with her illness.

"Let me go for the doctor," Levi said, his hand on the doorknob. "He's a friend of my brother's. I'm sure he would come as a favor to me."

He seemed to be implying that the doctor would come free of charge, but it no longer mattered. I thought of Elias sleeping while Elma suffered. Resentment stirred deep inside me, and something in my heart hardened.

After Levi left, I pulled the covers to Elma's chin and stroked her hair, which still smelled of lavender despite her illness. It was a soothing scent I had always associated with her. Feeling satisfied she was comfortable, I moved to the rocking chair. It was hard to say why I was so troubled by the attention Levi paid her. He was handsome and wealthy. Those were not flaws. Perhaps I was too cautious. I had wanted Elma to find a kind and humble partner, but I also knew I had a tendency to be overly protective when it came to her, my chosen sister. She was free to make her own match. As I drifted off to sleep, my thoughts roamed to Cornwall and what my aunt would say if she knew Elma was ill.

I woke with a start, aware of deep voices whispering near Elma's bed.

"The babbling is consistent with yellow fever," the doctor was saying.

I sprang from the chair but could not put words to my fear.

"I've never seen her so pale," Levi said.

"It's the tinge of yellow that disturbs me," the doctor muttered. "If it's the great sickness, she'll turn a most unnatural shade of mustard. There's no mistaking it."

"And then?" I asked.

"And then she'll begin to bleed."

"From the nose?" I said, recalling a young boy whose nose bled for days before his death from the fever. His mother tried everything to stanch the flow, propping him up in bed and stuffing his nostrils with torn rags. But when blood began to spill from his ears, nothing more could be done. I had heard that the sick were being quarantined at Belle Vue, a rustic estate along the East River that had been converted to an isolation hospital. It was reassuring, I supposed, to know that the ailing were getting medical aid, but the treatments sounded nearly as barbaric as the disease itself: ice-water baths, blood purges, sweating cures, metal rods, blistering the skin.

"Nose, eyes, uterus—I've heard of instances in which the pores themselves bleed."

There was a comforting weight on my shoulder. I turned and my chin brushed against Levi's warm hand.

"It is not yet the hot season," the doctor said, "and there have not been any cases reported this year."

Elma tossed her head, mumbling gibberish, and the doctor leaned over her.

"Mrs. Ring." He stood, tilting his head to the side and studying Elma. "Could she have a bit of water?"

"Certainly," I said, reaching for the pitcher.

"Boiled would be better."

"Yes, of course." Reluctant to leave, I looked over my shoulder as I stepped into the hallway and again as I started down the stairs.

The mood in the room was different when I returned minutes later. Both men were quiet, leaving the impression that I had interrupted their conversation. Elma was calmer too, but I had the uneasy feeling that she had been calling Levi's name again.

The doctor reached for his bag "Her eyes are clear, so I don't think she's in danger, but keep others away and take this." He pressed a clear glass vial into my hand. Impossibly light, it was smaller than a robin's egg, and as fragile. I could see that the liquid inside was the color of blood. "It's laudanum," he said, "to relieve her discomfort. Dispense only a drop at a time and only if she is in pain."

My palm grew warm and I shuddered. Derived from opium, laudanum was known to be addictive and potentially lethal. "Is it necessary?" I asked.

The doctor folded my fingers closed. "Have it on hand."

I have often wondered what would have happened if I had simply refused, pushed it back at him with a firm *No, thank thee.* After the men left, I went to Elma's bureau. The top drawer squeaked open as if protesting the intrusion. Pushing aside stockings and undergarments, I buried the vial deep in back, relieved to be rid of it.

Days passed and, like a lost soul who had innocently paddled into a riptide, I felt that I was on the verge of drowning. Yellow fever claimed its first victim of that summer: a prominent merchant and war hero. Days later, the midwife who helped bring Patience into the world fell ill. Doctors performed bleeding and purges but were unable to stop the flow of blood and bile. Both her children followed her to the grave. The following week, three cases were reported in a single night. The number doubled, and doubled again, until fever consumed the city.

The public was warned to avoid fatigue, hot sun, and night air, to walk in the center of the street away from infected homes, not to shake hands. The daily papers printed advertisements blaming the use of strong malt liquor and distilled spirits for weakening men's resistance. A leading scholar wrote a two-volume work claiming the epidemic was caused by volcanic eruptions in Sicily. Others said the poor were dying because they ate an abundance of watermelon. The Common Council faulted "manifold sins, immorality, and profaneness." Federalists labeled the scourge a foreign contagion, while Republicans cited abominable filth and the incompetence of Federalist magistrates.

The acrid stench of death filled the air as I entered the market. With its pyramids of ripe fruit, the Fly Market had always been lively and colorful. Now roosters roamed free, pecking rotting produce. People hurried through the deserted aisles. Most clutched garlic to their noses and mouths or wore satchels of camphor around their necks to ward off the fever. The coffee tents were gone, replaced by rows of caskets, the pine still green as if the trees could not mature fast enough to keep up with demand.

"Coffins of all sizes!" boys cried, hawking their wares.

"Where's your pretty cousin?" the fruit vendor asked as I chose berries. He was an Italian man with smiling eyes who had always paid special attention to Elma.

"She has been ill. Thankfully, it was nothing serious." Elma's fever had broken a week earlier, and yesterday she was well enough to share stories with Charles.

"Moral squalor causes yellow fever," said a slight woman sniffing tomatoes.

I wanted to ask her if a bad tomato had caused her pinched expression, but when she set it down, her features remained sour.

"Forty-five people died yesterday," she added. "The dead cart's overflowing and the pits at potter's field are full. 'Course, that's the only place families are allowed to bury fever victims."

I nearly dropped the berries as I silently vowed to keep the children inside, in my bedroom, if need be.

"Sailors are burning corpses at the Battery," the woman said. "At this rate, the city will soon be a ghost town."

The vendor looked past her, clearly eager for her to go. The macabre chatter was not good for business. "Isaac!" he called.

I caught a glimpse of a navy jacket. "Is that Isaac Hatfield?" I asked, because the man had not stopped.

"Do you know him?" He shook his head. "Of course you do, he's sweet on your cousin."

"Elma?" I said, as if there were any doubt.

"A pretty girl is like—" The vendor smirked, fanning gnats off the fruit.

Downy feathers landed at my feet, and I turned to see an elderly woman with cloudy eyes plucking a headless chicken. Stalls away, flies swarmed moldering slabs of meat.

Cannon fire pierced the air.

I jumped, knocking the vendor's stand, making berries spill and tomatoes roll. One hit the ground, bursting into pulp and seeds. "What on earth?" I asked, looking around the empty market for a place to seek cover.

"Some magistrate thinks firing cannons to concuss air will chase the fever away."

Sick to my stomach, I bought a few potatoes and a handful of leeks and practically ran home.

An earthenware water jug sat in the corner of our doorway. It was not one of ours, and it was not filled with water. As I picked it up, I noticed a slip of paper plugging the spout.

LIARS AND THIEVES was written across the top in stiff block letters. For the life of me, I did not know what to make of it. I turned to see if anyone was watching. Isaac Hatfield had been at the market. Was he watching me? I glanced up at our windows, but no one was looking out. Behind me, Greenwich Street, like the market, was deserted.

LIARS AND THIEVES. The cryptic message was printed on a torn newspaper scrap. The ink had bled, obscuring most of the story beneath, but my eye caught a familiar name:

It gives us pleasure to learn that measures for supplying the city with water are going into immediate effect. A number of laborers are busily employed in clearing out the spacious well at Lispenard's Meadows . . .

"Mama!" Charles said, flinging the door open so that it banged on the hinges.

"Charles," I snapped, "it's not safe out here." The empty streets seemed stalked, haunted.

"I thought Hamilton was for commerce," Elias complained as I entered. "Closing the ports is bad business." He and Levi sat at the dining table, exactly where I had left them an hour earlier.

Elma stood over Levi. Her lashes fluttered against her cheek as she gazed down at him. I was not insensitive to the affection between them. Nor did I consider it a small thing. I had lain awake every night since Elma's recovery, worrying that he would hurt her, and she already had a fragile constitution. It felt frivolous, almost unlucky, for them to so intensely focus on their dalliance when an invisible killer was consuming the city outside.

"There are those, including Hamilton's own doctor, who believe the fever arrived on merchant ships," Levi said.

"Well, it's here now. What's the point of closing the ports?" Elias asked.

"Perhaps we can prevent the scourge from spreading," Elma said.

Elias shook his head, making it clear he not only disagreed, he resented her input. "Without trade, we may all die of starvation."

While Elias's habit of prioritizing business over practically everything else was a constant source of worry, in this instance I did not disagree. Closing the ports would only add hardship to heartache.

Elma took my basket and began unpacking. "Were the streets very quiet?"

"Empty. People are afraid to venture out. Everyone has an opinion about what causes the fever, and rumors are spreading as fast as the disease. A woman in the market blamed it on sin."

"It is polluted water that's killing people," Elma said, "but Levi's going to fix it." She spoke as if Levi could single-handedly destroy the menace beyond our walls. And Levi did not disagree.

"Pipes have already been laid from Pearl Street down to Chapel," he said. "In less than a month, homes there will have water."

"A month?" I said, recalling Burr's plan to lay miles of pipes. "Surely it will take longer than that to tap water all the way from the Bronx."

"Our men are digging wells instead," Levi said.

"Wells?" The newspaper scrap fluttered in my hand. Somehow I knew it was meant for me. It was hurtful but ultimately harmless, mischief, the kind of thing meant to stir trouble. And it reeked of Richard Croucher. I was certain he had left it, though I was less sure why. If he had a bone to pick with Levi, he could do it himself. Still, there was something about Levi's arrogance that begged response.

"Thy men are digging wells at Lispenard's Meadows?" I asked. The disgruntled man named Lispenard who spoke at the water meeting had referred to his land as a swamp.

Levi's challenging gaze met mine. "Yes."

"But that water's filthy. Burr and thy brother promised freshwater."

Levi frowned, and for the first time I saw a clear resemblance to his older brother. "It can be fixed if street wash is kept out and people stop dumping garbage." He looked at me so severely, it was almost as if he believed I tossed the trash there myself.

"Digging wells is faster," Elias said. "Water could be available this fall."

Should I have been impressed? Digging wells in a teeming cesspool instead of piping in freshwater seemed like a major concession.

There was a knock on the door. When I went to answer, I found our neighbor Elizabeth Watkins wiping away tears.

"I won't come in," she said, twisting the top button of her dress until it dangled by a thread. "It's just that Lily Forrest died this morning. They're taking her out now. I thought perhaps Charles shouldn't see."

"Lily Forrest?" Charles was the same age as Lily, and the two often played together. I thought of her yellow ringlets, which we all admired, then shuddered, imagining them streaked red with blood. *Liars and thieves.* It was wrong to think the message was harmless. Polluted water was killing people. Not just people, but children. *Liars, thieves, and murderers.*

"It started early yesterday with hiccups, then the whites of her eyes turned yellow; her lips too," Elizabeth said, clearly savoring each gory detail. "After supper, the poor dear started vomiting black bile by the mouthful, and when she cried, her tears were as bloody as a demon's. Lorena was screaming loud enough to wake the—"

Mumbling an excuse, I shut the door in Elizabeth's face. To my eye, her complexion had a distinctly yellow hue.

"Elias," I said, turning to him, "it's high time we take the children to Cornwall; the sooner the better."

Elias rubbed his temples, where gray hairs were rapidly overtaking brown curls. "Every person with a dung cart or carriage has fled to Greenwich or Harlem Village. Next there will be vagrants on the streets, robbers looting and burning homes." He shook his head, gazing toward the store door. "Even if goods are rotting, I have to stay and protect what's left."

I was sympathetic to his plight, but I was also scared, frightened of vagabonds and disease. "Then I'll go with the children. Elma will come with us."

Elias scraped his chair away from the table. "It may be best."

"Elma," I said, breathing a sigh of relief, "if we start packing now, we can catch tomorrow's boat."

"Caty," she said, "I can't go."

"Why on earth not?"

"If I go, who will care for the men?"

I lowered my voice. "They'll make do. Even Elias thinks it's necessary."

"It *is* necessary for you and the children. But I will stay."

I understood her desire to prove herself but not her timing. "Elma, dozens are dying each day. Let's not argue—"

"I'm not arguing," she said, raising her chin. "I'm insisting."

If I could have left immediately, I would have. Concern for the children surpassed all other worries. Distracted by fear and grateful that Elma was charitable enough to remain behind and care for the men, I did not have time to question her motives.

—5—

Settling into Cornwall was harder than I could have imagined. I had never seen my aunt Mary without Elma, and the changes in her were troubling. They had once been as intertwined as our white picket fence and its rosebush; it was difficult to say who supported whom. With Elma gone, the answer was clear. Stripped of Elma's bloom, my aunt looked run-down and spindly. It was impossible to shake the sense that I had stolen her child away.

"News from New York," Aunt Mary called from our back porch, waving a letter so that it fluttered like a flag in the breeze.

Beneath a cloudless sky, a scattering of gold leaves foretold the end of summer—and, hopefully, the end of the scourge. Thanking my aunt, I found a seat in the shade of a nearby oak. It had been weeks since I had heard from Elias.

The letter was fastened with three drips of wax, more puddle than seal. Elias often performed two tasks at once but usually did both well; mess was unusual. With trembling hands, I tore it open and was startled by the scrawl that confronted me.

Elias wrote that the yellow-fever epidemic was mercifully mild. Still, many had fled the city and business was slow. His tone was alternately petulant and tender: "My shirts are soiled and need mending, and I miss the sound of the children in the morning and thy warmth beside me at night."

I rested my head against the tree, touched by his candor. It was unlike him to be affectionate, and I wondered if he had come to appreciate me in my absence.

Aunt Mary came and sat by my side. "What's he say?"

"Not much," I said, aware that she was really asking for news of Elma. Sun peeked through the foliage, and the sound of Charles's laughter as he battled imaginary foes warmed my heart. No matter how he grew, he would always be my firstborn, the tiny infant who had nestled by my side as I marveled at his perfection and worried after his needs. I wondered if my aunt felt the same way about Elma. What a mixed blessing her birth must have been.

"How is Gulielma?" Aunt Mary asked. I couldn't remember the last time I had heard her full name spoken aloud. I studied Elias's words, as if I might find a sentence or two about Elma if I just searched a bit harder. My eyes focused on the bottom of the page. "Caty," he wrote, "come home."

It was a direct appeal, but I read and reread the sentence as if it were written in code. The baldness of his plea mystified me. Elias had books to keep and orders to plan and had promised to fix the shutters, which were missing slats and rattled in the wind. He had been cold and standoffish since our move to Manhattan, and the situation had grown worse since Elma's arrival. Perhaps he felt threatened by our affinity, the sisterly bond he would never be able to replicate. He came to bed long after I had gone to sleep, woke before I rose, and passed whole days in the store, only returning for meals. We had a houseful of boarders, so I could not imagine that he was lonesome. I wasn't exactly alarmed, but I was troubled. Something wasn't quite right.

"Does he mention Elma?" my aunt asked again.

"Not specifically, but it sounds like the household is in order. I'm sure she is helping enormously."

Aunt Mary smiled wanly. "I worry about her, especially now that no one is there to look after her."

I watched Charles climb a discarded barrel. On warm summer days, we tied the barrel to the oak and floated it in the creek, where Charles rode it like a horse and called it Cider, in homage to its original contents. But while the sun was still powerful each midday, the nights had become brisk, and Cider had been retired for the season. I held my breath as Charles scurried over the slimy barrel, slipped down the side, and climbed up again. Worry is part and parcel of parenting. While the sight of Charles toppling headfirst into the grass made me want to leap to my feet and catch him, I also knew the importance of letting go; I would have thought my aunt understood that.

"Elias is there with her," I said.

My aunt's eyes followed a bumblebee as it hummed beside a scarlet rose. "You know Elma. Once she had her mind set on moving, there was no holding her back."

I was sympathetic to Aunt Mary's loss, but I could not understand why she wanted Elma to share her lonely fate. The town didn't openly gossip about the two of them anymore, but no one had forgotten. If Elma had stayed, her prospects for marriage were slim to none. I did not know what the city would offer, but I understood that Elma could walk down its streets in anonymity and peace. She would continue to help me with the boardinghouse, perhaps find work in a millinery shop, and one day, God willing, she would marry and have a family.

"There are opportunities for young and industrious people in New York," I said, aware that I was beginning to sound like Elias.

"Opportunities can be dangerous for a young woman. Elma wants to be accepted—and loved."

"Most girls dream about finding love." I thought about Elias romancing me on the breezy banks of the Hudson. I had been deeply moved the day we first kissed, but those feelings were now as distant as summer heat on a bitter winter night. I could recall my pleasure but not the sensation. Marriage was far different than I'd imagined it would be. We were both exhausted. Elias always worried about money. And I alternately resented his distraction and was relieved when he left me alone. But we had two beautiful children. Life was not a fairy tale.

Aunt Mary seemed lost in her own thoughts. "The man I fell in love with," she said, "Elma's father, was very kind. Elma has his eyes, and his stubborn streak." In a gesture I had always associated with Elma, my aunt tucked a loose hair behind her ear, and, for an instant, her expression was almost youthful. "Together, it was as if we were one. He made me feel more like myself than ever before but *better*. I wanted to be better, for him. I was sure we would share a wonderful life."

I could not recall an instance when anyone in my family had revealed a detail of Elma's birth. I wondered why my aunt was telling me these things now.

"What happened?" I asked, a breath above a whisper.

"The war happened. Perhaps we should have married before he left. He offered," she said, her tone challenging, as if she had imagined defending herself many times, "but I was convinced there would be plenty of time to wed under happier circumstances. Elma's father marched alongside General Arnold in Quebec . . ." Her voice trailed off. "He never returned."

"He lost his life," I said, filling in her words. Was she worried that Elma too would never come back?

"By the time word reached me, I was four months along." She smoothed her skirt. "A woman who gives birth out of wedlock is a villain, no matter the facts. Some part of me foolishly hoped his family would embrace Elma, that they would see his legacy in her. Maybe if she had been a boy . . . We went to live with them, but the situation was unbearable. As young as she was, Elma sensed their disapproval. One day I found her in the yard, picking dandelions. She was crying. When I asked what was wrong, she couldn't answer, as if sadness were a condition she had come to accept. That's when I left."

"And came here?"

"Yes. Your father's been very generous."

"But not Mother."

A single cloud screened the sun, darkening Aunt Mary's expression. "Your mother is frightened by what she doesn't understand. There was an incident after you left. Elma was quite taken with a man, and he seemed to return her affection. But your mother was convinced nothing good would come of it."

"Elma never breathed a word," I said, feeling stung.

"As I said, nothing came of it."

"Who was he?"

"A handsome fellow. But he was just passing through, and your mother didn't trust him. More than once, she pointed out that a man like that would never marry a girl like Elma. She practically chased him away. It seems my bad choices will forever color Elma's life." She shook her head. "Caty, I was frightened to let Elma go to the city. I thought she would be safer here with me, but I suspect you are right. It is selfish of me to hold her back."

"I never said that."

Aunt Mary smiled, or at least her lips curved upward. It was the saddest expression I had ever seen. "Not in so many words."

The wind blew, rustling the letter on my lap. I turned from my aging aunt to Elias's letter, and my concern for him began to fade. It would have been kind to include a word or two about Elma, but he was too focused on his own needs to consider anyone else. No doubt he had written late at night after a hard day's work. Candlelight and exhaustion make even the hardiest souls lonely. Maybe he did miss me, or perhaps he was simply suffering a moment's weakness. Elias and I had our entire future ahead. Aunt Mary would spend the rest of her life alone.

I folded the letter and tucked it in my pocket. I would return home sooner than later, but, in truth, I was in no great rush.

We remained in Cornwall three more weeks.

Elias met us at the boat slip. He embraced Charles and took Patience in his arms, more loving than he had been since the early days of our courtship.

"Caty," he said, when he came to me. His eyes, so full of pride while greeting his children, were mixed with an emotion closer to humility. He took me in his arms, and I smiled to think that perhaps he had truly missed me.

After weeks in the country, returning to the city was like waking from a gentle dream to a colicky babe. Harbor winds gave way to rancid smells as our carriage, rattled over each cobblestone. Others had come back to the city as the threat passed, and it was more congested than ever with hogs, dogs, and people vying for space. Elias turned toward Greenwich Street, narrowly missing an oncoming carriage. We bounced over a hole and swerved to avoid a peddler. The man shook his fist, sputtering obscenities.

Elma was leaning out our front door, craning her neck to see down the street, as we drove up. Levi stood by her side, their shoulders grazing in the tight doorway.

"Elma!" Charles jumped down before the carriage had stopped.

Elma twirled him around, and even Elias laughed. I bounced Patience on my hip. New York City was dirty and crowded, but in my absence it had started to feel like home.

"Elma, you'll strain yourself," Levi said, setting his hand on her shoulder.

The gesture was subtle yet intimate. Elma seemed to physically soften when Levi touched her. She lowered her chin, her expression all but hidden behind a curtain of hair. Graceful and mature, her beauty more ethereal than ever. She had not gained back the weight lost during her illness. Her expression was drawn and her collarbones jutted out under her dress. Oddly, her frail appearance was now in vogue. Elizabeth Watkins told us that the fashionable ladies who strolled the Battery promenade took laudanum to achieve the dainty femininity that came so naturally to Elma.

"Levi," Elias said, "come help with the baggage."

Levi hardly acknowledged him. "I'll return the carriage," he said.

Cradling Patience, I followed Elma inside. The house smelled like warm bread. Every chair, pot, and pan was in place and the hearth was freshly swept, yet something was wrong. I scanned the room—mantel, windowsills, and pantry—but was unable to find the source of my misgivings.

Richard Croucher shuffled into the parlor, breathless and flushed. It was as if he had walked up a flight of stairs rather than down. "About time you're back," he said. It was an odd greeting, but one typical of the man.

Elias dragged the trunk inside.

"Busy as usual, eh, Ring?" Croucher said, slightly too loudly. "Always running 'ere, scurrying there." Elias pointedly ignored him. Croucher widened his eyes at me, then turned to Elma, looking her up and down in a way that turned my stomach.

Elma scooped Patience from my arms. "Let me feed her. Charles, come help."

Charles shook his head. "She's messy."

"Come along now," Elma said. I waited for her to craft some kind of game to entice Charles, but she hurried away.

I turned to Elias. "I thought thee said the store was quiet."

"Quiet as the grave," Croucher said. He pronounced each syllable with care as if determined to convey his point. "But your *Husband* managed to keep active."

"Are the shutters fixed?" I asked, straining to sound light. Croucher enjoyed stirring up trouble, and I refused to allow it to spoil my homecoming.

Elias placed his hat back on. "I'll go help Levi," he said, though I had already heard the carriage drive off.

Elias came to bed late that night. Despite his warm greeting, I could tell he was avoiding me. Sitting close in the darkness of our room, I smelled his breath and listened for slurred words but found no evidence that he had been back at the bottle.

"I think Elma is in love with Levi," I said. I had thought of little else all day, and there seemed no point in mincing words. "And I believe Levi loves her too."

Time away had given me a fresh perspective. Elma had managed the house in my absence. While it was easy for me to remember her as the vulnerable child who stood at our doorway on a cold winter's night, I could see that she was truly a woman now, capable of making her own choices. If I questioned her judgment or held her back, I was no better than my aunt.

Elias dropped a boot to the floor. "Ezra Weeks will never allow it." He sounded resigned, not tipsy.

"Well, it is not his choice." I had my misgivings about Levi, but I was loath to see Elma impugned or, worse, heartbroken.

The second boot landed with a thud. "It may as well be. Levi depends on his brother. Ezra raised him and supports him to this day. He won't be satisfied unless Levi marries up."

"Ezra has a wife of his own."

"She's barren. That makes Levi and any of his future children Ezra's only heirs. He hasn't worked this hard to watch it all disappear."

"Elma may not be wealthy, but kindness and sincerity are worth far more than all the money in the world. Surely even Ezra sees that. Levi would be lucky to have her."

Elias pulled off his socks, wadding them into a tight ball and tossing them to the middle of the room. "Money is one thing, but Elma is disgraced by her birth."

A cart passed outside. I listened as its dull rumble faded into the distance. I could not recall Elias ever referring to Elma's past, and I had grown comfortable with his silence.

"Well, thankfully it's not his decision."

The bed creaked as Elias rocked forward. "Caty, listen to me." He sounded somber and all too sober. "We cannot afford to offend Ezra. He controls the purse strings of Burr's water company, and if he grants us even a little bit of stock, we'll be able to pay him back and then some."

"Pay him back?" A shiver shot through me. "We owe Ezra money?"

"It was a loan of sorts. Remember?"

"I thought he invested in the boardinghouse. That's not the same."

Elias clenched his fists. "Stop twisting my words. Everything is fine. All we need is a few shares. With Burr at the helm, that company is bound to succeed." He lay back in bed. "Now go to sleep. I haven't slept in ages."

"Why not?" I asked.

"Caty, it's late."

I was sure I would not sleep a wink. Elias's sentimental letter, peculiar yet touching, was now another brick on the barrier rising between us. My husband had turned into a stranger. "Did something happen while I was gone?" He did not answer, so I asked again, more directly. "Elias, what happened?"

"I wasn't going to say, but . . ." Elias kept his back toward me while he spoke. "I don't know. Maybe I don't want to know. A few weeks back, I woke in the middle of the night and heard talking in Isaac Hatfield's room, but Hatfield was out of town."

"It must have been Levi and Will."

"Why would Levi and Will be in Hatfield's room?"

"Why would anyone be there?"

The candle flickered and hissed as the wick sank into an oily pool. "Elma kept house."

"Elma wasn't likely dusting in the middle of the night."

"I didn't say she was."

"Elias!" He shot up. My harsh tone startled both of us. "I'm in no mood for riddles."

Elias shook his head. "I wish this were a joke. Caty, what I'm trying to say is that Elma was *with* Levi. When I went up in the morning, I found the sheets tumbled, and her clothes—the ones she'd been wearing the day before—were scattered about on the floor."

"What?" My head reeled as if I had been physically struck. "That's impossible."

Elias remained still. His silence was more unsettling than any accusation.

"What's more," I said, "why would they be in Isaac Hatfield's room when Elma's room is steps away?" I shook my head. "It makes no sense."

"Lust is reckless." Elias's voice dropped. "A man—men—they forget themselves."

"What? Did he force himself on her?"

"No! Not that. No."

I swung my legs over the side of the bed. I was filled with dread and anxiety. Elma's mother had planted seeds of doubt that were rapidly taking hold. I could not specifically say that Elma had taken advantage of my absence, but I felt betrayed. I needed to talk with her.

Not wanting to disturb the other tenants, I tiptoed upstairs. My concern turned to confusion when I cracked open her bedroom door and peered inside. The curtains were drawn and the lamp was on the bureau, casting a warm glow. Elma lay on the bed. Her back was propped against a pillow, her legs outstretched, and her feet bare. Levi sat by her side. His hair, which I had never seen untied, hung loose around his shoulders. He leaned protectively toward her, his head lowered as if to hear her better. I watched, enthralled. No one had ever listened to me with such intensity. I was just outside the door, yet neither noticed me.

"It's wrong," Elma said. "Dishonest, maybe illegal."

"It's politics."

"Men died fighting for our freedom. Women lost husbands and sons. Children lost their fathers. This is no way to honor them."

I thought of Elma's father, wondering if she knew what he really was. He had given his life for our young country. And she had sacrificed in countless other ways.

"I shouldn't have said anything."

Elma rested her hand on his and looked into his eyes. "I'm glad you did. It's too much to keep bottled inside."

I should have left or made my presence known. Instead, I held my breath and leaned closer. The pair sat in a silence so comfortable it was impossible not to admire it. Theirs was the kind of intimacy I had always craved. A tender awareness I had never experienced with Elias. I don't know how much time went by, a minute, maybe two. The air was heavy and time moved slowly.

"I'm not sure what to do," Levi said. "He's my brother. He raised me."

"Which is exactly the reason to speak up. You'll spare him a terrible mistake. How will he be able to live with himself? How will you?"

If it were possible to move closer without quite touching, Levi did.

"I wish we could go somewhere far away, where there was only you and me, alone." He reached forward, brushing the hair above her ear, and it was then that I noticed the ivory hair comb. I had not seen Elma wear it since the morning after she arrived, but I remembered it perfectly: bone-white, arched, and as delicate as she was, with a silky ribbon woven through the teeth to dangle against Elma's curls.

Slowly, Elma twirled the ribbon around her finger before unclasping the comb and holding it in her palm. "It's the most beautiful gift I've ever received."

Levi touched the soft skin above her eyes, then her mouth. "It's a promise," he said. "See your name? I carved it myself."

Lips trembling, Elma ran her finger over the inscription.

The bedsprings sighed as Levi tipped forward to stroke her cheek. His caress was gentle and slow. He said her name once, then twice. Elma responded with a soft moan, one so intimate that it made me blush. A small smile crept across the corners of Levi's mouth as his lips parted to meet hers.

"Elma!" I pushed the door open.

Levi bolted upright, looking entirely changed; his eyes blazed angry and menacing. I stepped back and the door slammed in my face. But not before I caught a glimmer of glass on the nightstand. It was the briefest of glimpses one fraught with the anxiety of the moment. Still, even in a court of law, facing the most distinguished legal minds of our time, it would be impossible to deny what I saw: a gemlike vial stained reddish-brown, the color of blood.

~6~

I was unsure what the morning would bring, but when Levi entered the parlor he was docile and obliging.

"Mrs. Ring," he said. "I lit a fire in my chamber last night. Would you be kind enough to check on it later and make sure it died out?"

"Certainly," I said, too troubled to say more. Thankfully, Charles was playing peekaboo with Patience, and their giggles filled the silence. I sifted flour and kept my eyes on the bowl, hoping Levi would leave. The other men had come and gone, yet he continued to linger.

"I rekindled it just before daybreak and am worried it's not properly extinguished," he said a bit too loudly, and I understood what he was explaining: He had spent the night in his own bed.

"Very well, Levi."

Charles stuck Patience's small hands in the flour and began to stamp ghostly prints along the table. Patience reached out and tugged his hair, hard.

"Ouch!" he said, swatting her away and knocking an egg to the floor.

Patience began to bawl.

"Charles!" I shouted, looking down at the mess. The sticky blob mirrored my mood.

He turned to me, wide-eyed and confused. "Where's Elma?"

"Fetch a rag," I snapped, unable to answer his question. Elma had managed to dodge me all morning, going to the water pump, the market, and Elizabeth Watkins's house. Aware that my anger was misplaced, I took a breath, turned back to Levi, and smiled tightly. I wanted to confront him, but it would be easier to face Elma. Or so I thought.

Half the day passed before Elma appeared. I cornered her toward evening, while she was in her room, washing her hair.

"Elma." I rested my hand on her shoulder and felt the warmth of her skin through her dressing gown. "Aunt Mary has entrusted thy care to me." My eyes scanned the nightstand. I had not expected to find the vial of laudanum, and I was right. It was gone.

Soapy hair hung over Elma's face, but I distinctly heard her sigh.

"It's wrong to entertain Levi in thy room," I said.

"Help me rinse?"

I reached for the pitcher and pulled it away, causing water to spill on the floor. "This is serious."

"Caty." She sounded mature, a bit thorny. "I can't talk like this."

I poured the tepid water slowly over her head while she massaged the soap out. When the pitcher was empty, she sat up, flipping her hair so that it fell across her shoulders and down her back. The room filled with the scent of lavender as she dried the ends with a towel.

"My friendship with Levi is not what you think."

"Elma, I don't know what to think." I took a deep breath, determined to speak my mind. "Elias told me that while I was out of town he found thy clothing on the floor in Isaac Hatfield's room."

The towel dropped to her lap. "And you believe him?"

I exhaled. I had wanted her to deny the accusation. It relieved some of my guilt at having left her alone, as well as the resentment I felt toward her for having betrayed my trust. "Then tell me what he saw."

Fan-shaped water stains spread across the shoulders of her dressing gown as she shook her head. "Don't believe everything Elias says."

I was both offended and alarmed. "Elias is my husband. He's the father of my children." No matter how much Elias changed as we adjusted to city life, it was essential that I remained loyal to him. I had thought Elma understood that.

"Of course," she said, as if reminding herself. She swallowed, then spoke in a rush. "I was collecting laundry and was not as tidy as I should have been. I must have dropped some clothing on the floor. I'm sorry."

My heart sank. I recognized her brisk tone. It was the same one she had used throughout childhood when she did not want to admit she had ripped a dress or lost a coin. "And last night?" I said before she could continue. I was certain we would both regret whatever half-truths escaped her mouth. "I saw it with my own eyes. When I went up to thy room—Elma, if it was innocent, why did Levi slam the door?"

"Caty, I am sorry. We were just surprised." She seemed as reluctant to betray Levi as I had been toward Elias. Her loyalty only increased my ire. "Levi can be impulsive," she said. "I'm sorry he behaved that way. There was nothing to be done at the time. I knew you and I would speak today."

"That doesn't explain why he was sitting so close." I blushed remembering how Levi had caressed her face hungrily.

Her eyes grew darker and more distant. "Levi's become a dear friend. He knocked on my door to wish me good night. We began talking. He's lonely and, well, I know what it's like to be alone."

I nodded; certainly that much was true. But as I thought back on how she had written without her mother's knowledge, asking to come to New York, I could not escape the feeling that she had taken advantage of me. "Elma, did thou know Levi before he arrived here?"

She took time answering. "Levi did pass through Cornwall on his way from New England down to Manhattan. We met one morning at the mercantile. I bumped into a sack of nails." She giggled, then covered her mouth, her eyes widening at the memory. "I was clumsy because I was looking at him. I'd never seen such a handsome face! He helped me collect the nails that had fallen. Afterward, he walked me home. We spoke for nearly two hours." Elma prattled on, more enthusiastic than I had ever heard her. "He stayed for a week longer than he had planned. One afternoon when it was breezy, he wrapped his coat around my shoulders and I knew what it would be like to feel his embrace. Caty," she whispered, "we fell in love."

There was that word: *love*. It was not that I didn't consider love when I married, more that I did not grasp its true meaning. Elias was a good match, a solid and pious man of whom my parents approved. As a mother, I now understood what it was to love Charles and Patience more than life itself. My feelings toward Elias had always been different. I respected his work ethic and valued his opinion. We had created a life together. What I felt was affection, not love. Taught to do what was proper, it hadn't occurred to me to want more.

"Why should it matter if we already knew each other?" Elma said, her voice rising in defensiveness. "It means our feelings are real. They *last*."

I felt numb. Was I simply disappointed in Elma, or did I resent her secret and envy her passion?

"No." I shook my head. "It means . . ." *Lie* seemed too strong a word, but I would have used it if I had known what other confessions lay ahead. "Elma, why keep this from me?" I asked instead.

Color rose in her cheeks. "From the instant Levi walked in to this house, you thought he was no good for me. The only reason he's still here is because Elias thinks he can get something out of him."

The charge was true enough. I did not bother denying it.

Elma nodded as if confirming what she already knew. "It is well and fine for me to help you cook and clean, but you've made it quite clear that I don't deserve happiness." Tears rose to her eyes.

"Elma." I reached for her hand. My fingers touched as they circled round her wrist. Once, as a child, I had rescued a sparrow chick that had fallen from its nest and placed it back in the tree. I had the same feeling now, as if Elma might easily snap. "Elma, why say such a thing?" I asked, recalling how, hours after I had replaced the chick, I found it shriveled and dead in the grass.

Elma looked down at our hands. "If it were up to you, you would have sent him away, just like your mother did. I wanted to tell you, of course I did, and I kept waiting for the right moment. But you never gave him a chance."

Elias had said that Ezra Weeks would never accept Elma as Levi's wife. I was the least of her obstacles. "Elma," I said gently. "Perhaps our concerns are founded in reality. Maybe Levi's not the right—"

She pulled her hand away from mine. "Because he's wealthy? Or handsome?"

"He is undoubtedly handsome. But, Elma, Levi is desperate for his brother's approval. Elias says he's completely dependent on Ezra."

"Not everything is about money."

"I didn't say anything about money. It's just—thy behavior affects us too."

"Us? You mean if Ezra Weeks doesn't approve of me, Elias might suffer. He may not be able to trade on *that* particular connection."

"Thou of everyone should know I'm not that cold or calculating," I said. "From the start, I've had a bad feeling about Levi. Did thou ever ask why he is living here in a boardinghouse rather than with his brother?"

"To be near me."

"Then he should make his intentions clear. He should have spoken to Elias or me. Sought our approval instead of hiding behind closed doors."

"But you do *not* approve! That is most evident. And Elias—" Elma held the towel to her face. Moments passed before she took a deep breath and lowered it. "Caty." She leaned toward me, and her anger, which had been so quick to flare, seemed to have subsided. "You are my best friend in the world. My true sister. Please try to understand: Things—people are not always who they seem to be."

"Elias?" I whispered, so dizzy that I had to sit down on the bed.

She grew busy again, folding the towel and hanging it over the back of her chair. "Ezra may be influential," she said, "but that does not make him good, and Levi is beginning to see that."

"Ezra Weeks, of course," I said, breathing a sigh of relief. Still, Elma's anger had troubled me; her sincerity was even more disarming. "See what?"

"The men who claim they are going to transform this city are nothing but"—her gaze met mine—"liars and thieves."

I had nearly forgotten the torn newspaper. "The note?"

She nodded. "The Manhattan Water Company." Her eyes, which

had been dull and dark with indifference, shone with secrecy as she lowered her voice. "The water company is an enormous fraud."

"That can't be. I saw their meeting with my own eyes, heard their plans. Elias was there, and Burr and Hamilton. Why would they do all that work for nothing?"

She bit her lip, choosing words carefully. "I didn't say it was for nothing."

"Oh, Elma, really! Those powerful men aren't just playing in the mud." Seeing her cringe, I lowered my voice to match hers. "Tell me. No more secrets."

She picked up a small looking glass and pinched her cheeks. I had never seen her do anything like it before. She looked different, womanly.

"Elma, what else did Levi say?"

"He said the Manhattan Water Company is about politics, not water. By pretending to provide water, Burr has become immensely popular, and he's throwing his support behind Jefferson. All of those lovely wells will never be connected to a water source."

I remembered the elaborate plans. The Greek god pouring chiseled water. The gateway leading nowhere. "All that hubbub? For nothing?" The idea was so far-fetched I might have laughed. Except instinct told me it was no joke. Somehow the water crisis and the election had become one and the same. I still did not fully understand how they were connected, but I was just now being introduced to Colonel Burr and his web of lies. It would take months for me to understand the connection between Burr's ambition, the Weeks brothers' greed, and Elma's undoing.

Worse yet, I still could not understand her silence. "But why leave a cryptic note? Why not simply talk to me?"

"I know it was silly, but I promised Levi I would not tell a soul. Still." She shook her head and her voice grew indignant. "What Burr and Ezra are doing is wrong. I told Levi to speak to his brother, but Ezra is his only living relative. Levi thinks he owes him respect and gratitude."

"Doesn't he?"

"Not if what Ezra is doing is dangerous. People will continue to die because of him! I thought if you understood what was happening, you would talk to Elias. He attends the meetings. I was sure he'd speak up."

"And what would I have said? Elias wouldn't have paid any attention to a torn newspaper scrap and an anonymous note."

"Elias has a lot at stake. I thought he would be up in arms. I thought you would see—these men are corrupt."

"Half the city was sick with fever. Lily Forrest had just died. All I could think about was the children. I didn't have time to decipher clues."

Elma nodded. "It's just as well. I should not have betrayed Levi's trust. You can't breathe a word."

"Elma, Levi lives in our home, which Ezra has *invested* in." Necessity—or a lack of choice—may have caused my principles to warp, but I still had trouble accepting Ezra's loan. It was a struggle to speak with conviction. "We owe them money. If Elias is mixed up in their crooked deals, I must warn him."

"No!" She caught my sleeve, pulling me closer. "Caty, I'm begging you. Give it a week, maybe less. Levi says the legislature will vote on Burr's company any day now. The fraud will be common knowledge soon enough."

The room had grown shadowy, and I lit a lamp as if it might illuminate her explanation. The bits of conversation I had heard seemed to support what she was saying. I looked down at the floor where the pitcher had spilled. Loose strands of Elma's dark hair floated in the murky puddle like tendrils.

"And then what?" I asked.

"And then Burr's sham will be clear. Elias, and everyone else, will know the truth."

"But will Elias suffer? I can't allow that. *We* cannot allow that. Our home is at risk."

She squeezed my finger and looked into my eyes. "You have always said I should listen to the voice inside me, the one that knows right from wrong. That's what I'm doing. This might not be the most expedient solution or the most obvious, but right will prevail. Caty, trust me. I am following my conscience."

The expression made me pause. Elma never attended meeting, and it was rare for her to cite Quaker principles. Part of me resented her for using them to defend Levi and his lies. Still, I did not doubt her sincerity. She believed in Levi and was following her heart. I vowed I would speak to Elias if the truth did not surface in a week's time. Until then, I needed to trust Elma. How could I deny her that?

The usual assortment of women, children, and servants of all color, shape, and size were gathered around the dilapidated pump when I went to collect water the next day. Elma normally fetched the water now, but I wanted to see the ruse for myself.

Elma's explanation was so outlandish, I'd been reluctant to believe her, despite my misgivings about the Weeks brothers. But I knew that even the most sinister imagination could never concoct such an elaborate scheme. Elma had deceived me by omission, but she would never truly betray me. I didn't fully understand the details, nor did I grasp their ramifications. And I certainly did not foresee the danger that would soon engulf our family. Trying to be optimistic, I told myself that confiding in Elma proved Levi's affection. Still, like a scratch in my throat, an irritant I could not swallow, I could not shake the notion that theirs was an intimacy built on lies.

"Well's dry," I heard a man grumble as I wound my way through the throng. People were milling about, as stagnant as the water. It had been an unusually warm autumn. Leaves were crumbling to dust on trees before falling into brittle heaps. Charles leapt from pile to pile, crunching foliage underfoot.

"How are we expected to live?" a woman beside me cried. She held an infant in her arms. He was quiet—sickly, not content.

"That one's working on it," said another woman, whom I

recognized from Greenwich Street. She pointed into the crowd and there, amidst the shabby group, stood Ezra Weeks.

Ezra was not tall, though he seemed to tower above everyone else. I hung back, observing, as he directed a dozen workers. Some were digging a trench the size and depth of a grave. Others tossed logs from a wagon, narrowly missing people.

"What's happening?" I asked the woman I recognized.

"Laying pipes," she said.

A haphazard assortment of misshapen logs lay scattered across the congested street. Some had large knobs or bits of bark reaching out like human limbs. They clearly would never be coaxed into forming a straight line to Greenwich Street or anywhere else.

"Wooden pipes?" I asked.

"Cheaper than iron," a man chimed in. "They hollow logs out, then seal them with tar."

There was no tar in sight, and very little water. "But the well is dry," I said.

"Pipes have to be connected so Burr can tell his stockholders that work's been done." He passed me a handbill.

To the Public, was printed in large letters on the top of the page. "Notwithstanding the intervention of a malignant fever, which occasioned so great and so large a desertion of the city, the waterworks have never been suspended. . . ." My eyes skimmed the page: ". . . a single well will yield a quantity excellent for drinking and good for every culinary purpose."

My stomach sank as I looked from the bold announcement to the dusty trench. So Elma had told me the truth. Sealing wooden pipes had to be exacting work, yet the workers tossed logs about with little care. The ones in the trench pitched shovels of dry dirt up onto the street, where it swirled in a funnel of dust and blew back into the pit.

Ezra stood downwind. He had tied a kerchief across his mouth, but that did not stop him from shouting orders. Levi was among the men, knee deep in dirt, nodding attentively at his brother's commands.

An older man, stooped and balding, shoved his way through the commotion. "They don't give a damn about water, just about fattening their purses, and to hell with the rest of us." His voice sounded familiar, yet I could not place him. "There's nothing here but pestilence and plague," he hollered, grimacing as if in pain.

All at once, I recognized the passionate voice and wounded expression. It was the man named Lispenard, the one who'd spoken so fervently at the water meeting.

Lispenard pointed to Ezra, then kicked a log. "You destroyed my land," he said, loud enough for all to hear.

People who had paid no heed stopped talking and looked. An angry crease formed across Ezra's brow and spread to the rest of his face as he turned around.

Fascinated, I edged closer. It was refreshing to see a man of modest means defend himself. Lispenard had lost most of his hair, his face was marred with lines, and his forehead was discolored with spots, but he spoke with conviction. His very presence seemed to confirm everything Elma had said.

"Left nothing but a maze of holes," he shouted. "Last week, one of my cows broke her leg and I was forced to put the poor creature down. Now I hear the legislature has approved Burr's company. Stock's trading and I've come to collect my due."

Levi pulled himself up from the ditch and went to his brother's side. "Stock's all gone," he said, grinning as if Lispenard should be pleased by the company's good fortune. "No one could have predicted its superlative success."

"No one?" Lispenard asked. "How much do you own?"

The workers, who had stopped digging, set their shovels down and watched with wary expressions. Some moved closer to listen.

"Take a break," Levi called, dismissing them with a wave.

Ezra Weeks pulled down the kerchief, revealing a frown. "Surely we would all be more comfortable discussing this matter in private. Perhaps over a bottle of Madeira?"

"Fresh air doesn't bother me," Lispenard said.

Ezra ran his hand over his mouth as if trying to sculpt his grimace into a more amiable expression.

"I heard the Manhattan Water Company raised two million dollars," Lispenard said. "You folks are getting rich while the rest of us don't have a literal drop in the bucket."

The crowd pressed closer. My eyes darted to Levi, wondering what he stood to gain.

"They're gambling with our livelihood!" hollered a man, tossing his empty buckets to the ground with a crash.

"They're gambling with our lives!" Lispenard said, jabbing a finger inches away from Ezra's nose.

Ezra shifted his weight onto his heels, and his voice became measured and low.

I crept forward and caught a few words.

"Damages," he said. "And rewards."

The lines in Lispenard's face softened.

Ezra pointed north, then made a wide arc with his arms that seemed to encompass a range of possibilities. "Albany . . ." His voice grew louder, although I still couldn't hear everything. "A prestigious position . . . forge valuable connections."

Lispenard watched Ezra intently, his gaze occasionally shooting to Levi, who nodded while his brother spoke. Gradually, he leaned toward the brothers, his shoulders softened, and he took a single step forward.

In one swift movement, Ezra Weeks wrapped an arm around his shoulder and the trio walked away from the crowd. When they were nearly at the carriage, Ezra turned to his workers. "Come back tomorrow," he said.

The men shuffled their feet. "Tomorrow's Sunday," one called.

"Then the next day," Ezra said. He seemed not to care. A dog barked at his heels and he kicked it away.

The crowd was not as easily dispersed. "What about our water?" the woman with the ailing baby cried.

I pulled my shawl up over my head and moved closer, ears primed to the men's hushed voices.

Ezra guided Lispenard into the carriage. "The Manhattan Company," I heard him say. It was impossible to ignore that this time he omitted the word *Water*.

Suddenly there were shouts on the outskirts of the crowd.

"There's been a duel! Colonel Burr has fought a duel at Hobuck Ferry!"

All eyes turned toward the new commotion. "Aaron Burr?" someone hollered. "Who'd he fight?"

A sole voice escaped the din. "Is he dead?" Ezra asked. "Is Colonel Burr dead?"

─7─

The days shortened. News reached New York that General Washington had died in his Mount Vernon home. The first snow of the season fell. The rooftops and streets were blanketed in white. When morning arrived, the sky was brilliant blue.

"It's too beautiful to remain cooped up," Levi said, stomping snow off his boots as he entered the parlor where Elma and I sat sewing. "Come along, Elma. I've harnessed Ezra's sleigh. Shall we go for a ride?"

"I'm not dressed for the weather," Elma protested, though she set the bonnet she was mending aside and allowed Levi to pull her to her feet.

Levi reached for her shawl, wrapping it, and his arms, around her shoulders. "There."

Elma laughed, looked at me, then bit her lip.

All at once, I felt old and matronly. Sour, like Elias, or Mother. Levi and Elma clearly cared for each other. Who was I to stand in their way? I smiled at Elma. "It's cold out there. Dress warmly."

Elma's eyes sparkled. It was impossible to deny: They were a beautiful couple, well matched in that regard. "I'll just be a moment," she said, hurrying upstairs.

Levi walked from the window to the hearth, then back again. He tugged at his collar, said he was warm, and went to wait outside.

When Elma came down, her hair was held back with the delicate ivory comb.

"Was that a present?" I asked, increasingly frustrated each time she wore it without revealing its provenance.

Elma put her hand to her head, dreamily running her fingers through the silky ribbon, just as she had the night Levi slammed the bedroom door on me. She nodded.

"From Levi?"

"Yes," she said, shutting me out just as effectively as he had. "Is he outside?" She went to the window, then took a step back. "Look at the women. They're all dressed in black."

"They're mourning General Washington," I reminded her. Had I been too judgmental from the first time Levi entered our house? Is that what drove Elma away and kept her from my confidences even now?

"But they're so fashionable," she said. Her skirt rustled as she smoothed it down. "Those feathers must have been dyed."

I joined her at the window. Despite the solemn procession, Greenwich Street was crowded with revelers enjoying the fresh snow. Sleigh bells rang. A group of boys tossed snowballs. Levi packed a handful and threw a ball at them, laughing when they returned fire. I had never seen him so handsome or so happy.

Spotting us at the window, he waved for Elma to join him.

She shook her head, more coquettish than shy.

"Don't worry about these ruffians," he called, firing a last shot at the boys. "I'll protect you." The wind colored his cheeks, and his eyes glistened as he came to escort Elma outside.

Harness bells jingled as a stylish black sleigh led by a handsome chestnut cut a path through the street. Runners whistled and snow sprayed. Elma was right in its path, seemingly oblivious.

I ran to the door and called, "Elma, watch out!"

The tall horse came to an abrupt halt. His nostrils flared as he tossed his head and whinnied in protest. With his statuesque posture, ginger coloring, and impatient manner, the driver much resembled his high-strung horse.

"Mr. Hamilton," Levi said, approaching the sleigh.

Alexander Hamilton raised the reins as if he would happily plow straight through him.

"Taking the fourteen-mile round?" Levi asked, tipping his hat at Hamilton's well- appointed companion. They sat snugly under a thick mohair blanket. The woman wore a black velvet helmet-like hat with a large red feather that protruded like a beak. I had heard many favorable things about Elizabeth Schuyler Hamilton. Her mother came from one of New York's most esteemed families; her father was a general and a senator in the first Congress. She was mother to five or six children. Instinct told me that the woman with the bouncing red feather and matching ruby lips was not Elizabeth Hamilton.

"We were heading that way," Hamilton said, looking past Levi, clearly ready to move along.

Levi blocked his path. "I'm surprised to see you out today," he said, "what with news of Washington."

"I'm much indebted to the general's kindness, but I don't believe he would have wanted us to sit inside on such a glorious day." The blanket rose and fell as Hamilton patted his companion's thigh.

"Will you be attending the funeral?" Levi asked.

Hamilton's mouth pinched closed, and for a moment it seemed that he might simply refuse to answer. "Our *esteemed* president has declared Washington's birthday a day of"—he lowered his voice in an imitation of Adams's New England accent—"'devotion and prayer.'" He cracked a whip, urging his horse forward. "I'll pay my respects then."

"Mind you pay the toll," his companion called over her shoulder, laughing loudly as the horse pranced off.

Elma stood a bit taller, but then her shoulders scrunched together and she shivered. Was it the cold, or had she drawn the same conclusion about Hamilton's cheerful companion?

"What toll?" she asked. "What did she mean by that?"

"Tradition says couples need to pay a toll at the Kissing Bridge," Levi said, placing a hand in the hollow of Elma's back and helping her into the sleigh. "Do you think you might pay?" he asked, hopping in beside her. I couldn't hear her response, but she laughed as a gust of wind tunneled down the street, swirling feathery-light snow, and the sleigh vanished in a cloud of white.

"Hamilton's on the warpath," said our neighbor Joseph Watkins, who had been eavesdropping as he shoveled his walkway. I turned toward him and raised my eyebrows.

A stout man with a gray beard that rose and fell with his heavy breaths, Watkins looked relieved to set his shovel aside. "Burr tricked every member of the legislature, and Hamilton to boot."

"What's that got to do with Levi?"

"Levi works for Burr and Burr's company."

A pair of dogs raced past us, scattering snow. One stopped to bury his muzzle in a drift, while the other wagged his tail and barked.

"But I thought Hamilton was for the water company," I said, recalling the boisterous toasts at the committee meeting.

"Hamilton supported the water company. But as soon as the legislature approved its charter, the Manhattan *Water* Company became the Manhattan Company," he said, stroking his beard and shrugging. "It's not a waterworks: It's a bank."

"A bank?" Still completely focused on the idea of freshwater, I pictured a bucolic riverbank before realizing what he meant.

"Money's more precious than water to our friend Burr. The country's only got two banks: Both were created by Hamilton; he controls them, and only his supporters get loans. But Burr managed to dupe Hamilton and create a Republican bank. That's what the duel was about."

"If Hamilton is so angry, why didn't he face Burr himself?"

"Hamilton sent his brother-in-law because he's a better shot."

"I heard Burr had a button clipped off his coat, the men shook hands, and they rowed back to town."

"No blood was shed this time."

Off in the distance, the tracks from Elma and Levi's sleigh blended into the wintery sky and disappeared.

I was clearing the supper plates when Elma and Levi crept inside. They closed the door so softly and stepped so lightly that had I not been listening for them, I would not have heard. I stood just off the entrance, inside the parlor and away from the light.

"You're in no position to judge us, Elma," Levi snapped. He was trying to be quiet, but there was more to it than that. He sounded angry. I tucked my hands in my pockets to stop them from shaking.

Elma sounded bewildered and a bit cross. "I was simply repeating what you yourself have said: Digging wells in the snow is useless."

"Our work doesn't concern you."

"It concerns everyone! Summer is around the corner, and with it comes fire and fever. Levi, you could die. Or I—"

"But to say that to Ezra. To his face!"

"Someone has to! I told you if you did not say something, I would."

"Elma," he said. His voice was low and cold, nothing like the caring man who had caressed her face so lovingly. "Don't threaten me." Steps creaked as he started upstairs.

Her footfalls trailed his. "If we don't do something, we're as guilty as they are," she said.

"Elma?" I called.

There was a perceptible pause.

"Elma, please."

Elma entered the parlor, looking distracted. Her eyes were red, and she twirled the comb's ribbon around a finger as if reassuring herself of its presence.

I waited for Levi's steps to grow faint. "It's late," I said, glancing across the entranceway at the store where Elias was working.

"Levi and I dined with his brother."

My heartbeat began to slow. A meal at the Weeks residence was a valid excuse for missing dinner at home. If Levi was introducing Elma to Ezra, it legitimized the attention he paid her and eased my concerns about her reciprocation.

"And?" I asked.

She did not look nearly as pleased as I would have expected. "The house is grand and the furnishings are fine. There are three Negro servants. One served us." Her voice had an edge, making her sound more slighted than sad.

"And Elizabeth Weeks?" I asked, treading as carefully as Elma had when she entered the house.

"She has a hooked nose and large earlobes."

I fought back a smile. "I wasn't asking about her appearance. What was she like?"

"She's from Boston and very well bred. The entire dinner, she addressed me as if she were speaking to a child."

"Perhaps she was being polite?" Like me, Elma was not accustomed to society, and her fear of committing blunders made her overly sensitive.

Elma stopped playing with the silky ribbon and her hand fell to her side with a dull slap. "Ezra hardly spoke at all. At least, not to me. All he did was criticize Levi."

"On what account?" I asked. Levi always struck me as annoyingly well mannered, at least in proper company.

"A thousand things. It was all I could do to keep quiet. Finally, when it seemed Levi would never defend himself, I simply said that the Manhattan Company really ought to uphold its promise and provide water. Ezra practically leapt from his seat, and Levi was furious the entire ride home. I thought he might even . . ." She trailed off. "It was as if he was doing everything he could to contain his rage. He said he told me about the company's plans in confidence and I should keep my opinions to myself."

The hair on my neck stood a bit straighter. I heard the frantic cries of the woman searching for her daughter as flames engulfed their home, and I saw Lily Forrest and her bloodstained curls, rotting in a pit in potter's field.

"He's wrong. Without the water we were promised, people—children—will continue to die in horrific ways, and he and his brother are . . ." I tried to make sense of everything I had heard. "Elma, what *are* they doing?"

"Levi is already livid." She hesitated and looked toward the doorway. "He swore me to secrecy."

"It's not a secret anymore. Joseph Watkins said the charter passed and that the Manhattan Water Company-m" I stopped and corrected myself. "The Manhattan Company is now a bank. But what does that mean?"

Elma walked toward the fireplace, nodding at me to follow. "Burr knows we are desperate for water, and no politician could afford to speak against him."

"This city is parched, Elma. That's why Hamilton supported the plan. Everyone did."

"But Burr never intended to provide water," she whispered. "The water company was a sham." She bit her lip, then spoke in a rush. "At the very last moment, when the legislature was about to approve the water company, he added one final clause. Levi said he wrote it in invisible ink."

"What did it say?"

"That the company could use its profits to start a bank. The problem is," she leaned closer, "there are no profits. All the money that was invested is being used to fund the bank."

"Why not just provide water?"

"Caty, don't you see? It's not only a bank, it's a Republican bank. The first of its kind. If people can borrow from a Republican bank, they can vote for a Republican president. Because of this, Jefferson may win the next election."

I was simultaneously impressed by the depth of her understanding and increasingly alarmed. "Why would Ezra Weeks risk his reputation to help Burr?"

"Levi says Ezra's been working toward this his entire life. If Jefferson becomes president, Burr will be his vice president. Ezra will be rewarded."

"So it's money again."

"And prestige. Ezra may meet Jefferson. He could become an ambassador or receive a cabinet post." Elma shook her head, smiling through her tears. "Fancy me at a state dinner! No wonder he thinks I'm a bad match for Levi."

"Oh, Elma." I took her into my arms. She came willingly and I rocked back and forth, stroking her hair while her tears soaked my dress. I wanted to comfort her, but I could not deny her words. It was exactly as Elias had said. Ezra Weeks was well enough acquainted with our family to know that Elma was practically an orphan, without fortune. That would be enough for him to write her off as unsuitable for his dashing and promising younger brother.

Elma wiped her eyes, pulling away as suddenly as she had submitted. "It's been a long day." She straightened her skirt. "I'm exhausted."

She did look worn out. "Go get some sleep," I said.

Elma went up to her room and I picked up my knitting, but I was too troubled to darn a single stitch. The politics, the lies, the money, and the ambition—all of it was wrong. I had never trusted Levi, and now he was confirming my worst suspicions, dragging Elma into a pool of ever more complicated lies. Perhaps Ezra's disapproval was for the best. Elma still had time to make a more appropriate match and get away from this political quicksand before she sank in deeper. I was considering how to broach the topic when I heard a loud scream and a thud.

Rushing upstairs, I found Elma lying unconscious on the third-floor landing. Levi was kneeling by her side and Croucher stood above them.

"How dare you speak to her like that," Levi said.

"You, Levi Weeks," Croucher said, pronouncing each word as clearly as I had ever heard him speak, "are an impertinent puppy. Mrs. Ring"—he turned to me—"don't trust this lout. He's up to no good."

Elma's eyes fluttered, and I knelt beside her. She was drifting in and out of consciousness yet her hands cradled her belly, gently rocking.

"She's been frightened nearly to death," I said. Though in truth, it was I who was suddenly afraid.

"You're a filthy old man!" Levi said. He was hovering so close to Croucher that, had they been outside in the frosty air, their breath would have mingled.

"You've fooled that girl into believing you're some kind of Adonis," Croucher said.

"Someone has to look out for her."

"I'd say you and Elias Ring have been more than obliging."

It was impossible to ignore Croucher's grating sarcasm. "Leave Elias out of this," I snapped. I meant to convey outrage, but the mention of Elias's name made me feel even more vulnerable.

"Levi?" Elma said. Her voice was as faint as a whisper, but he heard. He shot a final furious look at Croucher, before gathering Elma in his arms. She nestled close to his chest as he carried her into her bedroom.

I breathed a sigh of relief, thankful that whatever had passed between the two men had not turned violent. But when I joined Levi and Elma in her room, horror replaced fear. Though he had laid her on the bed, she continued to cling to him with her arms laced around his neck and her eyes fixed on his. Her dark hair fanned across the pillow, luminous and full, and her complexion glowed with a distinctly feminine beauty. After two babies of my own, I recognized her condition in an instant. Elma was with child.

—8—

First Day dawned bright, but when I stepped outside I was blasted by an icy gust, and not even the sun could warm me. The clear skies were a ruse, the kind of brisk stillness that precedes a bitter storm. I exhaled and watched my breath blow away, as fleeting as a midnight dream, then retreated to the warm parlor.

Church bells chimed. Elias and Charles put on their coats to go to meeting, but I lingered. I might not find a better time to talk with my cousin. Elma had pulled a chair close to the warm hearth. Her knitting lay on her lap, but she sat motionless as if deep in thought. I told Elias to go on without me, sat down beside Elma, then waited for her to speak. Without uttering a sound, she rose and, standing behind my chair, wrapped her arms around my neck and rested her head on my shoulder.

"Caty, I can't bear to make you sad." Her voice was so faint I could hardly hear, though she was practically whispering in my ear. She was clearly under some sort of spell.

"Nothing could make me love thee any less," I said, hoping she would speak frankly if she felt understood and safe.

Elma walked to the window. "Levi says it's not sinful to keep our love a secret for a little time."

The sky was darkening and a sprinkling of snowflakes had started to fall. I was waiting for her to confess her condition, and I had no idea how to respond. Disappointment and anger were irrelevant emotions, though I was not beyond them. Above all, I was scared.

"It is not much of a secret, Elma. He was in thy bedroom!" I tried softening my tone. "We've always told each other everything."

She nodded, though I had the impression she was reassuring herself, not agreeing. "Levi and I are to be married," she said.

"What?" I should have been relieved, but my frustration bubbled up again. "But why must thee stay silent all this time?"

The shadow of the winter sky through the window clouded her features. "Levi wants to tell the families, his and ours. He plans to tell you himself, but not quite yet."

My concern had transformed into exasperation. "What is he waiting for?"

Elma sighed. I forced what I hoped was a compassionate smile. "He doesn't want Ezra to know." Her voice broke.

I took a deep breath. "Regardless of what Levi may think of his brother, it's not right to deceive him."

Her response was as sharp and sudden as a slap to the face. "I'm respecting Levi's wishes. If you listened to Elias, perhaps this would be a happier home."

I was speechless. Eccentric behavior due to lovesickness was one thing, but it could not completely explain what was happening to Elma. I had never known her to be cruel or conniving. Saddened, I joined her at the window and gazed out. Snow was sticking to the windowsill, and the flakes, which had seemed so pure just minutes ago, looked menacing.

"Caty, I'm sorry," she said, taking my hand and squeezing with gentle insistence. Her skin was soft, but her grasp was as firm as when we walked down the streets of Cornwall as sisters. "This will be over soon. At eight o'clock we're going to the minister's house, at nine we'll be home, and then everyone will know."

"The wedding is tonight?" After these months of secrets and anguish, Levi would make an honest woman out of Elma. I embraced my cousin, but a shard of doubt still lodged in my heart. Such a swift resolution seemed too good to be true. Or perhaps it merely appears that way now. I have considered and reconsidered the events of that day so often that the only thing I am certain of is that the crystalline snowflakes collecting against the windowpane looked like a bleak, impenetrable wall between the outside world and us.

Elias returned with dire predictions of the impending storm, while Charles struggled to contain his excitement.

"I'm going to make a snowman," he said, "maybe a whole snow family!"

I stoked the fire, but it couldn't overcome the draft. My fingers were stiff with cold. I started chopping potatoes and the knife slipped, slicing my skin. A bead of blood dripped onto the table. I wiped it with the corner of my apron and it smeared into an angry crimson streak.

Charles rocked Patience in her cradle.

"Gently," I reminded him.

"She likes it," he said, rocking faster. Patience was giggling so I said nothing more, though I would have preferred for her to sleep.

The noon meal came and went. The snow continued to fall.

Elias went to secure the store windows, and Elma helped me clear the table while Levi entertained Charles by making shadow puppets on the wall.

"Here's a rabbit," he said, as his hand leapt through the air. "What? Who's coming?" Fingers misshapen and bent, his left hand crept up upon his right.

"Is it a wolf?" Charles asked.

"No," Elma said. "It's a lamb, and it has the softest fleece anyone has ever touched, whiter than the whitest snow."

Her words soothed Charles, and me. The fire finally warmed the room and cast a soft light. I picked up my knitting, nearly convinced that everything would turn out right, if we could all just make it through this evening. Then Levi stood.

"Headed out in this weather?" Hatfield asked.

"I'm going to call on my brother," Levi said, taking his hat and bundling himself for the cold.

Elma snatched up her knitting as well and concentrated on it intensely. It was not difficult to guess her thoughts. If Levi was going to consult his brother about their marriage, there was a good chance that Ezra might talk him out of it. I cleared my throat, trying to get her attention, but she bit her lip and ignored me.

"Digging holes in the snow?" Croucher asked. Like a rabid dog biting at Levi's heels, he grabbed his hat and followed Levi outside.

Stillness descended, as silent as the snowfall.

"Elizabeth Watkins says that Trinity Church is decorated with evergreen bushes," I said, trying to lift Elma's spirits.

"Can we go see?" Charles asked.

"I'll discuss it with thy father," I said. I did not think Elias would object, though lately we rarely found ourselves together: He came to bed after me, sometimes still holding a ledger and a candle, and began work in the store before dawn. Although he claimed to have missed me while I was in Cornwall, he had not reached for me in bed since my return.

The front door banged open and Levi came back into the parlor. There was snow on his hat and shoulders, and he was limping. Elma jumped from her seat and her knitting fell to the floor.

"What happened?" she asked, helping him into a chair.

My first thought was that he and Croucher had finally come to blows, but that was not the case. Not yet.

"It's nothing," Levi said. "I slipped and fell."

Elma knelt and examined his knee. His pant leg was torn, but he was more bruised than bloody.

"Charles, will you fetch the liniment?" she asked.

"You won't make it out today," Hatfield said, looking pointedly away from Elma. I cocked my head, wondering if Levi had mentioned their wedding plans.

"I'm determined to go out tonight," Levi said. His hand rested on Elma's as he spoke, and she smiled faintly, turning her face from the rest of us.

Charles returned with the liniment and a plaster. As Elma dressed Levi's knee, I could see warmth pass between them like a secret.

I waited until after candlelight, when the house was most quiet, before knocking on Elma's door. She answered immediately, dressed neatly in her pale-green muslin. Together, we had sewn the gown shortly after her arrival. It was her favorite, and she looked beautiful, but the fabric was too light for such a bitter evening.

"Shall I send Charles next door to borrow Elizabeth's beaver muff?" I asked.

Elma studied herself in the looking glass, smoothing the skirt and turning to both sides. "It would suit the dress."

Charles left and I sat on Elma's bed while she combed her hair. I was sorry that Aunt Mary would not witness her daughter's wedding, and I tried to ease my conscience by telling myself that she would be overjoyed by the match.

"Well, Elma," I said, "art thou ready for the march?"

"Yes, pretty nearly." She wrapped her shawl around her shoulders. "Oh—I almost forgot. In my top drawer. You'll find that comb. The one Levi gave me."

I went to the bureau. While part of me was happy she was finally confiding in me, there was another, louder voice still wondering why it had taken this long. The drawer stuck and I pulled harder, remembering the vial of laudanum I had buried there months ago. I rummaged past stockings and undergarments, hairpins and knitting needles, but the little bottle was nowhere to be seen. Elma, or perhaps Levi, had disposed of it after I saw it by her bedside.

"Is it there?" Elma asked, peering over my shoulder.

For an instant, I thought she was asking about the laudanum. I considered asking her where it had gone, but I did not want to dampen her mood and fresh trust in me.

"Why, here it is," she said, reaching past me. "Isn't it lovely?" She drew back with the ivory comb adorned with its single white ribbon in her palm.

A powerful curiosity, or some equally compelling force, made reach for the comb. I was sure it twitched or throbbed in my hand. I studied it carefully, running my fingers along the crest. There was an intricate design, a flourish of letters that twisted and curled like an exotic vine. Slowly, I traced each one. There, in soft swirls, was Elma's name.

Elma ran her fingers through the silky ribbon, as I had seen her do so many times over the past six months. The ivory shone against her dark hair as she set the comb in place. I straightened it and smoothed her curls. She was paler than usual, but some agitation was only natural.

"Don't be frightened," I told her, recalling my own wedding-day nerves. Of course, the circumstances were different. Elma had made her decision weeks or months earlier, when she allowed Levi into her bed. Was she regretting her choice? Her condition?

"Caty," she said, "do you think I'm being selfish? I mean"—she twisted the ends of her hair, curling what I had combed—"is it selfish of me to marry Levi? I love him so much. I couldn't live with myself if I harmed his prospects. . . ." Her eyes filled with tears.

Yes, Elma's wedding day was different than mine had been.

Charles raced up the stairs with Elizabeth's muff. "There's lots of snow!" he said, bouncing up and down.

Elma took the muff, but her eyes remained fixed on me. Was she waiting for my blessing?

"What's done is done," I said.

Did I sound like Elias? Would I have said more if Charles were not there? Part of me admired her for following her heart. But I didn't say so, to my eternal regret. I still felt slightly stung by her furtiveness since coming into my home and thought I was being instructive. She would have to be more careful when it came to sensitive matters in the future.

Shrill cries rang through the house, and Elma and I stood absolutely still, as if the baby's voice were the unspoken words between us. How had we come to this cold, impersonal place? In that moment, I blamed Elma—and Levi. Now I know that the fault was mine as well.

"Mama," Charles said. "Patience is crying."

Elma drew on her gloves. "Go to her," she said. "I'm fine. I'll be fine." Her tone was brusque, perhaps sad, perhaps resentful. I can only pray every day that she was not angry with me as she quickly kissed my cheek.

I went downstairs alone.

The clock was striking eight as I entered the parlor and went to soothe Patience. Levi nodded to acknowledge my presence. An instant later, he took his hat and went out into the entry. I heard footsteps on the stairs and then whispering. I tried to listen but could not make out a single word. The front door opened. They crossed the threshold. The latch fell. I took up the candle and ran to the door to see which way they had gone. It was moonlight, but having a candle made it darker.

The quiet house rattled my nerves. The children went to bed without protest, though I would gladly have told a story or cuddled under the covers. I tucked them in, allowing my lips to linger on their soft foreheads. The instant I extinguished the candle, Patience's eyes closed. Charles stifled a yawn, and before I knew it both were sound asleep. Patience lay on her belly with her tiny bottom jutting into the air, and Charles slept with an ease that I had always envied. The sweet perfume of their steady breath filled the room. I watched them for five minutes, maybe more, trying to absorb their calm before joining Elias in the parlor.

The mood there was starkly different. The fire was dying, orange embers disintegrating into ash. I tossed a log in the hearth and Elias looked up.

"I'm surprised Levi would go out on such a night," he said. He was sitting in a rocking chair, holding a book, though he was perched awkwardly forward and the book was closed. "Did he say where he was going?"

"Levi?" I shook my head. "No, he didn't say." My stomach fluttered. "It was Elma who told me. Elias, they're going to be wed."

The chair rocked back and the book fell to Elias's lap. "Why did no one tell me?"

I strained to make my voice sound more optimistic than I felt. "I only heard this morning, and Elma swore me to silence."

"No respectable woman gets married in secret," Elias said, seeming more bewildered than angry.

The skin on my neck prickled. I reached to scratch it and felt a chain of hives rising along my collar. I was not prepared to tell Elias that Elma might be with child. Even that would hardly explain why they decided to steal away on the darkest, coldest night of the year. The wind howled, blowing gusts through the desolate street. A sudden blast beat violently against the frosty windowpane, and the candle flickered. "What was that? Did someone cry out?" The snow had stopped falling.

Elias picked up his book. "I didn't hear a thing." His voice was hollow.

I went to the bedroom and looked in on the children. Patience's dark curls surrounded her pale face, and her tiny fists clutched the blanket. Not for the first time, I marveled at her resemblance to Elma. The sight should have warmed me; instead, an icy cold crept from my fingertips to my toes. I tried to picture Elma reciting her wedding vows, but the image was shrouded in haze. Where was this minister's house? She had neglected to tell me. I had failed to ask.

It was past ten when Levi returned. He was alone.

He took a seat at the table and rested his head upon his hands. His cheeks were red from the cold, but his hands were as white as if the blood had stopped circulating. When he saw me standing in the kitchen doorway, he started.

"Has Elma gone to bed?" he asked.

I looked from Levi to the front door and back again, wondering what game he was playing. He put his head back down. Moments passed, but Levi remained disturbingly still. It occurred to me that Elma had gone to return Elizabeth's muff. I sat down across from Levi to wait for her to glide in and share the good news. I even planned my look of surprise and how I would wake Elias and the children to celebrate. But seconds passed, then minutes, and Elma did not appear.

"Elma's gone out," I told Levi. I spoke slowly, as if he were confused. "At least, I saw her get ready to go, and I have good reason to think she went."

Levi's head sank farther into his hands. "I'm surprised she should be out so late at night and alone."

His words were clear enough, but I could not grasp their meaning. Elma had said they were going to be married. I had seen her dress. I was certain she had left with him, but I had not actually seen them together.

"I have no reason to think she went alone," I said, but even then I was beginning to doubt myself. Levi's cold stare made me shudder. His voice was steady, but I could hardly contain myself. "To tell the truth, Levi, I thought she went out with thee. She told me that she was going to, and I believe she did."

Levi sat watching the fire. "If she had gone with me," he said, his eyes fixed on the dancing flames, "she would have returned with me."

He stood and left. I sat too shocked to respond. I was as cold as I had ever been, shivering and weak. Waking Elias would mean admitting my fear, and I was not prepared to do that. I stirred the fire, swept the kitchen, and rearranged the chairs. The silence was oppressive. I turned the lamp low and resumed my seat near the hearth, jumping as the logs burned and buckled. The hives on my neck had grown into welts, and I scratched them until they bled.

Midnight struck. I took a candle and searched the house, praying Elma had come in unseen or somehow hadn't left with Levi and was reading or sewing in some little-visited corner of the house. My pace increased as I went from room to room. With each of my steps, the floorboards emitted a mournful creak. I approached Levi's door twice but did not knock. Desperate, I went to the window and looked out onto the street. Snow shrouded the city, making it look as peaceful as a graveyard.

—9—

The winter dawn broke slowly, as if it too were reluctant to face the day. I watched with glazed eyes as shadows lengthened along our bedroom wall: contorted figures, an elongated skull, a torso with a heart-shaped gap. The snow did not bring tranquility to the city; it crippled it. Greenwich Street was without activity or noise, except for a sharp wind that wrapped itself around our home and howled, making the shutters bang and windows rattle. I waited for the children to wake and call for me, need me, make me useful. I sat upright in bed, ears primed, eager for an excuse to take them in my arms and tell them that wind could not harm them and fear was the enemy of faith.

"Elias," I whispered. The sound of my voice confirmed this was no dream. A night so blustery and mean that every living creature had sought cover had come and gone, and Elma had not returned home.

Elias pulled the quilt over his head and groaned.

"Elias." I shook his shoulder. "Elma didn't come home last night."

He yanked the covers down and drew a deep breath, his eyes fixed on a point above my head.

"She and Levi left here together."

Elias was silent.

"But," I continued, though it was almost unbearable to say out loud, "Levi returned without her, and when I asked about Elma, he denied having seen her. He said that they hadn't gone out together at all."

"Perhaps thou misunderstood."

"He was very clear."

"Not Levi," Elias said, as if there were little doubt that Levi would speak clearly. "Perhaps thou misunderstood *Elma*."

Frustration coursed through me. "Speak with Levi," I said. "His behavior is odd. He's acting as if he knows nothing about where she is."

"What if he doesn't?"

"Elias, they left together. They were going to be wed."

"According to *her*," he spat, with an edge that seemed deeply wrong in the face of my clear and increasing distress.

"Elma told me they were going to be married, and I have every reason to believe her."

"That's what she said. I've never heard him say so."

"But I saw—" I stopped short. I had heard whispers on the stairs. The front door had closed. I had held a candle and looked out onto the dark street, but they had already vanished. "I'm certain they went out together," I said. I could hear the weakness of my argument and felt suddenly drained.

Elias turned back toward me, and now his voice was tinged with sorrow. He reached for my hand. "The only thing I saw was her clothing in a heap on the floor."

I pulled away, resenting him for dredging up such an ugly memory. The past was irrelevant. My sweet cousin was missing and it was my responsibility to find her. "That was laundry."

Elias tossed the covers away and sat up, fully awake. "Don't be naïve. Of course she would say that."

"Would thou punish Elma for her imprudence?" I asked.

"We should never have taken a girl like that into our home. Caty . . ." He clasped my hand again. I might have appreciated the gesture—it was so rare of Elias to show any sort of affection—except that his hands were as cold as his voice. "I'm sorry, but her behavior speaks for itself."

I was exhausted and bitter, but I felt a mother's urge to search every corner of the city until I found Elma and brought her home. I went to the bureau and hastily began to dress.

"It's a misunderstanding," Elias said again, as if that explained anything. "She probably went out visiting and the weather detained her."

The thought of Elma forging through icy streets or trapped somewhere unfamiliar did not alleviate my fear. Despite her brave face, she had always been fragile, and now, I believed, she was carrying Levi's child. The suggestion that she was out socializing was absurd.

"Who would she visit?" Elma had few friends, none—besides Levi—for whom she would risk going out on such an inhospitable night.

"What about Elizabeth Watkins? I believe she spent a night there last summer."

"Thou *believe*, Elias? Either she did or she didn't," I said. When I was away, Elias had been Elma's guardian, and his lack of attention to her whereabouts appalled me. Then again, I had left the city without any thought to Elma. Guilt lay heavy on my shoulders.

"She did," he said. "She and Elizabeth were constantly gossiping about something." Elias had always spoken highly of the Watkinses, so I was surprised to hear disapproval in his voice.

"Elma never said anything about it."

"Thou were away for six weeks," he said coolly.

"I wish thou were right, Elias, but it's ridiculous." I shook my head. "Elma would never want me to worry like this."

"Did thou have words?" Elias asked accusingly, as if he already knew the answer.

"Even so," I said, unable to deny the tension between Elma and me that had come to a head the previous day, "she wouldn't stay away this long."

"What now?" he asked.

"Well, Elias, that's quite obvious. I have to find Elma."

"It's going to have to wait," he said, swinging his legs over the side of the bed. "We have a household full of paying tenants who expect breakfast."

Breakfast was a sad affair.

Elma usually scrambled eggs, and I was reluctant to carry out her chores, offering only a stack of burned toast and strawberry preserve that was beginning to turn. She was conspicuously absent, yet no one referred to her. Levi chewed slowly and swallowed as if his throat were sore, pushing aside a tankard of beer as if it were poison. He was unshaven, and his dark-blue eyes sank into the contours of his face.

"Feelin' all right, Weeks?" Croucher asked eagerly.

Levi stalked out.

Croucher turned to Will. "Your master looks like 'e 'asn't slept."

Will sat forward as if he might speak, then seemed to think better of it and took another serving.

Charles ripped the crust off his toast, then tore it in half and half again until black crumbs sprinkled the table, chair, and floor. Patience began to fuss. Elias had ignored me, but the children sensed my anxiety. Charles would worry if I told him Elma was missing, further validating my own fear. I did not have the strength to comfort any of them. How could I explain Elma's absence when I didn't understand it myself? I just had to stay quiet until I found her, and then she could tell Charles herself about the adventure she had on such a snowy night.

I was preparing to go to the Watkinses' when the street door opened and a set of boots trod lightly up the stairs. I rushed out into the entranceway and was on the first step when Levi intercepted me. His broad shoulders spanned the width of the stairwell, blocking my way.

"Has Elma come home?" he asked.

It was no small effort to steady my voice. "I haven't seen her."

"I'm surprised. Where could she be?" He was twitchy, his eyes without their usual sparkle.

I tried to push past him. "She's upstairs. I'm sure I just heard her go up."

"That was me you heard."

I didn't understand how he could answer with such certainty. "Then thou moved more lightly than ever before."

Before the words were out of me, Levi was up the stairs. I followed on his heels. As we approached Elma's door, he stepped aside.

I knocked politely, then harder. Levi reached past me and flung open the door. We stood together on the threshold, surveying the empty room. The bed was made and the room was in its usual order, except for a discarded shawl, which hung lifelessly over the back of a chair, and an overturned hairbrush on the dressing table.

Levi sighed, though whether from distress or relief, I couldn't say. "She's not here," he said, confirming the obvious.

I looked at the brush. Morning light bounced off snowy rooftops and shone through the window, highlighting a few stray hairs, tangible proof of Elma's existence as well as her absence.

"Levi," I said, "this is too serious for me to keep quiet any longer. Elma told me she was going out with thee last night." His eyes flashed dark and furious, so I stopped short of mentioning their wedding plans. "Tell me where she is."

"Caty." His voice was as vacant as the room, and he looked through me with icy detachment. "I would not keep you in suspense if I knew."

We stood side by side in Elma's room, just as we had the night she was ill, except the bed was empty and Elma was gone.

"Levi," I pleaded. "Tell me something, anything at all. I no longer care what has passed between thee. Tell me where Elma is. Did she flee from fear or"—I lowered my voice—"shame?"

Levi paced Elma's small room as if he were eager to leave but reluctant to go. I wanted to shake him until he confessed the truth, but he was imposing and brooding, and I was frightened.

"Caty," he said, "I fear you are no longer my friend."

"Indeed," I said, "I shudder to think that I ever indulged a favorable thought of thee."

"Mama?" Charles raced into the room, positioning himself between Levi and me.

I was touched by his protectiveness and concerned that he felt I was threatened. Charles, who had always admired Levi, glared at him as if he were an intruder in our home.

"Where's Elma?" he cried shrilly, his voice filled with the panic I had been trying to suppress.

A gust of wind nearly toppled me the moment I stepped outside. The snow was as high as my shins, and the frozen ground sank and swelled, forming a treacherous path. The Watkinses lived next door, yet their house seemed hopelessly far. With each step, I prayed I would find Elma safe and sound. As my warm breath vanished and my chest began to ache from the cold, I made a thousand promises and bargains. I would be a more understanding wife, a compassionate mother, attend more meetings, and truly practice my faith. Most important, I vowed I would not scold Elma. She had used poor judgment. If she was safe, that was all that mattered. We would talk once tempers cooled. And if she was with child, we would handle that as well. No problem was insurmountable. I would forgive her. I already had.

Joseph Watkins answered the door after a few knocks. "Caty Ring?" he said, stroking his beard. "It's a cold day to venture out."

The front door opened directly into the parlor. My eyes searched the room. Joseph and Elizabeth had three grown boys, and the house looked orderly and tame. Pewter plates and candlesticks adorned the mantel. An open almanac lay on a bench by the window next to a fat calico cat. The sight sent my thoughts flying back to the mangy stray Elma brought home the afternoon Levi arrived. We had made him a warm bed in an old soapbox and fed him table scraps. But within a week, he had disappeared. Heartbroken, Charles had searched every corner of the house before losing hope.

Icy fear seeped into my bones as I faced Joseph Watkins.

"I've come to collect Elma," I said, as cheerily as possible.

Watkins's fingers closed around the end of his beard. "Elma?"

Elizabeth appeared by her husband's side. Buxom, and a bit of a busybody, she had a warm smile.

"Caty," she said. "Don't stand out in the cold!"

I allowed her to lead me to a fire blazing in the hearth. The room, which backed onto Joseph's workshop, smelled of sawdust. There were a handful of wood chips on the floor and dust in the air, which made the place cozy. A sanded piece of pine—the makings of a whistle or toy—lay on the table. Each item seemed a testament to contentment.

"Please, sit." Elizabeth stretched one arm out toward the room's most inviting chair and fixed her cap with the other. She wore a stained wrapper and tattered slippers. If I had not been so preoccupied, I would have felt embarrassed for intruding.

"Did Elma spend the night here last night?" I asked.

"Elma?" Elizabeth ran her hand over her chin in a manner very like her husband's. "Charles was here to borrow the muff. He's grown so! I told Joseph I thought he'd be taller than his father and—"

"Was Elma here?"

Elizabeth met her husband's gaze. "No. Caty, please sit. I'll make cocoa, or coffee?"

I was unable to stop from chattering. "Elias suggested she might have visited and spent the night. . . ." As the words tumbled out, I heard their hollowness. The Watkinses lived exactly one door away. Our homes shared a wall. If Elma were here, she could have banged on the partition and I would have heard. "The truth is," I said, "we had a bit of a quarrel. A small one, really, but, well, she's young." I sighed, hoping they would not ask any questions. "I'm afraid she may have taken offense. I thought in her anger she might have stayed last night, as Elias told me she did last summer."

Watkins's bony fingers dug into his beard. "What did Elias say?" His voice trembled. His sudden anger confused me and made me wary.

"Elma slept here while I was away during the yellow-fever scare. Elizabeth, remember?"

Elizabeth turned toward the hearth and began fiddling loudly with the kettle.

A kind man, Watkins seemed reluctant to deliver a blow. "Elizabeth and I are fond of Elma, but we've never had the pleasure of entertaining her overnight."

I heard myself gasp. I had trusted Elias's explanation. There was no other explanation.

—10—

A second day passed without Elma.

I searched every corner of her room, turning over and examining each hairbrush, ribbon, and doily as if seeing it for the first time. I looked under the mattress and in the wardrobe, rifling through dress pockets and rummaging inside shoes, and spent long minutes studying her knitting as if its pattern might reveal some clue. More than once, I pulled aside the lacy curtains and gazed out onto the snowy street, half-expecting to see Elma in her green muslin gown. I recognized her posture and dress in countless girls, but she was nowhere.

The temperature dropped and dropped again. Frozen sewage lay in the gutters. Sleighs that dared negotiate the treacherous terrain coated our home with a foul spray. As many times as I wiped the windows, the sludge returned, exactly like the bitterness that refused to leave my heart.

Restless and whiny, Charles roamed the house. It had been horrible enough when he asked about Elma and I had no explanation. Now he'd stopped asking, and it was worse. Patience refused to nap. I tried to mend a blanket but looked up at the door so many times that I pulled more stitches than I sewed. Beds were left unmade and dishes piled up. Shivering, I threw more logs on the fire, as if it might rekindle my hope. The fire hissed and smoke choked the room.

My eyes were teary from the smoldering ash and from exhaustion. I went to the door to get some air. It was a bone-chilling day. The snow, so pristine just nights before, was now pockmarked and gray. Wind stung my wet cheeks.

A faint sun poked through the clouds, dappling the street with spotty light. From the corner of my eye, I spotted the tiniest scrap fluttering inches off the ground. Stepping forward, I could see that it was a tattered ribbon, as weather-beaten as the snow. Without thinking, I followed as it danced in the breeze, leading me farther astray. It dodged and evaded me, drifting toward the center of the street. I pounced to catch it as if it were the most precious gift. The instant I had it in hand, I knew what it was: the silky ribbon that had dangled so seductively from Elma's ivory comb.

"Look out!"

A sleigh came barreling toward me. Hooves clamored and ice sprayed. I felt a horse's breath hot on me and heard blades inches away. Leaping out of the way, I slipped and fell. My skirt blew up, snaring me in fabric, and I lay on my back for what felt like minutes but could not have been more than a second.

"Caty!" Levi had jumped down from the sleigh and was panting beside me. "Are you hurt?" Bystanders paused to watch as he helped me sit up.

"I'm not sure." I had fallen hard. The collision had made my heart race and left me drained and confused. I looked into Levi's eyes, which were as dull as the sullied snow. My fingers closed on the discarded scrap of ribbon. In the absence of fact, it seemed vitally important.

Ezra shouted from the sleigh. "Are you insane? You could have been killed."

I pulled myself to my feet. "Ezra Weeks?"

Like a foreigner with no understanding of English, Ezra turned to Levi.

"Catherine is Elias Ring's wife," Levi rushed to explain. "Remember?"

Ezra's thin lips flickered in recognition.

"Caty?" Elizabeth Watkins was standing by my side. "I saw the accident. Can you stand?" She helped me to my feet, bending to brush snow off my skirt. "Oh, your dress is ripped." She glanced angrily at Levi as she tried to lead me away.

"I'm fine." The hem of my skirt was torn and dragging, but it was the ribbon that held my attention. I could not understand how it had become separated from the ivory comb. "It's E-Elma," I stuttered. "She still hasn't come home." I wove the soiled ribbon through my fingers, exactly as Elma had when it was new. Even now it was silky and smooth. She would never have discarded it intentionally.

"Perhaps you should lie down," Levi said. Though he sounded concerned, his demeanor was brusque as he took me by the forearm and began to walk purposefully toward our house.

I pulled away. "Ezra Weeks, it's important I speak with thee immediately," I said, hoping Ezra could inspire Levi to tell the truth.

"I'm afraid it will have to wait," Ezra said. "My brother and I have important business."

I thought about the water-company fraud. The Weeks brothers' business seemed more suspect by the moment. "It's of the utmost urgency," I said.

Ezra held a horse whip high in the air as if he might strike. "Very well," he said, though he barely lowered the whip.

Now that I had his attention, I hardly knew where to begin. "My cousin, Elma, a young woman who has dined in thy home—she's been missing for two days."

Bystanders, who had been watching since I toppled in the street, stepped closer to listen.

Ezra's expression remained inscrutable. "I am sorry for your worry, but I hardly see what that has to do with me."

"Thy brother," I said, my voice more strident than I had intended. "Levi knows where she is."

"Out of the way," shouted a chimney sweep, pushing a cart overflowing with ash. "Time and tide wait for no man!"

As if winding a clock, Elizabeth began twisting a button on her dress. "A young girl is missing," she said. The phrase *missing girl* rippled through the crowd, its anxious energy intensifying as it spread.

"Caty," Levi said. He looked sideways at his brother and began again, "Mrs. Ring, this is not the place for this."

"Where is the right place?" I asked. "I tried at home, but thou refused to answer."

"But, Caty—"

Ezra held up his hand and Levi bowed his head, hiding his face. "Mrs. Ring," Ezra said. "My brother and I will accompany you home and we'll get to the bottom of this." His voice was steady and confident, and he nodded at the sea of onlookers as if to assure them as well.

Charles was seated at the table, reciting arithmetic, and Patience was asleep in her cradle. Elias stood and opened his mouth to speak, surely ready to complain about my absence, but as Levi and Ezra followed me into the parlor, he stepped forward and offered his hand.

"Ezra, what a pleasant surprise," he said. I couldn't help but smirk. Elias hated surprises.

Ezra kept his hands in his coat pockets, and Elias, visibly taken aback by the slight, shifted his weight and rested his extended hand on Charles's shoulder.

"Mr. Ring," Ezra said. "Your wife made a scene in public not five minutes ago."

Elias covered his eyes. If he could have, I believe, he would have plugged his ears as well.

"I've asked Levi repeatedly about Elma's whereabouts, but he refuses to answer," I said.

"My brother knows nothing of your accusations," Ezra said.

I was on the verge of screaming—or crying.

"Friend," Elias said, "*accusation* is a strong word."

"Your wife accosted us publicly. What would you call it?"

Elias's brow furrowed. I had never seen him look so tired or so old. "Her cousin is missing, and she believes Levi knows where she is."

I took my first true breath in days. Elias was not exactly coming to my aid, but he wasn't discounting my fear. In his own systematic way, Elias was striving to get to the root of the mystery. And for that I was grateful. He recounted Levi's and Elma's friendship, explaining the attention Levi paid her. At a certain point, he stopped and looked at Charles. I could see that he was debating whether to mention the incident with Elma's clothing, but he skipped over it, merely concluding that the couple was "well acquainted."

Levi fidgeted while Elias spoke, but Ezra stood perfectly still. He held his hat behind his back with one hand, his other thumb hooked in his waistcoat pocket. When Elias explained that Levi and Elma had taken a drive together around the fourteen-mile round, Ezra's shoulders jutted backward and the fabric of his waistcoat grew taut.

"And," I added, "Levi has spent time alone with her in her bedroom."

An ugly smirk flitted across Ezra Weeks's features. "That tells you all you need to know about the girl, I should think."

"How dare thee." I raised my arm and might have slapped him but remembered Charles still in the room. Without taking my eyes off Ezra's, I said, "Charles, please go sit with thy sister." He scurried off without his usual protest.

The room was quiet for several moments before Ezra spoke. "Certainly," he said, his voice eerily calm, "the girl must be found." Like the politicians with whom he consorted, he managed to agree and disagree at once, acknowledging the urgency of the situation but not Levi's involvement. "Tell me, could she be visiting friends or family?"

My pulse raced at the realization that I would have to notify my aunt; somehow, I had avoided all thoughts of her until this moment. It was possible that Elma had returned to Cornwall, but not at night, during a snowstorm, without a word to anyone. No, there was only one explanation. Elma had told me that she and Levi were going to be wed. I had watched her dress, had heard her leave.

"She left here with Levi on First Day evening. See this," I said, brandishing the tattered ribbon as if it were proof.

Levi looked away, but not before I saw him flinch.

Elias lowered my arm. "Caty," he said, his voice filled with sorrow. "Thou have not slept in days."

Charles emerged from the doorway, where he had been hiding. "It's Elma's," he said, snatching the ribbon. "See?" He waved it as high as he could reach in front of Levi's startled face, and Levi stepped back as if it were a snake.

"Levi knows where she is," I said. "They left this house together the night of the storm ."

Ezra Weeks offered a polite smile, but it did not extend to his sharp gray eyes. "If you are referring to last Sunday, I can assure you that Levi was at my house. We were discussing the next day's business, as we often do in the evenings."

Panic rose in my stomach like bile and turned sour in my mouth. "That's impossible. Elma told me that they were going to be married that night."

"Elma and Levi are married?" Charles asked.

Ezra opened and closed his palms, Elias glared at Levi, and Levi stared down at his boots.

"She would not be the first girl claiming to be *involved* with my brother," Ezra said, as if this were a source of pride. Levi shot a sideways glance at him, but Ezra continued, unimpeded. "There was even an incident a few months ago that forced him to leave New England." He laughed. "He must be a fascinating fellow."

At his laugh, my distress turned to rage. "Levi is hiding something. The two of them have been keeping secrets from the start. They even knew each other before they moved here," I said, as if it were damning evidence.

"Levi was at the dock when Elma came," Charles said.

"That was Ezra," I said, remembering Levi's explanation. Now, as I gazed between the two brothers, their features and affects so utterly separate, I saw how flimsy the story had been. "Thou *were* at the dock when Elma arrived," I said to Levi, wondering why I had ever trusted his word over Charles's. "Thou lied this whole time."

"Elma forbade me to say anything," Levi said. "She said you would put her right back on that boat if you knew we had traveled together."

"And thou?" I said, turning to Elias. "Thou said it was Ezra who asked after a room for Levi."

"It was Ezra I spoke with," Elias said.

Was it my imagination or did he shoot Levi a challenging glare? I looked from Elias to Ezra and Levi. They were all liars. "Levi," Elias said with a sigh. "Where is Elma?"

"I miss Elma," Charles cried. He was tugging at his hair, combing it incessantly with his fingers. When I looked closely, I saw that he was pulling from the roots, and there was a bald spot above his left ear.

"Oh, my Charles," I said, leaning down to hug him. My pain was unendurable, but seeing Charles suffer was worse. "Charles, I'm so sorry."

Levi's eyes darted to and from his brother. "I don't know where she is, but—"

"But what?" I snapped, standing up again.

Elias put his hand on my wrist. "Caty, let him speak."

Levi looked down at Charles and his eyes glazed over. "I've often heard Elma say that she wished she'd never had an existence."

I drew a sharp breath. "It's an expression. I acknowledge that it is wrong, but I've said it myself. At this very moment, I could say, 'I wish I never had an existence to witness a scene such as this.'"

"Mrs. Ring." Ezra Weeks shook his head. "Sarcasm won't help us find the girl."

"Elma!" I said. "Her name is Elma."

"Caty," Elias said. "Ezra is right."

Bolstered by their defense, Levi continued. "Elma and I sometimes had occasion to speak of private matters. She told me more than once that she believed she was a burden, that her frail health was an imposition, and that she was more harm than help in your home."

"That's ridiculous," I said. I had never considered Elma an annoyance, but Elias was conspicuously quiet. I was once again reminded of all the people in Elma's life who had called her useless. Was it any wonder she had learned to believe it?

Levi sighed. "I once heard her—Elma—threaten she would swallow laudanum."

I shook my head. "She would never speak that way."

"It happened while you were in Cornwall. Others heard her as well." Levi's voice grew adamant. "Mr. Ring was there. Right, Elias? Do you remember what happened while Caty was in Cornwall?"

Elias was slowly shaking his head, though his eyes remained locked on Levi.

"Where on earth would Elma get—" I started to say *laudanum* but stopped short. "The vial thy doctor forced on us!"

"Once, she even took out the vial." Levi paused to watch me, and I flashed to the evening I walked in on them and saw the menacing little glass gleaming in the lamplight. "She said if the situation were dire enough, she would drink it full."

"That's ridiculous," I said again. "It would kill her."

"I sat with her late into the night until she was calm."

Our small parlor was smokier and more confining than ever. I sank into a rocking chair and my eyes settled on Patience's blanket. If Elma was carrying Levi's child, it was a dire situation indeed. Had she told Levi about her condition, or was it a burden she was shouldering alone? One she could not bear? If Levi knew of Elma's pregnancy, would he protect her—or his own reputation?

"Levi . . ." I wanted to appear bold and menacing, but tears were streaming down my cheeks. Elias remained silent. Sadness overwhelmed me as I realized he believed Levi's story. Charles's quiet cries grew into shrieks.

"Levi," I said, "from the bottom of my heart, please tell me what's become of Elma."

There was a flicker of sorrow in Levi's dark-blue eyes. Then they hardened. "Mrs. Ring," he said, "it's my firm belief that Elma is now in eternity."

~11~

Elias notified the police. We organized a search party.

On Christmas Day, the men assembled in front of our house: Some were concerned citizens wearing dark overcoats and boots; some sported their old military garb. Hats and scarves buried their faces, but nothing could obscure their prying eyes. Elma's plight was soon known throughout the city. The story spread rapidly about the raven-haired beauty who vanished into the night.

Reluctantly, I wrote my aunt a carefully worded letter. I struggled over the same phrases that unsettled my mind, vague expressions like *last seen* and *gone missing*. As tactfully as possible, I asked if Elma had returned home, praying that a misunderstanding, or desire to hide her pregnancy, had driven her away.

Each dreadful day, strangers appeared on our doorstep bearing found and bedraggled items: a stray scarf, a lost shoe, a button. One man brought dogs. He rapped on our door, asking for an article of Elma's clothing so the hounds could pick up her scent. I deliberated a long time, not wanting to part with a single item of hers, and finally handed over a pillowcase, one embroidered with irises. A lone strand of Elma's dark hair clung to a purple flower. I watched through the window as the keeper held the delicately stitched case to the dogs' wet noses. The pack looked wild. They barked incessantly and climbed atop one another, then started off in five different directions, as hopelessly lost as I felt.

More distressing than the strangers were friends and neighbors who arrived, expressing concern and offering help. It was impossible to look them in the eye. I was the one who had invited Elma to this mean city. I had promised to care for her, and I had failed. Church elders spoke of faith. But sitting in silence, waiting for a divine light within, seemed futile. When Lorena Forrest took my hand in hers, encouraging me to look within myself, all I could feel was sorrow.

Two more days passed, but for me time was suspended. The snow melted; more fell. The crowd on our doorstep ebbed and flowed, and I watched them with the same detached interest with which I observed the dismal weather. The house needed dusting, linens washing, men and children feeding. I went through the motions, cleaning, cooking, mending, and life assumed a false sense of normalcy. But the pounding behind my eyes and tremor in my hands never quite left me. I felt neglectful, almost cruel, going about my daily chores when Elma's fate was unknown.

Each evening at the stroke of eight, I heard footsteps on the stairs and playful whispers, and I stood perfectly still and listened, as if this time I might be able to make out what was said. The front door opened, the couple crossed the threshold, and the door shut. Too late, I held a candle and looked out onto the pitch-black street.

The cold spell broke and more men arrived, holding fishnets, weighed down with sandbags to drag rivers and poles to probe under docks. People volunteered their boats and their time, and when the river ice softened into slush, they strung nets between boats and slowly, painstakingly, rowed parallel lines along the shore, stopping to poke at the putrid muck. Elias accompanied them, carrying a map and meticulously marking sections of the waterfront where Elma was not found with a large, sickening X.

I watched with the wind in my face and my heart in my throat, but it was too awful, standing on the edge of the choppy river, squinting into the salty spray, as they pulled up garbage, dead dogs, even the bloated body of a frozen horse. After a few days, I stopped going, but Elias went dutifully. He had never spoken a kind word about Elma, nor did he say one now, but he did not complain. He returned home for dinner, his cheeks chapped, his lips dry and cracked, and his mood dismal. I was thankful for his help, though late at night I tossed and turned, wondering why it had come at such a high price.

My aunt's reply arrived all too soon. She must have received my letter and penned a response the same morning, trudging a mile through winter winds to the post in town. I tore it open, knowing it offered my last true hope. But the letter contained nothing but more questions, none of which could answer. In a shaky, childlike scrawl, Aunt Mary wrote that Elma was not in Cornwall, nor had she heard from her in over a month. Then I recognized, at the bottom of the page, Mother's practiced hand. I read on, trembling.

"Catherine," she wrote, her script sloping with weighty accuracy. "Where is thy cousin? Mary cannot eat a morsel, thy father will hardly speak, and I am extremely alarmed. Write immediately with more information." Her concern felt like criticism. Resentful, I threw the letter into the fireplace and watched the paper crinkle and ignite.

Early on the morning of the twenty-ninth, when Elma had been missing for seven days, the sheriff knocked on our door. His visit confirmed my worst fears. Elma's disappearance was now a criminal matter. My first impulse was to ignore him, but the rapping grew more forceful, until it merged with the pounding in my head. A crowd collected outside, Charles clung to my skirt, Levi paced upstairs, and I allowed Sheriff Morris into our home. Though I had not called for him, Elias joined us in the parlor. Days earlier, he had welcomed Ezra Weeks into our home; now, arms crossed, he eyed the sheriff suspiciously.

The questions were abrupt and painful.

"Describe Miss Sands," Sheriff Morris said.

"Her health was frail," Elias offered reluctantly.

The sheriff gazed doubtfully around the parlor. "Would you have a miniature? Some likeness I could show?"

Elias shook his head.

"What was her usual routine?"

"She helped my wife run the boardinghouse," Elias said. "Made breakfast, cleaned, sewed. And did laundry."

I breathed in sharply, certain he was intentionally reminding me of the morning he found Elma's day-old clothing on the floor.

"Was she a Christian woman?" the sheriff continued, seeming to have picked up on the tension.

"Yes, she was," I said.

"She did not frequently go to meeting, nor to any other church," Elias added.

Though it was almost unbearable not to defend Elma, I stood behind Elias and did not contradict him. His cursory knowledge seemed to satisfy, and I had no desire to divulge more. Elma was not here, and I did not think it was fair to let a stranger scrutinize her behavior.

"And her parents?" the sheriff asked.

I collapsed into a chair, dismayed that he had so quickly cut to the heart of the matter.

Elias sighed. "Her mother's not well. She lives in Cornwall, up the Hudson."

"And her father?"

"He was a preacher, but he died some time ago," I said, before Elias could respond. "In England," I added, so there would be little hope of checking the facts.

Elias and Sheriff Morris exchanged nods before the sheriff moved on to the next wrenching question. "Would you have reason to suspect that Miss Sands was unhappy?"

Elias rubbed his temples. "She was . . . temperamental."

I shot upright. "That's not true," I said. "Her health was delicate, but her mood . . ." My thoughts roamed to the missing laudanum and Levi's sorry accusations. "My cousin would *never* take her own life." Suicide was too desperate. Elma had options. She could have come to me. Why hadn't she come to me?

"Her mood was the same as ever," I concluded quickly, though I saw Elma's wet eyes as she called herself useless.

The sheriff nodded, but he looked past me toward Elias. "Would you have reason to suspect that she might have run off? Either by herself or with a lover?" he asked. I could hear Levi pacing incessantly in his room, making the parlor ceiling groan.

I knew Elias would be furious if I made unfounded accusations, but I had to convey my instinct. "My cousin did not know many men," I said. "She arrived in the city six months ago and has only associated with our tenants."

The creaking upstairs stopped.

"Several men live in the house," I said. "Isaac Hatfield travels often. Richard Croucher—" I shuddered at the thought of Croucher's distasteful manner, but he was not the focus of my indictment or fear. "And then," I said, hearing my voice grow louder, "there's Levi Weeks." Elias's eyes were boring holes through me, but I continued. "He and Elma were close friends. They were acquainted before she moved to the city."

Nodding, Sheriff Morris looked up the stairs. I was sure he would call for Levi, but he turned back to me instead. "Mrs. Ring, were you away from home last summer?"

I should have found his knowledge surrounding the intricacies of our home reassuring, but I was only more disturbed.

Word spread about the sheriff's visit, and the crowd outside that day was dozens deep, extending from our front door to the Watkinses' house and beyond. A man claimed to have seen Elma on the Battery promenade. She had been spotted on a ferry to Brooklyn, a coach to Connecticut, and a ship bound for Europe. She was alone. She was with a foreign gentleman. She was laughing. She was being abused. They all gathered on the pretense of providing help, but the truth was that they were hungry for slander. My family had been twisted inside out, and vultures were picking through our remains.

"What was Elma wearing?" a woman hollered when I went outside to fetch water.

Her familiarity shocked me. With her long gray hair and eager expression, she had a frantic look. I was sure I had never laid eyes on her before, yet she addressed me as if we were friends.

"Have you no mercy?" Croucher chided, appearing suddenly at my shoulder. Despite my misgivings about his character, he had participated in each search party with solemn dedication and canvassed the entire neighborhood, questioning shopkeepers and cartmen, children, even Negroes. "Leave the poor woman to grieve in peace," he shouted as I fled inside.

The same crowd—indeed, the same crazed woman—appeared the next day and the day after, and I became reconciled to the questions the way a wounded soldier learns to walk with a limp. I came to expect, even relish, the opportunity to discuss Elma. As many times as I related the details, I did not tire of defending her—or myself.

"It was a stormy night," I said. "I did not want her to be cold, so I told her to dress for the weather. I sent my son next door to borrow a fur muff to keep her hands warm."

"Was she alone?" someone asked, quieter than the rest of the mob. Unlike the other restless onlookers, who seemed desperate for every gruesome detail, this man had a curious but professional air. He was young, with kind brown eyes, a large nose, shaggy hair, and an eager expression. He reminded me of a faithful dog, a loyal companion I badly needed.

"Elma left the house with another tenant, Levi Weeks," I said.

The fellow cocked his head. "Ezra Weeks's brother?"

"That's right." I nodded.

"Was it a special occasion?" he asked.

I turned back toward the house and saw Elias standing behind the drapes, solemnly shaking his head. But I had to speak my piece, for Elma's sake and for mine. I lowered my voice and stepped toward the man with the encouraging gaze.

"Elma and Levi were to be married that night," I said slowly, aware of the implications.

The crowd buzzed.

"How was her mood?" the same woman shouted.

"She was cheerful, as she always was—*is*," I said, willing myself to look the same, but my throat was dry and my entire being ached. I was masquerading, acting confident for my audience when I wanted to melt like snow in the midday sun. I couldn't help but wonder if Elma had also been pretending. Had she told me that she and Levi were to be married because she knew that was what I wanted to hear? Had she only feigned contentment? Was it possible that she had planned her own demise?

I wanted Levi out of our home.

"I can't stand to look at him," I told Elias, late at night.

"Don't be willful," he said.

"He mopes around the house. He doesn't eat, and I can hear him pacing, always. I hear him now."

Elias looked unconscionably sad, though I could not say whom his sorrow was for. "I don't hear anything," he said, settling back into bed.

"Back and forth, day and night. Heel toe, heel toe." The steps were slow and rhythmic, crushingly loud. "He does it on purpose, so I can't think." The claim sounded absurd even to me.

"Control thyself. For her sake."

I was accustomed to Elias's reproaches—they barely made an impression anymore. Now I blamed myself. Elma was my ward, and I had failed her. I was sure she was in pain. If her anguish was half as great as mine, she was in agony.

"Levi knows more than he's admitting," I said.

Elias frowned. "It won't help to alienate him."

"Levi could be the King of France for all I care." Elias gave me a sideways glance, and I remembered that Louis XVI and his queen, Marie Antoinette, had lost their heads nearly seven years earlier. "The point is," I continued, "it makes no difference who he is or who his brother knows. He is guilty. He walks around the house as if he's in mourning. He lingers at the search parties. He is hiding something, I swear it."

Elias rubbed his chin. "Making blind accusations will not help. It may actually harm her."

"That is cruel, Elias. How could I possibly harm her more than whatever has kept her from home for nine days?"

Elias nodded, seeming to regret his words. "Caty," he said more tenderly, "I share thy concern, but I don't know what to do."

I had never known Elias to be without a plan, and his hopeless-ness left me shattered for the millionth time that day. "She left here with Levi that night. I know she did."

"Did thou see them leave?"

I howled in frustration.

I still hear the stairs creak and the intimate whispers. The front door opens, footsteps cross the threshold, and the door slams shut. Too late, I hold a candle and look out onto the deserted street.

~12~

A new century arrived, but my thoughts were mired in the past. Elma had been missing for ten days.

A second letter arrived from Cornwall. I recognized Mother's severe script and set it on the mantel, unopened. I was washing the floor, scowling at the unwanted missive, when it occurred to me that the letter might contain word of Elma. I tore it open and my eyes scrambled down the page, but there were only more questions and the news that my aunt had taken to her bed. I considered going to meeting to pray for Aunt Mary's recovery but did not want to go out in public or search within myself. I had reached the depth of my grief but had only stirred the surface of my anger.

I was trying to coax some food into Patience when Will came and sat by my side.

"I've been thinking a lot about Miss Sands." His Adam's apple bobbed as he choked out words.

"That's kind, Will. We all have." I raised a spoonful of barley to Patience's mouth, sure that Levi had asked Will to come speak with me.

"I made her sad once. It was the day she came to New York, and I feel really bad about it. Especially now."

Patience swatted the spoon and stuck her fingers in her cereal, but I turned to the boy. I remembered him standing on the dock beside Elma, and I saw her pinch the bridge of her nose to fight back tears.

"Why was she unhappy?" I asked, hoping Will's story would not match Levi's and I could finally find a chink in Levi's armor.

Will shrugged. "She thought my master would come here with her. But he couldn't, not right away."

"Why not?"

"He had some things to square away with his brother first. Ezra didn't want him here."

"Will—" My breath caught. I was the only person who had heard Elma say that she planned to marry Levi that stormy night. If Will could offer proof, perhaps someone would listen. "Were they planning to marry?"

Will fidgeted in his seat. "Once, I pretended to be sleeping when my master undressed. He came with the candle to see if I was sleeping or not. Supposing I was, he went upstairs in his shirt and—" Color splotched Will's blemished cheeks. "He didn't come back until morning."

Disappointment coursed through me. This wasn't proof of Elma and Levi's engagement; it was simply more evidence of Elma's loose morals.

"When was this?" I asked, though I already knew the answer.

"Last fall, when you were away."

Patience knocked down the cereal bowl, splattering cold barley across the floor. Neither Will nor I moved to clean it up.

"The night Miss Sands—" Will's voice cracked. "The night Miss Sands . . . disappeared, my master slept well, but since then he's been restless, and last night near day he called out in his sleep."

I sat up so quickly that Patience began to cry. "What did he say?"

Will's gaze shifted from the baby to me. "He said, 'Oh! Poor Elma!'"

It was proof of nothing, yet it augmented all my suspicions.

The stairs creaked. I was sure Levi would storm into the room and confront Will, but it was Richard Croucher. For a fat man, he walked with a light stride.

"Talking about Weeks?" he said.

Patience clung to my bosom, and Will looked almost as miserable. He seemed even younger than his years, and his position was difficult: He had a loyal disposition and a villain of a master. He turned to Croucher as if he might deny the accusation but seemed reluctant to lie in front of me. "I was speaking with Mrs. Ring," he said.

"About Weeks's peculiar behavior? Or was it about Miss Sands—or maybe the pair of them?"

Will shook his head, but he was protesting Croucher's meddling, not his words. "It's private."

Croucher raised a brow; the hairs were long and wiry, his eyes watery. "The sheriff's come. It's not private—" He began to cough, swallowed, and began again. "It's hardly a private affair."

"Will was speaking with me in confidence," I said, attempting an imperious tone.

Blood rose to Croucher's neck and ears. "And yet I couldn't 'elp but overhear, but my recollection is somewhat different. In fact, the night Miss Sands disappeared, and the next night, and every succeeding night, I've heard Weeks awake from eleven o'clock till four in the morning. A continual noise."

I might have asked Croucher what he was doing awake until four in the morning or why his story did not match Will's, but those things were secondary to my true concern.

"What kind of noise?" I asked, but the sound was already thrumming in my ears, endless pacing throughout the day and night.

"Moving chairs, throwing down fireplace tongs, crumpling papers—I thought he was drawing plans for his brother's next spectacular public works, but since then I've accounted for it in a different way." Croucher cleared his throat. "The man is riddled with guilt. That, and fear."

"He is hiding something," I agreed.

Taking my assent as an invitation, Croucher sat down at the table, leaning close enough for me to smell his sour breath. "He's done away with her."

Suddenly, Will's adolescent bumbling was replaced with a grown man's rage. He jumped to his feet, toppling his chair. "You're no friend of my master's!"

"Just a moment, Will," I said, standing to place a restraining hand on his shoulder. I needed to hear what Croucher had to say. In the silence, I could hear the beating of my pulse, accusations I longed to express, my simmering rage.

"Since the day she disappeared, I've been going around, asking questions. You weren't the only one to see them leave together that night, Mrs. Ring."

Richard Croucher was the unlikeliest of allies, but I was relieved someone shared my conviction. "Who else?"

"Your neighbor, Lorena Forrest. She did."

I do not remember arriving at Lorena Forrest's house, just being there. Perhaps there was the usual exchange of pleasantries, though I doubt it.

"Lorena, did thou see Elma the night she disappeared?" I asked as we stood in her open doorway.

Lorena looked past me to the crowded street, and I wondered why she had not come to see me during these interminable ten days. Like the customers who no longer frequented our store, our friends had started to avoid us.

"I saw something," she said. "A sleigh."

A strange sort of satisfaction washed over me. Far from happiness, it was more like affirmation that I was not entirely mad.

"When was it? What time?"

Lorena stepped back as if alarmed by the questions. Or perhaps it was my tone. "It was quarter past eight. I know the time because I had just returned from meeting. Of course, it was a stormy night, but I make it a point to attend."

Ignoring her reproach, I plowed on. "That's exactly the right time. Did Elma get into the sleigh? Was she with Levi?"

"I did not see her get in. There were not many folks about, but one woman had slipped on some ice and I was helping her to her feet when a sleigh went racing past us at full gallop. It nearly knocked us both back down."

"And Elma?" It was impossible to hide my impatience. "Was Elma in the sleigh?"

"There were two men and a woman riding in it."

"Two men?" The information made no sense. "Was one of them Levi? Was it Elma?"

"Oh, Caty, I wish I could say. It was dark. Moonlight plays tricks on tired eyes."

"What color was the horse?"

"Who can tell the color of a horse at night?"

"Was it dark bay? Levi's brother owns a dark bay."

"As does half the city." She took my hand as if to apologize. "It's why I haven't gone to the sheriff. Everything happened so quickly, I'm not certain what I saw."

"But Levi always uses his brother's sleigh, and so few were out that night."

"It doesn't prove it was him. Then again . . ." She stood absolutely still, as if struggling with her conscience. "There was something strange."

"What was it?" I snapped.

"The harness had no bells."

"No bells?"

"It's peculiar. As if someone were being intentionally quiet."

"Quiet and cunning," I said, "which was exactly Levi's plan. He lured her away."

The color drained from Lorena's face. "Then what?"

"And then—" I was at a loss for words. "And then I don't know," I admitted, unable to say what I truly believed. By denying that Elma had come to harm, I could hold out hope.

There was a commotion on the street. People's backs were toward me, but there was no mistaking Levi's broad shoulders and fashionable hairstyle. He was shoving Richard Croucher, pushing him forward with open hands, the way one might prod the flank of an obstinate horse. Croucher was nearly twice Levi's width but only as tall as his shoulder. To make up the difference, he was craning his neck, spitting, and shouting directly into Levi's enraged face.

"What do you think of yourself now?" I heard him sneer. His speech, which was perfectly precise, seemed to be directed at the crowd, rather than Levi.

"How dare you spread rumors about me," Levi shouted.

"What about her?" Croucher asked. "Eh, Adonis? What about your sweetheart?"

Levi looked helplessly at the throng, as if he wanted their support but could not bear their presence.

"What happened to her?" Croucher demanded without a trace of his former accent.

Levi looked so despondent that for an instant I pitied him. But as he stumbled to answer, my sympathy rapidly waned.

"Miss Sands was my . . ." Levi hesitated. "She was my friend."

"And where is your friend now?" the woman who had been keeping vigil outside our home shouted. Levi blanched. I fought the urge to run into the street and accost him myself.

Lorena stood by my side, fascinated by the chaos.

"Is this justice?" I asked. Levi was being punished, but Elma's reputation was being dragged down with him.

There was more shoving, and I wondered if the mob might take matters into their own hands. I was more alarmed by my own emotions than by any possible violence. I was not against making Levi suffer.

"I'd say you were good friends indeed," Croucher leered. "You paid her a good deal of attention alone in her bedroom."

Levi swung and struck Croucher with a blow to the face. Croucher staggered backward, flinching, and a thin trickle of bright-red blood bubbled from his nose. His lips moved, tasting, and he raised his hand to his face and pulled it away, startled.

At the sight of his own blood, Croucher grew enraged. "Murderer!" he cried, swinging left, then right, into Levi's chest and shoulder.

Levi grabbed Croucher by the scruff of the neck. He was raising his fist to take another punch when he caught my eye.

I met his gaze, surprised that he would seek me out.

Croucher tensed as they both turned toward me.

"Caty," Levi said. "If you can say anything in my favor, you would do me more good than any friend I have in the world. Please, help me clear my name."

"What?" It seemed an outrageous request.

"Caty," Croucher shouted, "don't listen to this maggot."

"Go to the sheriff," Levi begged. "Tell him I'm innocent."

I had never been so incensed. "I wouldn't do it even if I believed thee, and I don't."

Levi buried his head in his hands and his chest heaved. He may have been weeping. "I'm ruined."

His remorse fueled my fury. "Has thou no pity for Elma? Or are thou thinking only of thyself?"

"Elma is lost. Go with me and say that nothing passed between Elma and me."

"If I were to do that, it would be positive lies."

"No doubt you're right. I'm undone forever, unless Elma appears to clear me."

"Thou left this house with Elma, and I will continue to say so until she is found."

Levi's back straightened as he stepped toward me. "What of it if we left together? It doesn't mean anything."

It was not exactly a confession, but it felt like victory. "Where is she?" I demanded. "Tell me what happened to Elma!"

"Where's Elma?" shouted the woman with the wild gray hair.

Wide-eyed and frantic, Levi took in the angry crowd. "What are you accusing me of?" he asked.

"A guilty conscience needs no accuser," Croucher snarled.

Levi's eyes narrowed into slits. "I have friends," he said, "powerful friends, who will defend me."

"Find them," I called as he stormed away. "Thou will need their help." My head was reeling, but my eyes were dry. I was done with tears.

I was folding wash, a task I usually delegated to Elma, when the muff reappeared It was presented with trembling, outstretched hands. Led into my home by his father, followed closely by spectators, a young boy offered the putrid muff to me as if it were a sacrifice.

I took it, stroked it, clung to it. Frozen in places, bald in others, it reeked of mold and decay, yet at that moment there was nothing dearer to me in the world.

Elias was reading with Charles. At the sight of the muff, he closed the book and covered his eyes. "Is it the one she was carrying?" he asked, refusing to meet my gaze. Charles began to whimper.

Unable to find words, I nodded. I would have recognized the muff even if it had not had Elizabeth Watkins's initials printed on the lining.

"Where was it found?" Elias asked, his voice shaking.

The boy's father looked anxiously around the room. He was a farmer, in stained breeches, and his boots left cakes of mud on the floor. Strangers jostled in the entranceway, anxious to hear the news.

"Give him room. Let him speak," Joseph Watkins said.

The farmer set his hand on his son's shoulder. "My boy was playing by Lispenard's Meadows." He shook his head. "I warned him not to go up there in this weather, but boys . . ."

"When?" I asked, unable to hide my mounting panic. Though the muff was in tatters, it was possible that Elma had only recently discarded it.

The farmer looked at Elias. He seemed unnerved by the urgency of my voice. "The boy brought it home the day before Christmas. I told him to get rid of the filthy thing, but he hid it in the barn. I can't say why. Maybe he sensed there was something to it. Then, this morning, we heard about the girl."

"This morning?" I shouted, dimly aware that I was misdirecting my anger at him. "How can that be? It has been in all the newspapers!" Elma had been missing only two days when the muff was found, and it was now nine miserable days later.

The farmer shrugged, avoiding my gaze. "Don't read papers."

I studied the man's scruffy beard and worn clothes. His fingernails were filthy. No doubt he could not read.

He shuffled, looking as if he regretted coming at all. "We live north of the city. Keep to ourselves." The boy gazed expectantly at his father, who moved his hand to his son's head and ruffled his hair. I looked at Charles, seated at the table beside Elias, and was ashamed that I had accosted the poor man in front of his child.

"Did thou go to the meadow?" Elias asked.

"I did," said the farmer. He seemed relieved to be addressing Elias rather than me.

"Was there anything unusual?" Joseph Watkins asked.

The farmer nodded. "The snow was fresh and I saw a sleigh track. There is no road there so I thought someone had lost their way in the storm."

"Gather the search party!" Watkins called. He took the muff. The foul thing smelled like wet leaves and rank hides, yet I was loath to let it go.

I collected my bonnet and shawl. Elias scowled and Charles began to sob.

"This is no job for a woman," Elias said.

"Joseph," I said, tying the strings of my bonnet. "Will Elizabeth stay with the children?"

"Yes, yes, of course," he said.

"Don't go," Charles begged, throwing himself toward me. "Mama, don't leave me too."

His cries pierced my heart, but I had no choice. If there was a trace left of Elma, I would unearth it. I would find her.

—13—

It was what I had been waiting for. It was what I had been dreading. A dozen men assembled. Several brought sleighs and shovels. Too tired to argue, Elias helped me into Joseph Watkins's sleigh. I sat wedged between the men as the horse flew at a full gallop up Greenwich Street.

We crossed Canal Street, and the road narrowed into a farmer's lane. The path was ungraded. The runners whistled as we slid across patches of ice. More than once, the sleigh was thrown off-balance, forcing Elias to jump down and set it right. The winter sun was slung low on the horizon. My face was raw from wind and cold. My body was frozen with fear.

"This isn't right," I said more than once. "Elma would never have come this way."

Elias gazed at me with dull eyes and did not respond. Though the conditions were poor, the ride could not have taken more than ten minutes. We cut through fences, galloped up and down hills, and crossed over a small bridge. The ground grew low and swampy, and clumps of thick brown dirt splattered our clothing and flew into our eyes. In the spring, the trees and gently rolling hills made the meadow a popular picnic ground, and in wintertime, people often skated on the frozen marsh.

Now the fields were a patchwork of crusty snow and mud, deterring even the most devoted sportsman. Brush weighed down the twisted tree limbs with frost, and snowdrifts surrounded the fields. A pillar of smoke rose from the chimney of the nearest farmhouse. I took a deep breath and inhaled the sweet smell of fire as it mingled with the cold air. It was a scent I associated with Cornwall and home, but it no longer soothed me.

The party slowed as the tracks ended. The horses came to a halt, stomping and snorting. Steamy breath billowed from their nostrils. I knew logically that Elma might have come to some kind of harm. Still, I had held out hope. In my wildest dreams, I never imagined she would be found in such a godforsaken place.

Reluctantly, as if he shared my horror, Elias stood on shaky legs. I caught the tail of his overcoat.

"She's not here," I said, trying to suppress a mounting sense of doom.

Elias pried my hands away and climbed down from the sleigh. Watkins and his crew jumped down and began to examine the ground.

"This way," said the boy who had found the muff.

Half a dozen men followed him on a path that seemed to lead nowhere.

"No," I called, but Elias was trudging away across the barren field. As I stood to follow, I caught a glimpse of a distant home. If not for the bare trees, I do not think I would have spotted it. The house was grand, two stories, with a wide second-floor balcony. It was painted white and sat in a clearing.

"What's that?" I asked a man who had remained behind to look after the horses.

"The mansion?"

"Yes."

"Richmond Hill. It was General Washington's headquarters during the war."

I knew the name. And I knew the current owner. "Doesn't Colonel Burr live there now?"

"He does." The man glanced up to where I stood gawking in the sleigh and seemed to recall the purpose of our trip. "May I help you, ma'am?" He held my arm as I climbed down.

Alone, I forged through crusty snow and bramble. Twigs snagged my skirt and scratched my hands, as if trying to hold me back. Willowy weeds resembled skeletons. I walked about a hundred yards before joining the others in front of a knee-high mound. It was thicker than the other drifts and almost perfectly round.

"Here it is," said the boy's father.

"What is it?" Elias asked.

"They call it the Manhattan Well. My boy was fishing around in there and spotted the muff."

The men gathered round the abandoned well. Frozen boards lay across the top. A single plank was tossed to the side, leaving an opening so narrow that it was hard to believe even the muff had slipped through. The party grumbled and speculated. No one seemed eager to make the first move.

One man broke the silence. "My neighbor did some work up here. Water was supposed to run down to the city, but quicksand choked the pump."

"It ain't old," the boy's father said. "Manhattan Company dug it last fall."

"Now Burr's more interested in getting elected," someone added. There was a chorus of assent. Still, no one moved.

I studied the frozen mound with resolve. This hole in the ground did not look like much, nor would it ever amount to anything. It was exactly as Elma had said: The Manhattan Company was a fraud. My anger slipped into dread as I focused on the hellish pit. I had little doubt that this was the scene of terrible violence. A place born of such cutting deception could only yield misery.

Elias stood apart from the others, hat in hand.

"Elias," I whispered. "Ezra and Levi work with Burr. Their men dug this well."

Elias did not respond. I wasn't even sure he heard me.

"Elias," I said again, turning toward him.

His eyes were closed and his head was bent in prayer. "He visits the sin of the fathers upon the children."

I drew away, wondering how, even now, Elias could hold Elma responsible for the weaknesses of her forebears. She didn't deserve this. No one did.

Elias approached the well. He knelt down on hands and knees and peered into the abyss, looked left and right, then shook his head. "Too dark," he mumbled, grasping one of the boards with his bare hands. His knuckles grew red from the cold, then white from exertion. He applied more pressure, and the plank broke free with a crack, exposing a circle of rough-hewn bricks below. Elias punched his fist into the well to break the ice. His hand was bloody when he pulled it back. Bright-red droplets seeped into the snow as he braced himself over the hole and leaned down for a closer look. "Can't see much," he called out.

A man named James Lent—I knew him from Greenwich Street and as a friend of the Watkinses—lit a candle and knelt beside Elias. The thin flame flickered, then expired. Two others, wearing tall boots, advanced. More boards were removed, but the winter light was waning, the well deep and shadowy.

"We need to feel it out," Watkins suggested. "Does anyone have a pole?"

"That's Lispenard's property," the farmer said, pointing toward the house with the chimney smoke.

I remembered the man named Lispenard, who had challenged Burr at the water meeting and accosted Ezra Weeks at the pump. He had accused the Weeks brothers of digging useless holes. Now I stood helplessly in front of one, awaiting Elma's fate. Reaching deep in my pocket, my fingers grasped her lost ribbon. I had carried it with me as a talisman, never imagining it would lead me here.

The farmer's boy was sent to fetch Lispenard.

Ten frigid minutes followed, while the men made a show of studying tracks and footprints. Some bent over to examine the ground at various angles, squinting eyes and tilting heads. One paced back and forth to the wagons, counting strides. A man with overgrown whiskers and buckteeth tasted the snow.

My boots were wet, my toes frozen, but my thoughts were clear. If Ezra Weeks's men had laid the pipes for this well, there was no doubt Levi knew of its existence. It seemed proof of his guilt. I stared at the well and its impossibly small opening. A grave was more inviting.

The boy reappeared with the outspoken man I recognized as Lispenard. Each carried a long pole. A chubby woman waddled behind them.

"Mr. and Mrs. Lispenard?" Joseph Watkins asked. The couple nodded. "We're here to investigate the disappearance of a missing girl."

"I told you," Mrs. Lispenard said, wagging her finger at her husband. "I told you I heard something."

"You heard about the missing girl?"

Lispenard spoke for his wife. "Arnetta and I heard about a girl that ran off with her lover."

"Yes," Watkins said, taking care to avoid my gaze. "Blanck's boy found her muff in the well."

"I knew I heard shouting," Arnetta Lispenard said.

My stomach dropped.

Watkins held up his hand. "Slow down and tell us what happened."

"That was the night the chimney backed up." Arnetta Lispenard turned to her husband. "Remember, Anthony? It was that snowy day, and when you came back from town, the house was near filled with smoke."

"Mrs. Lispenard," Watkins said. "What about the girl?"

"I was about to tell," she said. "Anthony was out in the barn. I was fanning smoke but couldn't get nowhere with it. That's when he came inside. Said smoke didn't bother him and went to bed. But my eyes were stinging such that I couldn't sleep a wink, so I cracked open a window. That's when I heard her."

"Her?" I asked, though I can't say for sure that I spoke aloud.

"At first I thought it was a loon. Those birds have the sorriest cries. Then I leaned farther out. The snow had stopped, stars were out, but it was dark and the moon was dull. It was no night for birds. That got me thinking, it must have been a woman's voice. It was quite pitiful."

"Could you make out what was said?" Watkins asked.

Arnetta Lispenard nodded. "'Lord have mercy on me, Lord help me,'" she cried with theatrical drama. "A few minutes later I heard another cry, but it was not as loud as the first. The noise was strange, almost . . . smothered."

There was a loud, shrill scream. I could hear Elma pleading for life, choking and gasping for air, and, as clearly as I saw the gray sky above, I saw her at the bottom of an icy well, fighting to keep her head above water—and drowning.

"Help her! Someone help her!"

Elias was shaking me, and I realized the screams were my own. "Caty," he said, wrapping his arm around me. "Hush, now."

All eyes turned to Lispenard.

"Your wife heard screams and you did nothing?" Watkins demanded.

"That's what she heard. I didn't."

Arnetta Lispenard, happy enough to criticize her husband, seemed to take offense when others did. "He couldn't have known. It's been a peculiar winter," she said. "Few weeks back, there was a barn cat got itself caught in twine and was hanging from the rafters as sure as if it planned its own end. And before that, Abe—that's our beagle—poor Abe fell clear through the ice." She raised an arm and pointed toward the marsh. "He howled something terrible, but there was no getting to him. Then the calf got sick. I remember saying I'd be happy when this winter passed."

"Elma's a girl," I shouted, "not a barn cat or a beagle."

Lispenard shook his head, stealing looks at the abandoned well. "My wife's always hearing noises. I didn't think much of it. She got me up and I went to the window. There was nothing there."

Watkins's friend James Lent stepped forward. "There was no sleigh?"

Lispenard blew air into his cheeks. "Not that I saw. It was a starry night but, like my wife said, the moon was dull. It was difficult seeing. If I'd seen a sleigh, I'd have gone out," he said, with an apologetic shrug. "Boys come up here. They fool around."

"But your wife said the voice was female," Watkins said.

Lispenard shuffled and avoided Watkins's gaze. He was a shadow of the man who had spoken so fervently at the water meeting. "Her ears are old," he said. "Young boys, women, even the wind, it all sounds the same to her."

"Might there have been a sleigh on the far side of the well, down the embankment?" Lent asked.

"I suppose there could've been." Lispenard frowned and looked at the well. "If I'd seen it, I would have gone out," he said again.

"The girl disappeared the Sunday before Christmas," Watkins explained. "Was that the same night?"

Arnetta Lispenard stared into the distance. "Yes," she said, nodding slowly and then with more assurance. "I believe it was, because we'd been to church that day and the minister gave a sermon about sacrifice. Remember, Anthony?"

Lispenard grew pale and nodded as if he were only now realizing the gravity of his error. "We can feel out the well with these," he said, passing a pole to Lent.

Climbing the snowbank, Lent balanced on the rim of the well and sank the first pole. It was longer than a grown man, but once it was submerged, no more than a foot could be seen.

"Pass the other," Lent said, and someone handed him the second pole. Like a witch's cauldron, the well was stirred and poked.

For days I had thought of nothing but locating Elma, though I had never considered how she would be found or what would happen when she was. I wanted to find Elma. I needed to find her, but not here. Not in this lifeless, miserable place.

"I think I feel something," called Lent.

I covered my mouth so as not to scream.

The men's circle grew tighter. Watkins took hold of the pole and nodded. I watched as he directed the others.

"Grab it," Watkins said. His muscles flexed, and his face grew red and hardened into lines.

"Can you get underneath and hook it?" Lent asked.

Others tried. Some went down on hands and knees. But they came up empty-handed.

"See anything?" Watkins asked.

Supporting himself on a pole, Lent teetered perilously over the edge. "Looks like . . ." he said.

I staggered backward and opened my mouth, but the scream died in my throat.

"Dear Lord," Elias whispered.

Arnetta Lispenard appeared at my side. "Come along, darling, let me take you inside," she offered.

Eyes fixed on the well, I shook my head.

Watkins went to his carriage and returned with a hammer and nails. He rested the longer pole on the ground and drove a nail into its end, banging with full force. The fury of his blows matched the beat of my heart and echoed across the desolate fields. When the nails were in place, he handed the pole back to James Lent. "Try to hook it now," he said.

Again, Lent submerged the pole, applying his weight like a lever. "Help me," he said.

Watkins stood behind him and pushed the end of the pole down with the weight of his body.

A fistful of green fabric emerged, snagged by the sharp nail.

My knees buckled and, as if an invisible force had thrown me backward, I collapsed.

"Caty?" Elias stooped over and wrapped his arm around my shoulder. "Caty," he said again. "We must be strong."

I knew he was right. Yet the pain I felt was as real as any blow. I was breathless and stunned. My head was spinning and a wave of nausea rose within me. I had thought that Elma's absence was worse than death, that when she was found we would find some measure of peace. I was wrong.

"Up now," Elias said. He tucked his hands under my arms and pulled me to my feet.

The hope I had hidden deep inside was smothered as a nail and pole tore through the neckline of Elma's best dress, the one we had sewn so painstakingly, together.

"Draw her up," Watkins said. "Careful."

Elias pulled me close. I rested my head on his shoulder but could not look away.

"She's too heavy," said Lent.

The boy was sent to fetch a rope. He returned with a coarse, thick cord, the kind used as a noose. I watched in horror as Watkins and Lent steered the pole and shimmied the rope. Other men gripped the ends, pulling, chafed hand over chafed hand.

"Heave," someone cried.

The men tugged and panted. Some cursed. One gazed into the hole, dropped the rope, fell to his knees, and retched.

Lispenard, who had been so full of bluster, staggered backward, as pale as the snow. "It can't be, this can't be," he repeated like a vow.

"Pull together now," Watkins directed.

A chunk of thick snow slipped down the side of the well, exposing more bricks. The damp rope dragged against the icy grime and frayed until I thought it would snap. The men pulled.

Slowly, Elma emerged.

Her neck was limp, twisted at an impossible angle, and a shroud of wet hair obscured her face. The rope ran across her chest and under her arms. It took four men to hoist her up. Her back arched and scraped across the bricks and boards, and the rope grew slack as her body slid down the embankment and came to rest.

Elma had been eleven days in this gruesome place. Her hat was off. Her gown was torn open above the waist. Her shawl was missing. Her shoes were gone, and the tops of her feet were scraped. I went to her and knelt by her side. Frost had collected on her lashes. Her eyes were cloudy and vacant, open but unseeing. As I cradled her head and lifted it onto my lap, it rolled sideways as if no longer attached to her body. I brushed a tangle of hair off her face. My fingers caught in a hard knot. The ivory comb clung to her frozen locks, the ribbon gone.

I leaned my head down close to hers and kissed her waxy forehead. She had a loamy stench like a cellar. I closed my eyes but could not escape images from a lost dream: a swampy meadow, stagnant water.

"Elma!" I wept, shaking her until her head lolled forward and back.

-14-

E lias dragged me away from the pile of rank clothing and tangled
hair that once was Elma. His eyes looked bleary, or my vision had
blurred. He led me back to the road. I slipped in the snow. As he
helped me into Watkins's sleigh, I caught my heel on the runner and
tore the leather. Elias struck the horse with the whip, splattering us
both with icy mud.

"Where's Elma?" I looked over my shoulder to where the men
stood, stooped gray figures melting into the white snow. "She should
be home."

"Watkins will see to that."

"When?"

Elias mumbled into his collar. His eyes were fixed on the road and
his head swayed along with the pitching rig. I could tell that he was
in shock. It would have been easy for me to join him, but my senses
were rapidly returning, my devastation turning back into the rage I
had been nursing these long days. Elma was dead, but she had fought
to save herself. Her torn dress and scraped feet were proof of her
struggle. Her pain was my agony. Her fight was now my battle.

"She didn't do this to herself," I said. There was no way to reconcile the outward signs of trauma with self-inflicted pain. No one,
no matter her sorrow, would torture herself so horribly. A rancid
smell clung to my clothing, and one thought gripped my mind: Ezra
Weeks's men laid the pipes for the well, and Levi knew the location.
It was likely he oversaw the project himself. "Levi did," I said.

The reins grew taut in Elias's hands, and the horse pinned his
ears and whinnied. "Why?" he shouted over the wind. I couldn't tell
whether he was questioning me or the unjust workings of the world.
Either way, I had a response.

"Elma was carrying Levi's child."

Elias spun toward me, the horse balked, and the sleigh swerved off the narrow path. Surrounded by brush, the horse pulled up. The harness was tangled and the sleigh tipped at a menacing angle.

"Damn!" Elias swore. He jumped down and tried to pull the rig forward, but the horse flared his nostrils and tossed his head. Elias slapped the horse's flank, but he only backed farther into the thicket. "Get down," Elias hollered, though he didn't offer a hand.

I lowered myself into spiky bramble I more convinced than ever that Elma would never have come here alone.

Elias righted the sleigh and coaxed the horse back onto the road. I waited until we were moving before speaking again.

"Elias." It seemed essential that he acknowledge Levi's guilt. "Ezra didn't approve of Elma. He would never have condoned their marriage."

"Let it rest," he said.

"So he lured her from the house on the pretense of a wedding, and then he—" I grew queasy again, thinking about what Levi had done, how Elma had fought to save herself.

Elias snapped the reins. "Let her rest!"

"I can't," I said. "I won't," I swore.

We turned down Greenwich Street. Men, women, and children were gathered on the sidewalk in front of our house, and more spilled out into the street, making it impossible to approach. Three boys, not much older than Charles, tossed a ball. It was well past candlelight and frigid on the street, but the crowd closed in as we arrived, eager for news.

"Where's Elma?" called the woman who had become Elma's most ardent supporter. Other shouts drowned her out. Everyone had a question. None of which I could answer.

One of the Forrest boys pushed through the crowd to take the horse and sleigh.

Elias wrapped an arm around my shoulder and ushered me inside. His shoulders were shaking, his chest convulsing.

Through the dimness, I could see the children perched halfway up the stairs with Elizabeth Watkins. Their white nightgowns shone in the darkness like a modest beacon of hope.

"Caty?" Elizabeth rushed downstairs the moment the door closed behind us.

"She's been found," I said, then shook my head, imploring her not to ask more in front of the children. "Thy husband and the others are bringing her home and we'll be able to lay her to rest."

Charles ran down, hugging my legs. "Elma's coming home?" he asked.

I stroked his hair. It was silky and soft, though not as thick as Elma's. "Elma is in heaven now," I said, trying to compose myself.

"No!" he screamed, and his tiny fists punched against my skirt.

"That's enough," Elias said. He took Charles by the collar and pulled him away so forcefully that his bare feet dangled momentarily off the ground.

Elizabeth began to sob, and so did Patience. My stomach clenched. I had been unable to save Elma and I could not even comfort my own children. I knelt and took Charles's hands in mine.

"Heaven is a beautiful place. There are green pastures and clear, flowing streams—" My explanation sounded like one of Elma's stories, and I choked on my words.

"The Lord has summoned her," Elias said. Perhaps he regretted handling Charles so roughly, because his tone was unusually gentle.

I turned, hoping Elias had returned to his senses, but my relief was short-lived.

"Why?" Charles cried. "Why now?"

"Charles!" Elias exploded. He had always been quick to anger, but I had never seen him so volatile. "Off to bed. And mind thy sister."

Charles's eyes widened as he looked past the dark parlor toward the bedroom. "What if the Lord calls Patience or me?" He stepped backward. "What if we don't want to go?"

At her name, Patience began to shriek.

"The innocent will be spared," Elias said.

I spoke sharply, without considering Charles's fear. "Elma was innocent!"

"Caty," Elias said, "let the children go to bed."

"I'll take them," I said, scooping Patience into my arms. She was hiccuping, and I hugged her warm body until I could feel her heartbeat in my chest.

Elias clutched my arm. "The men will be returning, and someone has to see to her. Let Elizabeth put them to bed."

"Of course," Elizabeth said. She wiped her tears and smiled at Charles, though she had no words of consolation. No one did.

Elias's fingers dug into my flesh. I kissed Patience's soft forehead before handing her back to Elizabeth and following Elias into the parlor.

The fire was low. The room was empty, or so I thought until I saw a dark shadow in a rocker. The chair was pulled close to the hearth, tilted forward, and Levi was resting his feet on the grate. His body was doubled over, and he hugged his knees as if in pain.

"They found her," he said, not bothering to turn.

"Yes."

"At the Manhattan Well?" Levi asked.

Elias's head snapped up. "Why did thou say that? How did thou know?"

"Be-because of the muff," Levi stuttered. "Because of where it was found."

"The farmer's boy named Lispenard's Meadows. They never mentioned the Manhattan Well," Elias said, clenching his hands into tight balls.

"How would thou know where she was found?" I asked. "Unless thou put her there."

Levi jumped to his feet, pointing out the window. "Those people outside told me. They said the muff was found at Lispenard's Meadows."

"They named the Manhattan Well?" I'm not sure I would have believed him if he said the sky was blue.

"Yes," he insisted.

I shook my head and was about to say more when Elias shoved a chair so forcefully that it banged into the wall, broke a leg, and fell over. "Why weren't thee part of the search party?" he asked.

"I just returned," Levi said. "I only now heard."

"Yet thou knew exactly where she was found," I said.

"Tell us what happened to Elma," Elias demanded.

Levi took a step backward. There was little room between him and the fireplace, and his eyes flashed with fear. "I swear I don't know."

"Liar!" Elias shouted, rushing toward him.

"Caty?" Levi looked desperately at me, as if I would ever come to his defense.

"Elma was expecting a baby," I said.

Elias stopped in his tracks, and Levi blinked hard.

"She told you that?" he asked, looking from me to Elias.

"Not in so many words, but I guessed—"

Elias spun toward me. "I thought she confessed."

"She didn't have to; I could see. Isn't it obvious?" I asked, because I was the only one who seemed to understand. "He killed her to protect his inheritance."

There were shouts outside. I watched through the window as a sleigh drew up and the crowd grew silent. The front door opened and Isaac Hatfield entered.

"Watkins is here," Hatfield said, eyes downcast. "He has . . . He's brought—" He shook his head, running a hand over his forehead. "Dear God, what's the world come to?"

Elias glared at Levi. "If I were to meet thee in the dark," he said, "I wouldn't think it wrong to put a loaded pistol to the side of thy head."

I wanted to feel grateful that Elias was defending Elma for once, but his vehemence seemed reckless. Throwing chairs and spewing threats would not avenge her death.

Hatfield took stock of the dark room and splintered chair and stepped between Elias and Levi. "Your cousin is lying outside in a wagon bed. Let the law see to him."

Turning away, Elias kicked the chair before stepping back from Levi. His arms were folded across his chest, stiff and unnatural, but Hatfield stared at him and then exhaled, seemingly satisfied that the worst of the tension had passed.

"Mrs. Ring," he said, addressing me with awkward reverence, "would you please get the door? Elias"—his voice hardened— "Watkins needs help."

I followed Hatfield outside. A crowd had collected around the sleigh and Watkins was trapped in the bed, standing and shouting orders, until they cleared a path.

"Elias," I said, turning. I had thought he was right behind me, but a moment passed, then two, and he did not appear. I hurried back inside, worried that he and Levi had come to blows. "Elias?" I stood on the threshold, peering into the dark room.

Elias stood between Levi and the doorway, with his back toward me. "It's high time for the truth," he said. "She's dead. What happened to her?"

Levi sounded exhausted. "I told you. I don't know."

"The sheriff is on his way. I won't keep quiet."

"Accuse me"—Levi's voice grew sharp and menacing—"and my brother will take your home. You'll lose everything, including your name."

"My silence can't be bought. She's dead!"

"You're not innocent," Levi said. "Remember, Croucher saw you."

Elias laughed. He sounded deranged. "Richard Croucher will be happy to see thee hang."

My confusion about Elias's erratic behavior soured into suspicion. I stepped into the room. "Elias?"

There was banging at the front door.

"Ring," Hatfield hollered. "Come help."

I hurried back to the entrance, unfastened the latch, and stepped aside.

Watkins and Lent carried Elma inside. They had laid her on one of the frozen boards. Watkins had tried to hide her battered body with his overcoat, but her hair hung over the coarse fabric, and her bruised feet were exposed. The house took on a musty smell and I gagged, aware that the putrid stench came from her.

"Oh, Elma." My entire being shook. Nothing would ever be right again.

Sheriff Morris followed the men, trailed by a watchman. The sight of a uniformed officer with his leather helmet and heavy bat added to the unreality of the moment.

Watkins kept his eyes trained on the makeshift bed. "Where shall we put her?" He sounded angry, almost betrayed.

Elias, now quiet, deferred to me.

I gazed at the body. It was Elma, yet it wasn't. I pictured Elma's face, gentle and sweet as she was as a child, then my eyes returned to the foul lump before me. A feeling much like exhaustion, but more profound, overwhelmed me.

Levi stood in the dark corner, his lips twitching as he muttered to himself.

"Bring her upstairs to her bedroom," I said, leading the way.

Sheriff Morris followed on my heels, directing the men. James Lent negotiated the stairs backward, stooping down low so the warped plank would remain level. Elma's arms hung off both sides and scraped the stairwell's narrow walls like a last desperate plea.

In Elma's room, they laid her down on the bed and slid the plank out from beneath her. The movement upset her body and I went to her side, wanting to set her right. I touched her wrists, intending to place her arms flat, but they refused to bend. Her hair was frozen stiff. I brushed a lock and it snapped off and fell to the floor.

Elias stood next to me, his face nearly as white as Elma's. Watkins and Lent hung their heads. Levi hovered in the doorway. His shoulders were hunched and his eyes looked haunted, with none of their earlier fury.

I pulled back Watkins's coat. Someone had closed Elma's eyes, but she did not look the least bit peaceful. The waxy skin on her shoulders beneath her green dress was exposed. I tugged the fabric together in a futile effort to protect her modesty. The sour smell intensified, and I flung Watkins's coat to the corner as if it were the cause of the sickening odor. That's when I saw the bruises: discolored spots in a chain around her neck. I pressed my fingertip to one. The impression was larger than the tip of my index finger, but not by much.

"What's this?" I traced the spots with my finger. There were a half dozen, maybe more.

Elias grabbed my hand and held it back. "Caty, stop."

The sheriff stepped closer. "Mrs. Ring," he said. "May I ask you a few questions?"

"My wife's too distraught for questions," Elias said.

"The sooner we know the facts, the sooner justice will be served," Sheriff Morris said.

"Yes." I shared his sense of urgency. "I'm ready."

Sheriff Morris launched into his inquiry. "When was the last time you saw your cousin, Gulielma Sands, alive?"

I had never heard anyone but Aunt Mary refer to Elma by her Christian name. The knowledge that I would have to soon explain Elma's fate to my aunt made me dizzy. I was certain the news would kill her. I stumbled backward. Elias helped me into a chair, and someone brought a glass of water. I stared at the cloudy liquid. It was nothing like the pristine water that flowed readily from the streams in Cornwall, and I had no desire to drink it. Elma died in this city's filthy water. Levi had put her there.

"How long has it been since you saw Miss Sands alive?" the sheriff asked again. I knew the question was a mere formality, as the timing of her disappearance was public knowledge.

Elias stepped between us. "She's in no condition to be interrogated."

I took a deep breath. Elma would never again experience the colors of autumn or hear a robin sing in early spring. She would never hold her baby to her breast, never marvel at her child's laughter. No one would inherit her playful smile or gift for storytelling. Levi had stolen her future.

He would pay for his crime.

"It's been eleven days," I said, feeling more clearheaded. It seemed like a long time for Elma to have been gone and a short time for my fortune to have changed so completely.

Sheriff Morris stated the date that Elma had vanished as if he had given the matter considerable thought. "December twenty-second. And what time did she leave here that night?"

"Shortly after eight." I recalled the stormy evening, remembered brushing Elma's glossy hair, the lifeless remnants of which lay scattered on the floor. I pointed at Levi. "She left with him. They were to be married."

Levi was motionless on the threshold.

"Levi Weeks," Sheriff Morris said. "Do you know the young woman who lies there a corpse?"

Levi stepped backward. "I think I know the gown."

"That is not the question. Is there no mark in that countenance you know?"

Levi covered his eyes with both hands. "It's too hard."

"Answer him," Elias demanded, his voice rising. I set my hand on his arm, praying he would not threaten Levi in the sheriff's presence.

There were shouts on the street, but in Elma's room, we were still. Now that their mission had ended, Watkins and Lent stood awkward in their idleness. Hatfield was biting his lip as if holding back words, or tears, and I could see the blue veins in Elias's neck throb.

The sheriff kept his eyes on Levi. "Do you know this girl?"

Levi was shaking his head. He managed to maintain his composure, but he kneaded his rigid white hands.

Anger surged through me and I rushed to Elma's side, struggling to free the ivory comb from the weedy tangle that had been her silky hair. "What about this?" I said, holding the bone-white comb under his nose so the sharp teeth nearly scraped him.

Levi's mouth fell open, but he still did not answer.

There was huffing on the stairwell and Richard Croucher burst into the room, shoving Levi aside. He marched up to Elma's bed and shook his head. "A fallen woman, indeed." His gaze was spiteful as his eyes met Levi's. "Found 'er in the Manhattan Well. What do you say to that, Adonis?"

"I have nothing to say to you," Levi spat.

"But you know the place." Croucher looked knowingly around the room, his eyes landing on the sheriff. "'e did a bit of work up there, you know."

No matter his previous indiscretions, I felt a swell of gratitude toward the bizarre Richard Croucher, the only one who shared my instinct. "Levi *did* help build that well," I emphasized. The disclosure seemed so incriminating, I imagined the sheriff immediately dragging him to the hangman's scaffold.

"I was by that way myself that night," Croucher continued. It was a strange admission.

I thought of the narrow road and deep snow.

Sheriff Morris turned, his eyebrows raised. "You say you were by the Manhattan Well that night?"

Pleased to be the focus of attention, Croucher did not seem to grasp the implication of the question. I wanted to gag him, but he continued. "Several times. Unfortunate I wasn't there at the right time. I might have saved her."

"What time were you there?" the sheriff asked.

Croucher's chest deflated. "I can't say exactly."

"So how do you know it was the wrong time?"

"I didn't 'ear nothing.If that poor girl was being murdered—" He removed his hat and ran his hand across the balding patch at the crown of his head. "My regrets, ma'am," he said, glancing at me, but he kept on speaking. "If someone 'ad been doing 'er 'arm, I'd 'ave 'eard something," Croucher spat, his speech failing as his temper increased.

"Where were you exactly?" Sheriff Morris asked.

Croucher's face grew ruddy and he wiped his brow. "I supped at Ann Ashmore's on Bowery Lane." He looked over his shoulder. "Ask 'er."

Sheriff Morris nodded at the watchman, who took note.

Croucher cocked his head toward Levi. "It's this man needs questioning. Ask 'im where *he* was."

"I dined at my brother's," Levi said sharply. His eyes darted around the room, avoiding mine.

"Why not lay your 'ands on 'er?" Croucher said. It was believed that if a killer set his hands on his victim, blood would flow from them, making his guilt manifest.

While I did not believe that blood would rush from Levi's hands, I was curious to see his reaction. My fingertips nearly matched the impressions on Elma's neck. I was certain his would be a perfect fit.

"Have him put his fingers on the spots around her neck," I said.

Elias stepped closer. "If thou are innocent, thou need not refuse."

Levi had taken another step backward and was now standing in the hallway.

"I'd sooner die than gratify your curiosity," he said, but his voice was void of emotion.

"Mr. Weeks," Sheriff Morris said, "I believe you should come with us."

Levi balked. "What charge is brought against me?"

"Thou can't be ignorant of the charge," Elias said.

Levi backed farther away; one more step and he would topple down the stairs. "I swear I am." His eyes were wide and his lips trembled.

"Mr. Weeks," said the sheriff, "I ask that you come peacefully."

"I'll come," Levi said, "but I insist you notify my brother, Ezra Weeks."

"We all know who your brother is," Croucher called as the sheriff led Levi downstairs.

The front door banged open.

"That's him!" someone shouted.

"That's Elma's killer!" an angry voice roared.

"Levi Weeks is a blackhearted murderer!" the mob bellowed. "Hang him!"

I allowed myself a fleeting smile.

⏤15⏤

The pounding on the door began early the next morning. Long minutes passed while I held my breath, praying the trespasser would leave. The knocking kept pace with my throbbing temples, announcing our new reality. Elma was dead, and an early-morning visitor could only mean more misery.

The previous night had been long and painful. Charles and I nestled together in his rickety bed. He sobbed while I choked back tears. Just before midnight, he drifted off, and I lay motionless, gazing at the starry night through the frosty window. Too troubled to sleep, I wandered into the parlor, lit a lamp, and confronted the inevitable. For the next few hours, I struggled to put words to this disaster.

> My Beloved Aunt,
> Our darling Elma was found dead yesterday. The circumstances are a mystery, but Elias and I are determined to discover the cause. She is home now, resting peacefully. Final preparations are being made. She will be buried at the Friends burial ground, a picturesque place with a rolling lawn, a short walk from our home.
> Please know that I loved Elma as if she were my own child. God willing, she has gone to a better place and, one day, we will join her in eternity.

The letter felt cruel in its brevity. Spilled ink and tears dotted the page. With bitter pleasure at the frivolous waste, I crumpled the thing and threw it into the fireplace. The cinders were hardly burning, and I squashed the page with a poker and buried it under the ashes. My second draft, and third, were just as pathetic. It was impossible to convey my sorrow, and I kept imagining my aunt's bony hands shaking as she unfolded the page. I cringed recalling that first letter I had written to Aunt Mary nearly a year ago, inviting Elma to visit. I had promised to care for Elma, and she had died a nightmarish death. I may as well have killed her myself.

Pushing the pitiful missive aside, I struggled to make sense of my emotions. I felt sadness and grief, resentment, guilt, and anger. Why did Elma trust Levi? Why did she leave me? Why did I allow her to go?

I found myself on the landing outside Levi's door. I had stood in the very same spot the night Elma vanished, too hesitant to knock. Fear no longer held me back. I had combed through each and every one of Elma's possessions, but this was the first time I had set foot in Levi's room since the sheriff had led him away. At first glance, nothing looked unusual. The bed was made, the wardrobe empty. Poor Will, who had fled after Levi's arrest, must have packed his master's things as well as his own. I opened each dresser drawer, beginning at the bottom and working my way up. I had rummaged through Elma's bureau countless times. Unlike her drawers, Levi's slid easily open. I heard a soft rolling noise before I saw it: The small gemlike glass was empty. Only a blood-red residue remained. Had Levi fed Elma laudanum before throwing her down the well? Why hadn't he destroyed the vial?

I was trying to collect my thoughts when I noticed the spilled remnants of a candle on the nightstand. It was a miracle the house had not caught fire. Furious at what I was convinced was Levi's final act of destruction, I went to the table, wanting to be rid of every last trace of him. When the wax proved too hard to scrape away, I lowered my lamp and lit the charred wick. The flickering light gave off an otherworldly glow, illuminating scratches in the puddle of wax. As the wick flared, letters came to life, twisting and turning like a vine seeking sunlight: *Elma.*

Elma's name had been etched by the same hand that had carved her ivory hair comb. The same fingers that had made the discolored imprints in the crooked chain around her neck. The same ones that had killed her.

My breath grew shallow and I sat heavily on the bed. I do not know how much time passed. When I looked again, the wax was dripping down the side of the nightstand, and the letters had melted into nothingness. Who could say if they had been there at all? My head was filled with a loud, persistent drumming.

The noise increased until it occurred to me that someone was knocking on the front door. I sat perfectly still, praying to be left in peace. Moments passed. Birds were chirping, but their chatter only emphasized the racket. I pulled my shawl around my shoulders and went downstairs to answer.

"Mrs. Ring?" A distinguished-looking gentleman, tall and slender in a dark overcoat, stood, hat in hand. "My name is Dr. Prince. The sheriff sent me."

A pack of wolves would have been more welcome. Wintery air flooded the vestibule, but it was the doctor's presence that made me shiver. He barely registered my distress. He had the seasoned eyes of a physician, one who had seen countless births and deaths and learned to reconcile the two.

"I've come to conduct the coroner's inquest," he said, brandishing a large black case with shiny clasps. I was certain the brass was as cold as his demeanor. I imagined his apathetic fingers probing Elma. "I apologize for the hour, but I wanted to get here as soon as possible." He glanced over his shoulder at the street, which was mercifully empty.

Elias shuffled out of the bedroom, looking as haggard as I felt. He tensed up at the sight of our visitor. "Please let us bury our kin in peace," he said.

"Mr. Ring," Dr. Prince replied, "I respect your grief, but I am afraid Miss Sands cannot be buried until I have conducted an exam."

"She's dead," Elias said. "What's left to examine?"

"Miss Sands's death is now a matter of law, and the sheriff has requested an inquest."

"The dead should be allowed to rest in peace," Elias said. "That's God's law."

"We can't bury her?" I asked. There seemed no end to the horror.

"After I present my findings to the coroner's jury." The doctor's voice softened. "If the death is determined to be unnatural, there will be a trial."

"Of course her death was unnatural," I said. "She was murdered."

Dr. Prince tugged at the chain of his pocket watch. "It's impossible to say what the evidence will prove, until after my examination."

Elias crossed his arms and positioned himself at the base of the staircase. "And if we don't allow it? What then?"

"Mr. Ring," the doctor said, "if you don't step aside, I'll be forced to summon the sheriff."

"That won't be necessary." Unable to predict how he might react, I placed a tentative hand on Elias's arm and spoke gently. "Anything the doctor finds will only help convict Levi."

Elias hung his head in concession, but his eyes trailed me as I led Dr. Prince upstairs. The climb had never felt so long or tiresome. The steps creaked. My legs ached and my temples pulsed. When we reached the third-floor landing, I stood back. Dr. Prince and his black bag appeared out of place in Elma's room, with its eyelet curtains and lace doilies. He seemed to agree, holding the bag high, as if he did not know where to set it, and finally settling on the table beside the washbasin. My stomach lurched as he snapped open the clasps. Knives, scalpels, and a miniature hammer with a pointed head clanged against a cold metal tray. The last item he removed, more dreadful than all the others, was a cloth mask, which he tied around his mouth and nose.

It struck me that Elma was nothing more to him than a job, a pile of rotting flesh like any other, which he was commissioned to examine too early on a cold winter morning. He would never know her, never admire her grace or hear her laughter.

"Wait," I begged. I took a deep breath, went to Elma's side, and ran my hand along her cheek. The stench was horrible, but touching her was worse. Her skin puckered and, when I pulled away, it refused to plump back into shape.

"Mrs. Ring, is there any information you may have neglected to tell the sheriff?" Through the mask, his voice was as sharp as the blades on his tray.

"Is it possible . . ." I began, gazing down at the lifeless creature that had once been Elma. "Could one tell if she used medication?"

The doctor looked up from his instruments. "What sort of medication?"

"Laudanum."

"Miss Sands took laudanum?"

"No!" I shook my head. "Just the opposite. There are those—Levi Weeks said she took it to do away with herself. But I know she never did."

"It is impossible to say until I've conducted my exam."

I smoothed down Elma's dress below the bodice, where it stretched across her belly. For the hundredth time since she came home, I considered changing her dress. The muslin was thin in places, ripped in others, and the green fabric was now the color of mold. But each time I reached toward the shredded collar, my eyes locked on the bruised spots around her neck. I was petrified to see what lay beneath the tattered dress.

The doctor straightened, holding a scalpel in one hand. "It is surprising what a body will reveal even after its demise. One can tell, for instance, whether an infant was stillborn or a victim of infanticide, whether a body found in water was someone who drowned or a victim of a disguised homicide, even if a young woman was a maiden." He held it to the light, running his finger along the blade.

It seemed like a direct appeal. I considered feigning offense, but his assumption was not wrong. What's more, I was tired of hiding the truth. If I had spoken out when I first suspected that Elma was pregnant, maybe I could have saved her.

I took a deep breath. "Actually, I've reason to believe . . . It's possible Elma was—"

Elias came rushing into the room, brandishing a torn newspaper. "Says right here she was 'willfully murdered!'"

I snatched the paper out of his hands. There it was: our tragedy reduced to a paragraph of print.

Thursday afternoon, the body of a young woman by the name of Gulielma Elmore Sands was found dead in a well recently dug by the Manhattan Company, a little east of Anthony Lispenard's farm. The circumstances attending her death are somewhat singular. She went from her cousin's house in Greenwich Street on Sunday evening, December 22, with her lover, with an intention of going to be married, from which time until yesterday afternoon she had not been heard of. Strong suspicions are entertained that she has been willfully murdered.

"Where did this come from?" I asked.

The question seemed to take Elias by surprise. "It was outside the front door. This one too." Elias read out loud: "'Little did Miss Sands expect that the nuptial arrangements she had been making with so much care would direct her to that bourn from which no traveler returns.'"

Elma had left a cryptic message in the water jug what felt like ages ago. This time the message was clear. "Why must Elma suffer any more?" I said, waving at the scalpels and knives. "It's obvious that Levi murdered her. Her life was stolen—will her body now be desecrated as well?"

There was an angry thud on the side of the house.

"What on earth?" Elias went to the window and began to furiously wave his arms. "This is private property. Get out of here!" he shouted through the closed pane.

"What is it?" I asked, not daring to approach the window.

"Those lunatics have put up a ladder," Elias said, frowning at Elma's lifeless body as if she were still causing trouble.

"Mrs. Ring, were you about to say something before your husband came in?" Dr. Prince's eyes settled on mine.

"The sooner we get this over with, the sooner we'll be left in peace." Elias's words were clipped and sounded like a warning.

"Mr. Ring," the doctor said, "would you draw the curtains and perhaps bring me a second lamp?" I had the impression he wanted Elias to leave so he could speak with me alone.

"I'll fetch the lamp," I said, suddenly eager to go. I had been ready to tell Dr. Prince everything, but Elias's interruption gave me time to reconsider. I had already said too much. Suggesting she was expecting might help convict Levi—or simply incriminate Elma. While every kernel of my being knew her condition, I did not have any real proof. If I was wrong, I would have needlessly sullied her name. Better to let the doctor conduct his investigation than to prejudice his results.

Desperate for air, I fled the house. Elma was being sliced apart, and I needed to know that Levi was suffering for his crime. *An eye for an eye,* I told myself, twisting Christian doctrine to accommodate my malicious thoughts.

Greenwich Street looked as dreary as I felt. People dressed in thick layers inched cautiously over deep ruts and mounds of filth. Each afternoon the snow melted, then froze again overnight, fortified with mud and waste. Sun peeked through the clouds, and the ice turned to slush as I walked, saturating my boots and numbing my toes. The deadening of feeling came as a relief. If I thought it would have helped, I would have immersed myself. Was that how Elma felt? Had she been desperate enough to throw herself into an icy grave? As quickly as the idea entered my head, I dismissed it. Levi wanted me to believe that Elma had killed herself, to absolve his own role in her death.

Despite the cold, street traffic grew as I walked toward City Hall Park. At the corner of Broadway and Warren Street, I stopped and stared. A three-story masonry building, Bridewell Prison sat squarely between the poorhouse and the old town jail. Angry cries and a general air of sickness and misery emanated from its depths. I could see men pacing along the rooftop. Women and children huddled together outside, awaiting any opportunity to speak with their fathers, husbands, and sons. Behind thin iron grates, the windows were exposed to the elements. Dagger-like icicles hung side by side with the bars, as if nature itself were conspiring to keep the criminals imprisoned.

A horse auction was taking place on the street between the prison and common. Men called out bids, and their shouts echoed across the open space and bounced off walls. I gazed into Bridewell's gaping windows, imagining Levi squirming in his cell, surrounded by violence and pain. No doubt he had imagined riding off on a handsome steed, a dark bay stallion very much like the one his brother owned. The one he had used to snatch Elma away.

"There's no escape," I murmured, taking solace in the imposing fence.

A horse trader, holding a feed bag in one hand and the reins of two steeds in the other, flashed me a sideways glance. "Here for the hangings?" he asked.

I looked around, suddenly aware of a commotion beyond the auction. The common had a festive air. Beggars and performers were taking advantage of the crowd. An old woman with leathery black feet limped through the muck with her head down and her hands out. A man with a fiery-orange beard that reached past his belly juggled three, then four, eggs while holding a fifth in his mouth. One industrious merchant was selling tiny wooden replicas of the gallows, demonstrating how the trap gave way by flicking his index finger at the miniature floorboards.

"Some say it's a merciful end," the horse trader said. One of the animals, a hulking chestnut with a white blaze, nuzzled the feed, and the trader pushed his nose away. "It beats starving or freezing to death in Bridy, and it's better than the Hangman's Elm." Taking my cringe as interest, he continued. "It's the tall elm up by General Washington's old parade ground. They hanged plenty there, but lots of times they got the rope all wrong, snapped heads right off. You'd better hurry or you won't be able to see."

In the center of the common, people had begun gathering around the gallows. Some stood with hunched shoulders, as if bracing for pain; others pushed eagerly forward. There was a macabre energy in the air. Small children climbed atop the whipping post to get a better view.

"Why are the gallows painted red?" I asked. I had passed them many times without giving it much thought. It had never been relevant to my world. Until now.

"It's meant to look like a pagoda," the horse trader said. He elaborated, "An Oriental temple." This time he chuckled. "Hell must be ruled by heathens."

A father walked with his son perched on his shoulders. "Two burglars and an arsonist," he said.

"No murderers?" the boy asked. He sounded disappointed.

"Soon enough," the father said. "That wretch who murdered the girl will swing for sure."

A foul taste collected in my mouth.

There were jeers in the prison yard as the condemned men climbed into a cart to be taken to the executioner's platform. From a distance I watched their lips move and thought I could hear them pleading innocence. I looked up at the windows again and imagined Levi, bones protruding, body riddled with lice, watching the ghastly scene and dreading his turn in the shadow of the gallows' crossbeams. It did nothing to relieve my sorrow, but I did feel a hint of retribution.

The crowd grew thicker. One voice rang out.

"Come shake Colonel Burr's hand," a barker called. "Meet the war hero and statesman who will save our city."

It was the second time I had set eyes on the man. Impeccably dressed, wearing high-heeled shoes with brass buckles polished to a shine despite the slush, Burr stood out in the shabby throng.

Echoing my thought, a man to my left said, "Look there: the emperor mingling with his subjects. A Bonaparte in the making."

"He's short enough," another joked.

Burr held his hat in one hand and greeted men with the other. "Why's he out here in the cold?" I asked the man next to me.

"Burr's campaigning night and day for Jefferson. Opened his own house to anyone working for the Republicans. He feeds them, even brought in mattresses."

"If Burr can turn a water company into a bank, he'll make Jefferson president and himself vice president," someone added.

"They make an unlikely team," said another.

"Burr's a crooked gun," the first man said. "You can never be sure of his aim."

Off in the distance, there was a loud bang and cheers as the first criminal fell through the trap. I had another vision of Levi, this time on the hangman's scaffold, standing ten feet above the same blood-thirsty crowd, confessing his guilt, begging for mercy. A blindfold covered his eyes; a thick noose circled his neck. I heard the lever bang and the trap give way.

A somber set of eyes met mine, then shot away. "Anthony Lispenard?" Although I had not thought about him since Elma was found, it suddenly seemed essential that we speak. "I'm Catherine Ring. It was my cousin, Elma Sands, who . . ." I lowered my voice to a whisper. "My cousin was found in thy well."

Lispenard appeared to know exactly who I was, and his reply was slow and deliberate. "The land is mine. The well belongs to the Manhattan Company." He nodded toward Aaron Burr.

Burr was shaking hands and warmly clasping forearms as if reeling men in. The man who moments earlier had referred to him as an emperor stood by his side, laughing collegially. The colonel chuckled and offered up a cigar. I watched with grim fascination. It seemed Burr could win anyone over.

I turned back to Lispenard. "Why did the Manhattan Company dig a well on thy property?"

Lispenard eyed the crowd warily, refusing to meet my gaze. "I'm not sure I understand the question."

"I—my husband attended the water meetings. I recall him naming several men who were opposed to Burr's plan. Thy name was among them."

"Opinions change."

"Thou spoke so eloquently about the injustice of Burr's plan, how the Manhattan Company would not benefit anyone except Burr and his wealthy investors."

"When did you hear me speak?"

"The point is that thy concerns are valid. Burr's company is not providing water. The rich are getting richer while others grow sick and die. Thy son and my cousin . . ."

Lipsenard shifted his weight. He seemed as uncomfortable as he had been the afternoon they dragged Elma's body from the frozen well. "Mrs. Ring, my son died of yellow fever. The circumstances of your cousin's death are—a mystery."

"Elma's death is no mystery at all," I said. "Tell me, did Levi Weeks work at the well on thy property?"

Cheers and gasps filled the common as the second condemned man was hanged. Men were dying, yet I hardly registered their suffering. My heart was filled with poison.

"Anthony Lispenard," I said, grasping his arm. "I have reason to believe that Levi wanted my cousin dead and that he brought her to *thy* property to have his way with her, knowing it was isolated."

He held up his hand as if to physically block my words. It was then that I noticed he was clutching a fistful of flyers. "Republicans," one read, "Turn out and save your country from ruin! Elect Jefferson and Burr!"

"What's that?" I asked, pointing to the flyers.

He lowered his hand. "Campaign literature."

"Supporting Jefferson—and Burr?"

Lispenard did not respond. He did not need to. If he was working for Burr, it meant he was also working with the Weeks brothers.

A roar cut through the crowd as the final criminal met his end. People jostled me, but I stood, leery of Lispenard's change of heart. A hand thrust a flyer toward me. I looked down, expecting to see more campaign literature. I couldn't believe what I held instead.

> Ghosts and Goblins at the Manhattan Well: The misty form of
> the raven-haired beauty, Miss Gulielma Sands, rises from the
> Manhattan Well at midnight. Her emerald dress is dirtied by
> moss. Wet weeds hang from her hair . . . .

Indignation pulsed through me. It seemed particularly cruel that
Elma's suffering, and my grief, were being exploited. I released my
grasp and watched the pamphlet flutter to the ground.

Lispenard was tipping his hat, bidding me farewell. It was an especially fine tricorn hat with a handsome felt brim. I noticed that
his ragged jacket had been replaced by a mohair overcoat with shiny
brass buttons as if his affiliation with the Weeks brothers had changed
his circumstances along with his opinion. By the looks of him, he
was providing a valuable service. Something far more essential than
passing out flyers.I was done mincing words. "How is it possible thou
heard nothing the night my cousin was murdered?" I asked.

Lispenard straightened his hat.

"Answer my question," I said. "Thy wife was very specific. She heard
a woman—Elma—begging the Lord for mercy. Anthony Lispenard,
have mercy on me now, please tell me what though knows.

"Mrs. Ring," he said. Though he addressed me by name, he took
care to avoid my eyes. "I'm afraid I must be on my way."

The word *afraid* hung in the air between us like a swaying corpse.
Lispenard was pale and appeared frightened. All at once, I understood his urgency. He was not simply running from me, he was flee-
ing the hangman's scaffold. Lorena Forrest had said she saw a woman
riding in a sleigh with two men the night Elma disappeared. The
woman was Elma. One of the men had been Levi. As for the other—
they were going to Lispenard's Meadows. Who better to drive them
there than Anthony Lispenard?

~16~

A third day passed while we waited for permission to bury Elma. Elias opened the windows in her bedroom, those on the second floor, then every window throughout the house. Drapes fluttered and doors slammed as icy gusts funneled through our hallways and through my veins. I scrubbed the floors with pine oil until my knuckles were raw, then doused them with too much lye, making my eyes and throat burn. Still, nothing could mask the rank, sweet odor coming from Elma's room. A relentless reminder of the violence that had been pre-determined under our roof, it clung to furniture, clothing, even skin. Dry-eyed and stoic now, Charles stood shivering by the fire, his arms wrapped around his narrow body, chin in his chest. I gathered him and Patience on my lap, tied a blanket around our shoulders, and buried my nose in their hair. Charles protested that he was too big, and Patience whimpered and squirmed, but I refused to let go.

Elma smells of lavender, Elma smells of home, I told myself, hoping that, in time, I would remember her as she was.

Friends gathered in the parlor, joined in a search for truth. "Seek and ye shall find," a church elder counseled, but he was not able to meet my gaze, and his words were faraway and hollow. Well-intentioned visitors expressed sorrow and shock while I sat in silence. Though I knew it was expected of me, I did not have the strength for small talk, let alone prayer or even a polite smile. The tender feelings I had always reserved for faith and family had been replaced by seeth-ing hatred. All I had now were questions—*Why was an innocent life cut short? Why do good people suffer?*—and doubts—*Why was that poisonous vial in Levi's drawer? Why was it empty?* The only thing I knew with cer-tainty was that Elma's death needed to be avenged. Levi deserved the ultimate punishment.

Four miserable days after Dr. Prince's examination, the coroner's jury announced its verdict: Elma had been "murdered by a person or persons as yet unknown." An hour later, an indictment was issued against Levi, and it left no doubt as to the horrors Elma had suffered.

Levi Weeks, laborer, late of the seventh ward, not having the fear of God before his eyes, but being moved and seduced by the instigation of the devil, on the 22nd day of December, in the year of our Lord 1799, did make an assault on one Gulielma Sands, feloniously and willfully, and of his malice aforethought, did strike, beat, and kick, with his hands and feet, in and upon the head, breast, back, belly, sides, and other parts of the body of her, and did then and there feloniously, willfully, and of his malice aforethought, did throw the said Gulielma Sands, down unto and upon the ground, giving unto the said Gulielma Sands several mortal strokes, wounds, and bruises, in and upon the head, breast, back, belly, sides and other parts of the body of her, and did then and there, feloniously, willfully, and of his malice aforethought, cast, throw, and push Gulielma Sands, into a certain well wherein there was a great quantity of water; by means of which Gulielma Sands did then choke, suffocate, and drown; and then and there, did instantly die.

Arraigned and imprisoned, Levi was left to await trial. And at last we were allowed to bury Elma.

Word arrived saying that my aunt was too weak to attend the funeral. "Mary has not been out of bed since thy letter arrived," Mother wrote. Normally the implication that my letter, rather than Elma's murder, had made my aunt ill would have left me feeling ashamed, but now that Levi was finally facing justice, I felt only the comforting pulse of my hatred.

Since Elma's mother was absent, Friends and neighbors assembled to perform the last sad duties. We transferred Elma to a plain pine casket. With painstaking precision, Elias hammered the lid shut. Richard Croucher and David Forrest carried the coffin downstairs and out onto the street.

"There she is," someone called. People closed in rapidly, making it impossible to proceed.

"We demand to see Elma," the crazed woman with unruly hair shouted, as if Elma, in all her former beauty, would appear.

"They're mad," Elias said, visibly shaken.

As the knot of people grew tighter, Watkins directed the procession back inside. "I don't know that we can get through," he said. "I'll get the sheriff. Perhaps he can order them to disperse."

Watkins left while the rest of us stood restless and rattled. The clock struck ten and the pallbearers squirmed under the coffin's weight, turning their heads in a useless attempt to seek fresh air. It had been difficult getting the casket down the narrow staircase, and no one wanted to take it back up. Setting it on the floor seemed disrespectful. Finally, I suggested they rest it on the dining table. Everyone looked toward the table with distaste, but there were no other options.

"Where's Elma?" the same woman shouted. Though she was outside, I had learned to recognize her high-pitched voice.

A fist banged the window, making us all jump.

"Levi's innocent," a man hollered. "And plenty of respectable folks say so!"

"Crock of bull," Croucher spat.

"It's that article," Hatfield said, "from today's *Gazette*. Said there was '*universal testimony*' in favor of Levi's character and cited a '*respectable authority*' as saying he's innocent."

"What respectable authority?" I said. Levi had bragged about his powerful friends, and I had challenged him to summon them. I knew he would have sought aid regardless of my threats, but I still regretted my words.

Elizabeth Watkins rocked Patience in her arms. "It can't possibly be referring to Ezra Weeks. That wouldn't be fair."

"What's not fair?" Charles asked, his young ears finely tuned to all things right and wrong in his cloistered world. "Is it about Elma?"

Without a glance at the children, me, or the coffin on the table, Elias chose this moment to flee to the store.

"Yes," I said, turning back to Charles. Over the past weeks, he had grown stoic under our new reality. His eyes had lost their luster. "But that man is wrong. We live in a country where brave men—" My thoughts roamed to Elma's dead father. "Men sacrificed their lives so the rest of us would be treated fairly by our system of justice."

Charles shook his head. "Negroes aren't."

"Well," I sighed. "Let's pray that will change soon."

"How can I pray if we don't go to meeting?"

"Prayers are inside a person," I told him without conviction.

Charles looked as if he might speak again, but I was in no mood to be challenged. I asked Elizabeth to watch the children and went to find Elias. Since the morning I saw Lispenard at the gallows, I had been trying to speak with Elias, but he had steadfastly avoided me, citing work, children, and fatigue as reasons not to talk. Now, on the cusp of burying Elma, my concerns were all the more urgent. She would not rest in peace until the mystery of her death was solved.

Inside the deserted store, Elias sat idle at the till. The cursed circumstances surrounding Elma's death had driven even our most loyal customers away, and he was struggling to salvage our dying business. A constant crowd of curiosity seekers passed our home, but not a single one approached. The shelves were fully stocked, their contents rotting.

"Elias," I said. "It doesn't matter how much we owe Ezra Weeks or if we lose our home or even our name. Levi must be punished."

Elias rested his head in his hands. He may have been covering his ears.

Beating, kicking, pushing, choking, suffocating, and drowning: The indictment's violent accusations rang in my ears like a siren. How could anyone question Levi's guilt?

"Elias," I began cautiously. "Levi killed Elma because she was carrying his child, but maybe there's something else. Another reason we haven't considered."

Elias pulled an accounting log from the shelf, opening it to a random page that he scanned with blind eyes.

"Levi wanted to protect his inheritance," I said, "but he didn't have to murder her. He could have denied the baby was his or simply refused to marry her."

Elias slammed the book closed and pushed it away. "There's no proof she was even with child."

"A woman knows these things, and I knew Elma," I said, a bit too defensively. "That doctor seemed to think the same thing."

"Well, then, that's why Levi killed her," Elias said. "He had no intention of fathering a bastard."

The insult no longer stung. "That's what I thought, but I'm starting to see things differently. Elma's word would have meant very little next to Levi's. If he said the baby wasn't his, Elma would have been just another disgraced girl. It's happened before and it will happen again."

"No one but Levi could have fathered that child!" Elias's eyes dropped to a shelf under the till. He grabbed a half-empty bottle of whiskey, poured himself a glass, and drank it down.

I couldn't muster any outrage at the sight while Elma lay dead in the next room. "Elias, there was some other reason. Maybe Levi told her a secret of some sort. I know he told her that the Manhattan Company never intended to provide water."

"Everyone knows that."

"They do now, but Levi told Elma before anyone knew. If word had gotten out, if people understood that the water company was a hoax, the charter never would have passed. Which would have been a disaster for Levi."

"Who told thee this?"

"Elma told me." I spoke with conviction as if Elma had shared every secret with me, but deep inside I cringed, aware of how much she had kept to herself. "But the Manhattan Company charter did pass, and Levi, Ezra, and Burr got exactly what they wanted."

"So far."

Elias cocked his head, studying me closely. "They got their bank, which is exactly what Burr needs to win the election. Isn't that enough?"

"Greedy men—ambitious men—always want more. What if Levi told her something else? The election is only a few months away, and Levi is privy to all his brother's business. They have already carried off one terrible fraud. Who can say what else they plan to do and what Elma may have known?"

Elias shook his head slowly, as if considering my argument, not ruling it out. "Why would Levi tell her anything so important?"

"Because he's impulsive and selfish. He doesn't think rules apply to him." I pictured Levi and Elma sitting alone together in her room, the candlelight casting a warm glow on her face as he caressed her cheek. "Perhaps he shared something late one night when they were alone, to impress her. He told her a secret, then regretted it."

Elias's eyes met mine and, for an instant, I felt that we were truly partners, as I had imagined we would be all those years ago in Cornwall. "What secret?" he asked.

My heart sank. "I don't know."

"Caty." He sighed, reaching for another drink. "No one can say what Levi may or may not have told Elma in her bedroom. Any secrets died with her."

"But we can't let those murderers get away with it!"

"*Murderers?*"

The word hung in the air like a banner. "Elma was killed at the Manhattan Well for a reason. She was found on the Lispenard property. Elias, Anthony Lispenard was against Burr from the start; now he's working for him. Why did his opinion change?" I took a deep breath, recalling Lispenard's tormented expression. "Elias, I think Lispenard is guilty—guilty of something. Lorena Forrest saw two men and a woman driving up Greenwich Street in the storm."

Elias scoffed. "Now Lispenard is the murderer? What about Levi?"

"I can't say anything for sure, but the sheriff is coming back here. Can't we ask him to question the man more thoroughly? I'm sure he's hiding something."

"Anyone else I'm supposed to implicate baselessly, then?"

I stared at the golden liquid at the bottom of Elias's glass and expressed my deepest fear, one I had buried in my heart since the afternoon Elma was found and Elias's behavior turned so peculiar. "When the men brought Elma home, while I was waiting in the vestibule for them to bring her inside, I overheard Levi say something to thee that I didn't understand. He said, 'Croucher *saw you.*' What did he mean by that?"

The ledger fell to the floor as Elias stood. "Levi, Lispenard—and me?"

"Elma won't rest until we punish her killer." I would not rest either.

"Now thou are trusting the words of Levi Weeks over thy own husband?"

My voice lowered to a shaky whisper. "Answer me this time and I will never ask again."

Elias pulled me toward him so that my head rested against his shoulder. I could not remember the last time he had held me, but this was not intimacy. "I asked thee to come home from Cornwall." His body shuddered. "Remember, Caty, I begged."

I pulled away. "Cornwall?" The conversation's turn made my stomach drop. "That letter?"

"Yes!" he said, as if I had struck upon the most relevant of points. "I wrote thee. Caty, please try to understand. Levi was telling the truth about the laudanum: She had a vial. She refused to part with it." Elias held his hands to his face, covering his eyes and shaking his head. "She was hysterical when I told her I'd found her clothing on the floor." He dropped his hands. "No doubt she was ashamed. One night, after dinner, she took out the vial. She held it up for everyone to see. Levi was there, and Hatfield, and Croucher. She said she would drink it all."

Elias was painting a picture of someone I did not recognize. "I refuse to believe it."

"She was entirely changed."

"What did Croucher see? What did Levi mean by that?"

"Elma was crazed. I didn't know what to do. That night I went to her room and demanded she hand over the laudanum. She started to cry and mumbled some gibberish about being useless. Then she went to the bureau, pulled off the stopper, and raised that foul thing to her lips. Caty—" He sobbed outright. "Caty, forgive me. Please forgive me. We have a life together. The children . . ."

"Elias." It felt as if my heart would not beat again until he answered. "What happened next?"

"I—I struck her."

"What?"

"I slapped her. I don't know what came over me. I've never done a thing like that before. Never been violent to a woman, a girl. Lord help me." He shook his head, and a tear slipped down his weathered cheek into frown lines and stubble. "I lost my head."

I tried to imagine the scene. Elma hysterical, Elias furious. Elias had a temper, but in nearly eight years of marriage he had never raised a finger to me. As for Elma, she withdrew when she was sad; she didn't turn her self-hatred outward. Then again, it was clear that I had not known my cousin as well as I thought.

"It's this poison," he said, swiping the whiskey bottle with the back of his hand so that it fell to the floor. Rather than breaking, it spun round, spilling alcohol in its wake.

I could see now that, in his own way, Elias had drowned as well.

"What about the vial? What happened to it?" I asked.

"I don't know."

"Why not destroy it?" As the words left my mouth, I realized I could have asked myself the same question. As if in a dream, I saw myself burying the fragile vial deep in the back of Elma's drawer. Why hadn't I shattered it?

"I'm so sorry," Elias said. "I will never forgive myself."

"That's what Richard Croucher saw?" I swallowed and asked my true question. "Thou had nothing to do with Elma's death?"

Color drained from his face. "Why say such a thing?" He didn't wait for me to respond. "I was here that night, reading in the parlor."

I nodded. Of course it was true. Elias and I had been together until he had gone to bed, and I had sat up waiting for Elma to return. Elias's behavior may have been peculiar, but Levi was the murderer, awaiting trial for his crime, I reminded myself. He would say anything to save himself.

There were shouts outside.

"Ring," Watkins called. "The sheriff is here."

"Let's see to the burial," Elias said. He sounded relieved.

The parlor was as dismal as I had left it. Elma's coffin lay on the table. Charles sat with Patience weeping in his arms. Elizabeth Watkins stood helplessly behind them. The men were idle and awkward, clearing their throats, dusting lint off their pant legs, and looking everywhere except at the coffin on the table.

"They will not move," Sheriff Morris said, referring to the crowd. "They demand to see her."

"What?" Elias snapped.

Sheriff Morris removed his hat. "I suggest we set the casket on the threshold so they might have the opportunity to pay their respects."

"Impossible." Elias shook his head. "I refuse."

"Then we might have to bury her at night." Sheriff Morris suggested.

"Like a common criminal," I protested. "Elias . . ."

Elias turned helplessly toward me, then back to the sheriff. "Laying her outside will satisfy them?"

Sheriff Morris shrugged. "It may."

Elias approached the coffin, hammer in hand. Listening to him seal the box had been heartbreaking, but watching him tear the nails away made me wince in pain. The men lifted the lid, and I pulled Charles close.

"Don't look," I told him, burying my face in his hair. "Remember Elma as she was."

The dining table and coffin were carried outside. Sheriff Morris supervised the watchmen, and they directed the crowd. Despite the cold, people began to line up, assured that they would get to pay their final respects and that Elma would not be taken from them until the very last person had gazed upon her.

A pair of watchmen stood guard while mourners filed by. People reached into the casket to touch her. Some prayed. Many held handkerchiefs, small satchels, even evergreen sprigs to their noses to mask the cloying stench. The gray-haired woman sobbed, threw herself on the open coffin, and had to be dragged away. A rough-looking man in farmer's gear stooped and kissed her brow. Elma, unseen and unwanted while she was alive, was now in the hearts of strangers.

Hours later, after the last stragglers had gone home, their curiosity satisfied, our sad procession was able to leave. Elma's coffin was placed in the back of Joseph Watkins's wagon, led by a lone gray horse. Our family walked behind. Elias carried Patience. Charles clutched my hand.

We buried Elma on a shadowy knoll. The lawn was barren and cold, and the men had a difficult time digging the frozen ground. I marked her grave with a plain white stone.

~17~

Monday, March 31st: More than three months had passed since the stormy night Elma had kissed my cheek that final time and I had long since stopped marking the horrific events according to the Quaker calendar. Religion did not apply to brutality and murder. That morning, I heard the wind rattling the windowpanes before I opened my eyes. Then I remembered: It was the day of reckoning. I threw off the covers and pulled on my best dress, the one I wore to meeting. Levi's trial was to begin at ten. I considered praying but did not trust the words that might escape my mouth. I hoped that once he was punished, the hatred within me would diminish, my faith would return, and my heart could rest.

Elizabeth Watkins came to collect the children.

"Don't go," Charles cried, clutching my skirt with surprising strength.

"No, no, no," Patience wailed, then went abruptly quiet. Her tiny head fell backward and her lips grew slack and turned blue.

"Patience!" I screamed, shaking her with too much force. An instant later, her cries resumed.

"Let me," Elizabeth said, taking her from me and stroking her hair. "Children hold their breath. Mine did."

I struggled to regain my composure. With her dark hair and eyes, blue lips, and lolling head, Patience had looked just like Elma did when she emerged from the well. Or perhaps that's what I saw because I could no longer think about anything else.

Two watchmen came to escort us to the courthouse. Damp gusts tunneled up Broadway as Elias and I made our way south in a lonely procession very much like Elma's funeral. The wind picked up as the island narrowed. We passed Trinity Church and turned in to Wall Street. My eyes were dry, but the salty mist that blew off the harbor settled on my lips and tasted like tears.

Federal Hall appeared around the corner, as hallowed as a church. George Washington had delivered his first inaugural address here, from its massive stone balcony, in 1789. Crowds had gathered that day and people hung out of nearby windows, waving flags.

At first glance, the scene looked as I imagined it had on that triumphant day a decade earlier, with hundreds of people gathered in front of Federal Hall. Women were dressed in their holiday best, and men wore frock coats or uniforms. But no one was celebrating. In spite of their fine attire, they shoved one another, shouted obscenities, and waved fists instead of flags.

"Weeks is a murderer! Hang him!"

The savage cries penetrated the walls as the watchmen guided Elias and me through a side entrance. The hallways were full, and officers were stationed outside the courtroom doors.

"Family of the victim," one of our escorts informed his colleague. He had guided us through the crowd, but now that we had arrived, he seemed uncertain how to proceed.

Strangers shoved against us, vying for a seat inside.

"Take them in," the court officer said, looking anxiously at the swelling crowd. "There won't be space left." He pushed people aside and pried open the door.

My eyes adjusted with a blinking awkwardness, as if sunlight had infiltrated a dark room. The ceilings were higher than any I had ever seen. The floors were marble. The only familiar features were the dozen or so rows of long wooden benches that flanked either side of the room. They reminded me of our meetinghouse, and I wondered if they had been crafted by the same hands.

"It's chaos," Elias said. His eyes were bloodshot, drawn, and sad.

The high ceilings made the room appear large, but there was little space for the public. People were squeezed five deep into every corner, all eager to voice their opinion. The papers had appealed for calm, asking the public to suspend their prejudices. Few took heed. Some parroted a recent editorial calling Levi "sober, industrious, and amiable." Others branded him a cold-blooded killer.

I was gazing at the crowd, wondering where to go, when my eyes settled on a familiar face. The man with the caring expression who had addressed me weeks ago outside the boardinghouse was seated left of the center aisle, several rows back. He nodded to me, making room on the packed bench. I fought my way toward him, and Elias followed. People grumbled as we wedged ourselves into the cramped space, but I was buoyed by his small kindness.

"That's the prosecuting attorney, Cadwallader Colden," he said as an unwieldy gentleman lumbered past our row. We were seated so closely that I could feel his chest rise as he spoke. "He's a bit green, but his family is well known."

Elias leaned across my lap. "I thought Colden was a *British* governor. Patriots burned an effigy of him and smashed his coach to kindling to build a bonfire on Bowling Green."

"That was the grandfather," the man said, his voice as comforting and steady as his demeanor. "The family remained in the country after the British fled. Did some work with the Iroquois."

"An associate of the British *and* the Indians," Elias said. "That's bound to make him popular with the jury."

Colden was clumsy in his height, as if he were still growing. The soles of his large shoes slapped the marble as he made his way to the front of the room. His hair was closely cropped and a few were standing on end. He looked a bit like Charles after a restless night's sleep, and I fought an urge to wet my palm and smooth his cowlick.

Colden stooped to release the latch to the gate that divided the benches from the rest of the court, then swung it open with such force that it banged against the rail. He approached the attorneys' table, towering over it for several moments before sitting opposite the judge's bench.

There was a commotion in the back of the courtroom. Elias's shoulder brushed mine as he turned.

"Burr . . ." The name drifted through the room. Some stood to see.

Aaron Burr marched up the aisle as if stalking an enemy camp. Each time I saw him, he seemed more imposing.

"Colonel Burr," someone called, "how's the campaign?"

"Where's our water?" a woman shouted.

And then: "Why are you defending that murderer?"

Though there was little room on our bench, I managed to slide closer to Elias. "Colonel Burr is defending Levi?"

Elias did not need to answer. Burr had taken a seat at the attorneys' table, one that faced the jury box.

"They say his speeches have the sting of vinegar and the smoothness of oil," the man beside me said. I turned, assuming he was talking about Burr, but he was looking to the back of the room. I gasped.

A second wave of whispers rippled through the crowd as Alexander Hamilton proceeded up the aisle. Like Burr, he was small in stature, though nothing else about the two men was similar. Burr was dark and brooding, while Hamilton's features were delicate, almost feminine. Unlike Burr, who had stormed the room, Hamilton strolled past our row, assessing the crowd like a fox sniffing the wind.

"What's he doing here?" I asked.

Elias did not answer, but the fellow beside me did.

"Burr and Hamilton are working together," he said, "to defend Mr. Weeks."

Hamilton approached the attorneys' table and rested a hand amicably on Burr's shoulder, making Burr flinch.

"But they hate each other."

"Politics makes strange bedfellows, as they say. Voting in New York begins in less than a month."

"So why aren't they out campaigning?"

"They are. Their names will be plastered on top of every paper. It's all anyone is talking about."

"Burr's an opportunist," Elias grumbled. "Hamilton's no better."

"It's publicity they're after," the man said, waving toward the attorneys. The side of his hand was stained black with ink. "They're here to solicit votes."

Over the crowd's rumbling, a coarse, guttural noise stood out. I turned and my eyes locked on Richard Croucher. He was at the back of the room, half a dozen rows behind us, nodding assuredly at me.

The crowd began whistling, impatiently calling for the proceedings to begin. Elias fidgeted as he struggled to remove his heavy coat.

"Place the prisoner at the bar," announced the court clerk.

People drew a collective breath as a door within the bar was opened. Spectators in the back rows stood. Two officers entered with Levi between them. The trio walked deliberately— Levi especially, who seemed take each step with care. His dark-blue eyes were glassy, his lips pressed together. He avoided looking at the crowd and instead stared at his defense lawyers with a haughtiness that was easy to hate.

"Handsome," a woman clucked.

I had been so intent on Levi's affectation that I had failed to notice his appearance. He was dressed in clothes I did not recognize, his dark hair tied back with a sky-blue ribbon. He was freshly shaved, his cheeks ruddy. He looked clean.

"He looks well," I said, surprised and, Lord help me, disappointed.

"Scoundrel," Elias sneered. Elias was not nearly as becoming as Levi. With his overcoat gone, I could see circles of sweat under his armpits. "But the prison windows aren't even covered, except for the bars. It must be freezing. And the food—"

"Prison? Levi spent a day in Bridewell, maybe two. No doubt Ezra greased someone's palm to get him out."" I followed Elias's gaze and recognized the silvery hair and commanding posture of Ezra Weeks. I would have expected him to position himself close to Levi, but Ezra was seated across the courtroom, beside the witness stand, as if to influence their behavior with his proximity. Somehow he sat in a space wide enough for two. He must have arrived hours early to get such a favorable seat or paid someone to hold it. He face remained expressionless as the officers led Levi to the prisoner's dock, a railed pen five feet across.

"Silence! Hats off, the Honorable Chief Justice John Lansing," hollered the court clerk as a middle-aged man with receding snow-white hair entered through the same door by the front. The room fell silent, and Lansing's robe rustled like a lady's skirt as he settled into the bench.

The man beside me removed a leather-bound notebook from his jacket pocket and began to scribble.

"What is it?" I asked, because it was impossible to read his scrawl.

"Lansing served under General Schuyler during the war."

"The judge reported to Hamilton's father-in-law?" My voice was as small as Charles's. "Is that legal?"

"Not that long ago, people didn't get representation at all. Just twenty lashings."

My gaze settled on his ink-stained fingers and the notebook balanced precariously on his knees. "Thou are a reporter?"

"A humble scribe. Call me Hardie."

I did not bother to introduce myself, sure he knew full well who I was.

We turned back to the front as a door at the side of the jury box opened and several dozen men followed a clerk into the room. They wore polished shoes or soiled boots, jackets of coarse cloth or fine overcoats. Some were freshly shaven. One had a thick tomato-red beard.

Colonel Burr removed a pair of eyeglasses from his jacket pocket, pushed them to the crown of his head, sat back, and squinted. The jurors were led to their seats on a raised platform behind a railing. There was not enough space for them all and many stood, shifting uncomfortably, as the clerk called the roster.

"Garrit Storm, dock builder; Simon Schermerhorn, ship's chandler; Robert Lylburn, merchant." The list went on and on. When every man had answered, the clerk turned to Levi. "Levi Weeks," he said, "prisoner at the bar, hold up your right hand, and hearken to what is said to you."

Levi's eyes had been trained on the floor, but he looked up, past the attorneys' table, toward his brother. He raised his hand. Even from a distance, I could see it tremble.

The clerk nodded. "These good men who have been last called, and who do now appear, are those who are to pass between the people of the State of New York and you upon your trial of life and death." The courtroom was humming, but the word *death* made everyone still. "If, therefore, you will challenge them, your time to challenge is as they come to the book to be sworn, and you will be heard." The clerk paused before calling "Richard Ellis."

A short man in ill-fitting clothes and tall boots approached the clerk. Hamilton moved to the edge of his chair as the man walked to the center of the courtroom.

The clerk held out a Bible, and Richard Ellis set his right hand on top. "Juror, look upon the prisoner," the clerk said. "Prisoner, look upon the juror."

The man glanced uneasily toward Levi, who seemed to shrink, alone in the prisoner's dock.

The clerk continued, "You shall well and truly try, and true deliverance make, and a true verdict give, according to the evidence, so help you God."

The juror gazed into the crowd. "So help me," his voice became lower, "God."

A second juror inched forward, and each in turn rested his hand on the Bible and acknowledged the oath.

Midway through the line, though, one man declined. "I am a Quaker," he said, "and I ask to be excused because my religion prevents me from sitting in judgment of life and death."

The attorneys conferred, then nodded, and the court clerk let the man leave, while I sat mourning my own lack of scruples. I had no qualms in my judgment that Elma's killer deserved to die.

A bowlegged man in farmer's dress approached the clerk. Hamilton stood before the man had the opportunity to set his hand on the Bible.

"Were you a member of the party that searched last December for

Gulielma Sands?" Hamilton asked. Elma's name rolled fluidly off his lips.

The man's eyes grew wide and he nodded.

Hamilton walked around the table toward the judge's bench. "I ask that this gentleman be excused."

The farmer retreated to the back of the courtroom, pushing others aside to sit on one of the long benches.

The panel of jurors proceeded. Hamilton objected to another man, who worked for the *Commercial Advertiser,* and to several more, for reasons that were obscure to me.

"Why is he allowed to decide?" I asked.

Elias shrugged.

Five more jurors were seated before Colden stood. "This man has done work for the prisoner's brother, Ezra Weeks."

Judge Lansing frowned. "Are you currently employed by Ezra Weeks?" he asked.

The man shook his head. "No, sir."

"Mr. Colden," the judge said. "If we were to ask each juror where and how he has formerly been employed, we would be here for days."

Colden looked crestfallen. "I disagree. There is a direct relation."

Judge Lansing was shaking his head even before Colden finished speaking. "Save your arguments for the trial."

Colden resumed his seat and did not object again.

The bells at Trinity Church were striking one when the last juror was seated.

"Gentlemen of the jury," the clerk called out, "the prisoner at the bar stands indicted for the murder of Gulielma Sands. He has been arraigned, pleaded not guilty, and is now to be tried by his country, which country you are, so that your charge is, gentlemen, to inquire whether the prisoner at the bar is guilty of the felony whereof he stands indicted, or is not guilty, so sit together and hear your evidence."

~18~

Cadwallader Colden rose for his opening statement. Neither youth nor height worked in his favor. A boyish grin made him appear inexperienced. His towering presence left him clumsy. Hamilton and Burr gave off a glow of experience and righteousness; Colden had no such charm. His voice had the flat, nasal inflections of the upper class.

"In a cause which appears so greatly to have excited the public interest, in which the prisoner has thought it necessary to employ so many advocates distinguished for their eloquence and abilities, so vastly my superiors in learning, experience, and professional rank"—Colden paused, smiling at the defense attorneys—"it is not wonderful that I should rise to address you under the weight of embarrassments which such circumstances excite."

Hamilton was perched attentively at the edge of his chair. To his left, Burr huddled over his notes. Neither man acknowledged Colden's praise.

"But, gentlemen," Colden's voice lost its cordiality as he continued, "although the abilities enlisted on the respective sides of this cause are very unequal, I find consolation that our tasks are also so. While to my opponents belongs the duty to exert all their powerful talents in favor of the prisoner, as a public prosecutor, I think I ought to do no more than offer all the testimony the case affords and draw from the witnesses all that they know, the truth, the whole truth, and nothing but the truth."

The words were fluent enough, though they lacked passion. No one was more interested in the outcome of the trial than I was, but I found my mind drifting as I searched the crowded courtroom for sympathetic faces.

"Levi Weeks, the prisoner at the bar, is indicted for the murder of Gulielma Sands. We are aware," Colden said, "that you will not readily be convinced that one so young has already imbrued his hands in the blood of the innocent." He walked across the room to the jury box, looking determined and righteous. "The deceased was a young girl who, until her acquaintance with the prisoner, was virtuous and modest and, it will be material for you to remark, always of a cheerful disposition and lively manners."

I nodded, vigorously enough for the reporter beside me to take note.

"We expect to prove that the prisoner won her affections, that her virtue fell sacrifice to his assiduity, and, that after a long period of criminal intercourse between them, he deluded her from the house of her protector under a pretense of marrying her and carried her away to a well in the suburbs of this city, and there murdered her."

Abruptly, Colden ceased speaking. He rested his hands on the rail of the jury box and bowed his head as if overcome by emotions.

Elias sighed, while I sat bewildered, floating outside myself.

Colonel Burr propped his eyeglasses on top of his head and crossed his legs, while Hamilton watched Colden as if awaiting an opportunity to pounce. A full minute passed before Colden spoke again. When he did, he apologized for the interruption and gallantly continued.

"I will not say, gentlemen, what may be your verdict, but I will venture to assert that not one of you, or any man who hears this cause, shall doubt that the unfortunate young creature who was found dead in the Manhattan Well was most barbarously murdered."

"Catherine Ring." A chill shot through me as the clerk called my name.

I had known that I would be a witness but was unprepared to be first. I reached deep into my pocket, running my fingertips over each point of the delicately crafted ivory comb. Although it had been a gift from Levi, I could not part with it. Its elegance recalled Elma's. I had even retied the lost ribbon, imagining a world in which I could just as easily repair the harm done to her.

The clerk repeated my name. I stood on shaky legs and, stepping on toes, proceeded to the end of our row. The audience chattered while I concentrated on keeping my back straight and head up.

"Her cousin," a woman said loud enough for the entire room to hear. "She was her *guardian*."

The words stung. I turned, expecting to confront anger with anger. Instead, I saw wide-eyed fear. The women before me were frightened by Elma's senseless death. They were equally powerless. But there was an explanation: If I had neglected to set my impressionable cousin on an honorable path, it mitigated the horror. They watched with something more than sympathy as the clerk approached me, Bible in hand.

"Catherine Ring is a Quaker," Judge Lansing instructed the clerk.

The clerk eyed me skeptically before stepping aside. As a Friend, I was not required to take an oath. We were thought to be guided by our own quest for truth. But as I took my place on the witness stand, looking at a courtroom full of doubting eyes, it seemed no one, least of all me, believed I was impartial.

Hamilton was on his feet before I had collected my breath. His eyes caught the light and glimmered like the sea. "Your Honor, defense counsel respectfully requests that Elias Ring should withdraw out of hearing during his wife's testimony." The speed of his objection suggested he had planned this first assault.

Judge Lansing's answer was also swift. "It's within the prisoner's rights."

The crowd parted as Elias stood. There were sneers as he wound his way up the aisle. I watched the courtroom door close behind him, confused by my relief.

"Pray begin by telling the court what occurred in your household from the time the prisoner came to board with your family," Colden said, his voice unduly loud.

I had never gone to the theater but knew that the groundlings pelted actors with rotten fruit if their performance proved disappointing. And here was high drama. I half-expected a disgruntled spectator to toss a bruised apple. Instead, what I saw was row upon row of somber faces. Ezra Weeks studied me over the steeple he had formed with his fingers. Behind him sat our neighbor Joseph Watkins, and several rows farther back were Anthony Lispenard and his plump wife.

As if on stage, I took a meaningful breath and willed my expression into a mask. "Levi Weeks came to board with us last July." My hands flew to my mouth as I realized I had breached Quaker practice and spoken the month's pagan name. I looked around the courtroom, glad Elias was not present to hear my lapse. The audience seemed mercifully unaware. "Levi was always attentive to Elma," I continued. "She once said—"

Colonel Burr stood. "Your Honor, we object." Though he was addressing the court, his eyes were trained on Hamilton, as if he was keeping a tally of points scored. "This is hearsay testimony," Burr said. "The declarations of a deceased person against a prisoner can only be admissible when they are made *after* the fatal blow, in the last moments, when the individual must be supposed to be under an equal solemnity with that of an oath."

Burr seemed to be suggesting that Elma should have accused Levi *after* her death, but that couldn't be. Troublingly, though, Colden was arguing as if Burr had made a legitimate point.

"Catherine Ring's testimony is proper to show the disposition of mind in the deceased when she left the house on the night of the fatal accident," Colden said. "It is the only way to discover whether Elma was sound in her intellects." He walked back to the table and began flipping through papers, citing precedents to support his position. His words sounded like gibberish. The jurors started to fidget.

With the ease of a man in his drawing room, Burr repeated his point. "The argument carries no weight in this court. In the first case, no ruling was made, and the second case took place in Scotland and is not valid."

Nodding, Judge Lansing upheld the objection.

Noticeably diminished, Colden approached again. "Mrs. Ring," he said, sounding almost angry, as if I had violated courtroom etiquette. "You may not repeat what Elma has said to you in private conversation."

I sighed. The trial was supposed to determine the force behind Elma's death, yet no one wanted to know the least bit about her. Hesitantly, expecting Burr or Hamilton to leap from their seats, I explained how Elma came to live with us and spoke of the attention Levi showed her. Reluctant to sully her name, I proceeded with caution. "I often found them sitting together, once on her bed."

A heavy silence settled over the court. Men looked at their shoes, but it was the women who interested me most. One in the third row, who was wearing a gray flannel dress buttoned to her chin, was wringing her hands. Another bit her lip until it grew red. Both looked guilty.

"When I was in the country—" I started. Feeling a set of eyes boring through me, I looked up and saw that Elias had crept back into the courtroom. He was standing to the side of the door, slowly shaking his head.

Turning to follow my gaze, Hamilton was quick to object. He pointed out Elias, and Judge Lansing reprimanded Elias and had him removed. I watched the doors close, thankful again.

"On the tenth or eleventh of Ninth Month," I resumed, "Elma and Levi were left together with my husband—"

"Which room did Elma sleep in while you were away?" Burr interrupted.

Hamilton and Burr interjected as questions occurred to them, but no one other than me seemed bothered. Burr's query was not overtly crude, but his tone made me blush. I looked at Mr. Colden, who nodded.

"She slept in the back room on the third story."

"During the period that you are describing, were there any other women in the house?"

Shame coursed through me. I shook my head.

"Out loud please, madam," Burr said.

"No."

Colden tried to mitigate the damage. "Pray, Mrs. Ring, has Elma not always borne a good character, I mean that of a modest, discreet girl?"

"Very much so," I said. This was the moment I had been waiting for, my chance to defend Elma. I closed my eyes so I could fully remember her flowing hair and easy laugh. She had been so eager to come to New York, to create a new life for herself, and she had fallen in love—with the wrong man. My anxiety began to abate, replaced by indignation. "I have known Elma since childhood. She is—she was—kind, loyal, responsible; to say otherwise would be wicked."

Ezra Weeks shifted in his seat, examining his nails.

Colden assumed a more confidential tone. "Would not the conduct between the prisoner and Elma have been considered improper, if it was not supposed they were soon to be married?"

I frowned, taking care not to look at Ezra Weeks. I did not want to insinuate that Elma's behavior was wrong, but it was difficult to excuse, even in light of their engagement.

Burr did not wait for my response. "Are Miss Sands's parents living?"

"Elma's mother has been gravely ill," I said, reaching deep into my pocket and squeezing the ivory comb until the teeth bit into my skin.

"And her father? You say he died in England?"

Panic shot through me as I recalled the lie I had told Sheriff Morris. "Yes," I said, nodding for emphasis.

"Elma took her mother's name of Sands?" Burr said, waving his hand as if brandishing a cigar.

I nodded.

"Out loud, please, madam. Pray tell us why Elma did not use her father's name." Burr watched Hamilton while he waited for my response.

The room was silent. I could hear my own shallow breath. Burr's satisfied grin proved he already knew the answer. I struggled to keep my voice level. "Her mother never married," I said.

There was a tremor through the audience and I had little doubt that its reverberations would reach Cornwall, where my poor aunt lay dying.

"If the mother had no scruples, one can't expect much of the daughter," a woman said.

"Bastard!" someone called.

"Quiet," the judge admonished, but it was too late. All eyes were fixed on Hamilton, though the man himself hardly took note.

In a wave of despair, I realized that Elias had been right. Hamilton and Burr were campaigning. Even in their defense of Levi, they remained adversaries, striving to outshine each other. In one fell swoop, Burr had managed to discredit Elma and, by extension, Hamilton.

"Is it true that Elma's father was a loyalist who fled the country during the war?"

I clutched the rail in front of me as if a trap had been released beneath my feet. "Certainly not." Aunt Mary had spoken so lovingly of Elma's father. "He was a hero who fought with—" The words died on my lips. Aunt Mary had told me that Elma's father marched alongside Benedict Arnold, which had not seemed wrong to me until this moment.

"A British war hero," Burr announced to the room.

"No," I said, though the denial sounded halfhearted. I looked out into the audience. Elias was gone. Hardie was taking furious notes. Only Croucher's eyes met mine. He nodded. "He was an *American* war hero," I said, steadying my voice.

Burr scoffed. "One who fled to England, deserting his comrades, abandoning a woman he disgraced, and forsaking his unborn child?"

I had no response.

Hours passed. I was asked to remain on the witness stand while the defense conducted its cross-examination. A chair was brought for my comfort. I gazed down at the attorney's table, wondering which of the powerful men would question me. Both looked formidable, but it was Hamilton who stood. His pearl buttons gleamed along with his eyes.

Hamilton paced the floor between the jury box and me, not deviating from a precise path.

"What was the state of Elma's health?" he asked.

"She was of a delicate make."

"Had she any habitual illness? One that might require medication?"

There was a pain in the pit of my stomach. "No."

Hamilton stopped pacing, then looked to the public. He stood for a long moment before moving on to his next question. "Where were her usual lodgings?"

"In the back room, on the third story," I said, mindful of the attention being paid to this point.

"Was it next to Joseph Watkins's bedroom?" he asked, as if the notion had just occurred to him.

I shook my head, confused. Watkins was our neighbor, not a member of the household. Hamilton waited until I gathered his meaning.

"Her bedroom wall backed onto his house—"

"Were there any other females in the house when you went to the country?"

It was the second time the defense had asked the question. "No," I said quickly.

"Elma said that she and Levi were to be married. Did you ever ask Levi whether he was engaged to her?"

The questions were coming so quickly, I could hardly follow. "After her death—"

"Had you ever any reason to suspect that any other person but Levi had an improper intimacy with Elma?"

"What?" I felt a stab of panic. "No. Never."

Colden stood. I held my breath, praying that he would object to Hamilton's lewd line of inquiry, but he asked a question instead.

"Catherine Ring, do you know of what materials the wall between your house and Watkins's is composed?"

"No," I said. "I don't." I turned back to Hamilton, dreading an influx of more furiously paced questions, but he had resumed his seat and was making copious notes.

─19─

Gray veins darkened on the marble floor as twilight fell. Our benches were low and the windows were high, making it impossible to see more than a patch of dwindling sky. The jury demanded a break and the judge reluctantly agreed to a short recess. Like a river breaching its banks, the narrow aisles overflowed with restless, hungry people.

"Levi Weeks is the picture of innocence," one woman declared. Others spoke of Colonel Burr's eloquence and Hamilton's fine manner.

My knees buckled the instant I reached the hallway, and I was abruptly aware of the tension I had been suppressing. Desperate for air and anxious to avoid attention, I decided to use the back entrance the watchmen had led us through hours earlier. I inched open the door and tiptoed onto the landing. Halfway down, I noticed two figures. One was Ezra Weeks; the other, Anthony Lispenard.

Ezra's voice was low and impassive. Though I could not see his face, I imagined his stony expression. With each rebuttal, Lispenard grew increasingly animated, until his protests echoed up the closed stairwell.

"No," he said. "I don't want any part of this."

"You took the job." Weeks's voice rose to an angry growl. "It's your responsibility as a Republican."

"Jefferson is the Republican candidate," Lispenard said.

"Jefferson doesn't understand New York."

"And if I refuse?"

"Think of the girl."

"What?" Lispenard sounded stunned and hopeless. "As if I could ever forget that poor creature."

"You made your choice," Ezra seethed. "There's nothing more to say." Shoes squeaked, and a rush of air blew up the stairwell as the door opened and slammed shut.

My thoughts raced, trying to make sense of the conversation. Praying for courage, I took a few tentative steps and saw Lispenard, looking utterly defeated. "Anthony Lispenard?" I called before he had a chance to flee.

A flicker of recognition crossed his lined face.

"What were thee discussing with Ezra Weeks?" I walked down, close enough to hear but out of arm's reach.

Lispenard nodded to the spot where Ezra had stood. He seemed reluctant to offer as much as a greeting. "It's private."

Privacy was a luxury I could not afford. "That man's brother murdered my cousin. She was killed on thy land." I took a deep breath and glanced over my shoulder. I wanted to make sure we were not being overheard, and I needed to confirm my escape route. "Why?"

Lispenard, so outspoken and brash the first time I'd laid eyes on him, was a shadow of his former self. "I have no idea why she was murdered."

"Not why she was murdered. Why was she killed at Lispenard's Meadows?"

"It's remote," he said, "but it could have happened anywhere."

"Does thy business with the Weeks brothers have to do with Elma's death?"

"What?" Lispenard shuddered, and his tired eyes surveyed the steep stairwell as if contemplating the effort it would take to walk away. "It's complicated. You would never understand."

"That well was never anything but a grave. What did thou know about it?"

"Mrs. Ring, I'm sick over what happened to that poor girl, but my quarrel with Weeks is about money, not murder." His voice rose and, for an instant, he spoke with the indignation of his former self. "Ezra Weeks promised me stock in the Manhattan Company. Instead, he and Burr pocketed the profits. When I threatened to expose them, they tried to buy my silence. They dug that well and swore the value of my land would double, maybe triple." He shook his head. "Now all I've got is a hole that will haunt me forever."

"Then speak up!"

"You saw me arguing with Ezra."

"He said something about a job. What job? Murder?"

Lispenard shuffled backward as I stepped forward. "I'm a victim too," he said. "Weeks dug that well to keep me quiet, but it wasn't long before I understood it was worthless."

"Elma's the victim," I said. "She lost her life. Tell me about thy argument."

"Ezra had me appointed to the Electoral College. That's the job. It's politics." He spoke with regret, not pride.

It's politics: Levi had used the very same words the night he slammed the door in my face. "When was this? Does Levi know?" I asked, wondering if this was the secret Elma took to her grave.

"It's a public position," he said, bowing his head like a dog that had been scolded. "Ezra said it was prestigious, that I would forge valuable connections."

"Then why argue with him?"

Lispenard pressed his fingers to the corners of his eyes. "Ezra thinks he can twist my arm and tell me how to vote. Mrs. Ring, you're right. It's no coincidence your cousin was murdered on my land. It's a warning."

"A warning to whom?"

"To me. The well where Elma died is still there. It always will be."

Court resumed. Elias was called to the witness stand. Dressed in a somber coat and wide-brimmed hat, he looked like a relic from the past century. Hamilton stood as Elias passed. The gesture, seemingly respectful, only called attention to the discrepancy in their attire. Hamilton looked educated and refined, while Elias's dark clothes and refusal to swear the oath made him appear nefarious.

"Levi Weeks," Elias began, "was a lodger in my house, and in Ninth Month—"

"What month is that called?" Burr asked, as if disputing the standards we Friends lived by.

Elias shifted his weight. "I don't know it by any other name." From a distance, I could see that Elias looked pale, all but green. He had lost weight and his drab clothing draped over his stiff limbs like a shroud..

Burr shrugged at the jurors, his eyes full of mirth.

"At this time, when my wife was gone to the country," Elias said, "Levi and Elma were constantly together in private. I was alone and lonesome."

I sat up straighter, unable to understand why he would offer up such personal information.

"Strange disclosure," Hardie mumbled.

Elias stood in the center of the witness stand, avoiding my gaze. "One night when our tenant Isaac Hatfield was out of town, I heard talking and noise in his room. In the early morning, after twelve o'clock, I went up and found the bed tumbled, and Elma's clothes, which she had worn that afternoon, on the floor."

One of the younger jurors spoke. "Did Elma go away naked?"

People laughed outright. More audible than their laughter, though, was a sorrowful moan from the prisoner's box. Levi looked distraught. Ezra stared at him.

"She left part of her clothes," Elias said. "The dress was her best, which she had on the day before, being First Day."

Levi was clutching the rail. I studied him as I might a vicious animal snared in a trap. I pitied his pain but would not have set him free.

Looking as confused as I felt, Colden tried to restore order. "Did you see anything improper in Elma's behavior before the prisoner came to live in your house?"

It was a full minute before Elias responded, "No." He did not elaborate, nor did he sound convincing.

A flash of color rose in Burr's cheeks as he stood for the cross-examination. "Did you ever know the prisoner and Elma to be in bed together?" He may as well have been holding court in a tavern, telling a bawdy joke.

I covered my eyes, imploring Elias to honor Elma's memory.

"No." Elias's denial sounded as if he were refusing to answer rather than refuting the charge.

"Did you ever speak to her about her improper intimacy with Levi?"

"I never did."

Burr squared his shoulders. "What is the wall made of between Watkins's house and yours?"

Like me, Elias seemed baffled by the references to Watkins and his home. "It's a plank partition, lathed and plastered," he said.

"Could you hear voices through the wall?"

Elias cocked his head. "Not as I can recollect."

Burr stood an arm's length away from Elias. "Is Joseph Watkins a decent man?" he asked.

"Mr. Watkins is a good neighbor." Elias looked out into the audience to where Watkins sat directly behind Ezra Weeks. He seemed to be pondering Watkins's proximity to Ezra, as was I. Watkins stared ahead, astutely following each line of testimony, and did not appear surprised to be the source of so many questions.

"Have you not threatened Levi?" Burr asked.

Elias shifted, unnerved by Burr's abrupt change in topic. "I never threatened him that I know of. The day Elma was found—" Elias looked directly at Levi. "I had a conversation with the prisoner and he asked if I had said certain things about him and Elma."

I remembered the afternoon the men brought Elma's body home and how Elias swore he would put a pistol to Levi's head. Elias had been at the edge of his wits. Was it possible he didn't remember?

"Did you tell the prisoners that you thought he was guilty?" Colden asked.

"I did," Elias said, nodding too emphatically, "and he appeared as white as ashes and trembled all over like a leaf."

Burr walked to the rail that divided the audience from the rest of the court and gazed toward the back of the room. "Was Richard Croucher's name mentioned?"

Elias faltered, seemingly thrown by the reference to Croucher. I rested my head in my hands as Levi's cryptic words again came to mind: *Croucher saw you.*

"Was Richard Croucher mentioned?" Burr asked again, his voice even but firm.

Elias gazed down until one could see nothing but the crown of his hat. "I can't recall."

The clerk called Richard Croucher twice before he was located in the hallway. He had both the limp and the hungry-eyed look of someone who had seen battle.

"May it please the court and the gentlemen of the jury," Croucher began, "I was at the Ring house during the time of Catherine Ring's absence in September." His gaze met mine before his eyes narrowed and shifted to Elias. "I paid particular attention to the behavior of the prisoner and the deceased, and I was satisfied from what I saw that there was a warm courtship going on. I have known the prisoner to be with the deceased in private, frequently and at all times of night." Croucher craned his thick neck. His face grew increasingly flushed and his speech slipped with each damning statement. "I knew 'im to pass two whole nights in 'er bedroom." Assured the room was listening, he leaned forward and continued, "Once, lying in my bed, which stood in the middle of the room, in a position so I could see 'ho passed the door, I saw the prisoner come out of 'er room, wearing only 'is shirt—" Although the tirade had left him breathless, Croucher sounded as if he would go on..

Colden cut him off. "Did you tell anyone what you saw?"

Croucher stared toward us, though I couldn't tell whether he was watching Elias or me. "I never said a word to no one."

Hamilton stood. "Have you ever had a quarrel with the prisoner at the bar?" he asked, rocking forward onto his toes as if Croucher's testimony was nothing short of fascinating.

Croucher appeared to collect himself. "I bear him no malice."

"But have you ever had words with him?" Hamilton's eloquence magnified Croucher's shabbiness.

"Once. The reason was this: Going 'astily downstairs, I suddenly came upon Elma, who stood on the landing. She cried out and fainted away. On 'earing this, the prisoner came out of 'is room and said it was not the first time I'd insulted 'er. I told him he was an impertinent puppy. Afterward, being sensible of 'is error, 'e begged my pardon."

Hamilton was absolutely still, seemingly mesmerized by the story. Burr too was watching appraisingly.

"Yet you say you bear him no ill will?" Hamilton asked. He shook his head, making his dubiousness clear.

"I bear 'im no malice," Croucher said again, "but I despise any man who doesn't behave in character."

"Do you know the Manhattan Well?" Hamilton asked. His voice had lost its geniality and was now clipped and purposeful.

Croucher leaned forward, resting his elbows on the rail, his manner forcedly casual. "It's one of Colonel Burr's dry wells, collateral for his bank."

"Got that right!" someone called out.

Hamilton neither smiled nor winked, but he may as well have. His features relaxed and he paused a full moment as if encouraging the audience to go on.

"Did you pass by the Manhattan Well on the evening of December twenty-second?" Burr interjected.

Croucher was not nearly as brash as he had been the afternoon Sheriff Morris first questioned him. He raised his fist to his brow and muttered. "I didn't—I wish I 'ad—I might, perhaps, 'ave saved 'er life."

Hamilton made as if to check his notes, but it was a cursory glance. "Did you not tell the sheriff you passed that way that night?"

Wiry hairs fell across Croucher's forehead as he shook his head. "I might 'ave said I *wished* I'd been there."

"How near the well do you think you passed that night?"

"Maybe the glue factory."

"What route did you take?"

"I can't say for sure. I might 'ave gone one way or another, seeing as I go sometimes by road, sometimes across the field.

There wasn't much moonlight. The going was very bad."

Hamilton raised his hand to his chin, posing his fine-looking profile atop his fingertips as if sitting for a portrait. "Mr. Croucher, were you ever upon any other than friendly terms with Elma?"

Croucher chuckled. It seemed no one but I took offense at the lewd line of questioning. Elias sat perfectly still. Ezra Weeks nodded knowingly. Then I saw that Levi was trembling with rage.

Croucher seemed to relish his discomfort. "After I offended the prisoner at the bar, I never spoke to her again."

As evening descended, candles were placed in front of the judge's bench and on the attorneys' table. Sconces were lit along the walls, creating more shadows than light. The jurors were wilting in their seats, but Colden continued to call witnesses as if he could persuade them through volume rather than substance.

Lorena Forrest described the galloping horse and the sleigh without bells. An elderly woman who lived across from Ezra Weeks recounted the "rumbling noise" of a sleigh that left Ezra's yard about eight in the evening on "the night the deceased was lost." Curiously, she said, the sleigh had no bells. I nodded wholeheartedly.

"When was this? What month was it?" Hamilton asked in quick succession.

The woman cupped her hand to her ear. "I don't know the month, but I know it was so."

"Was it after Christmas or before?"

"It was after, I believe." Her wrinkled lips quivered. "It was January."

People began to whisper, "She's confused. Senile."

A wooden gavel lay on the bench in front of Judge Lansing. His fingers opened and closed on the finely crafted handle as if marking time.

Arnetta Lispenard was called to repeat her sorry performance. "'Lord have mercy on me, Lord help me,'" she cried, imitating Elma, while the audience gasped.

My expectations were as low as they'd been all day when Anthony Lispenard exchanged places with his wife.

"On the Sunday that the girl was missing," Lispenard began, "my wife woke me up to look out the window. It was a clear night, starlit, but the moon was dull. I got out of bed to hear and see what I could. When I looked out, I saw a man walking near the well."

Colden was visibly startled. He checked his notes, walked to the witness stand, then returned to his notes. "How was this man dressed?"

Seated next to me, Hardie flipped to a fresh page, energetically scribbling.

"As near as I could tell, he had on blue breeches, white stockings, and a red jacket," Lispenard said.

Lispenard's story had changed by leaps and bounds. And the vivid details were bewildering. Countless witnesses had testified about the dull moon and dark night. It would have been impossible to make out the color of anyone's clothing, yet Colden nodded as if he were satisfied by the improbable response.

His voice dropped. "Was he alone?"

Lispenard listed to one side as he braced himself against the rail. "Who can say?" His gaze shot from Ezra to Burr. "The land is sloped. It's impossible to see the far side of the well from the house."

"So there may have been someone else? Someone you failed to see?"

"Might've been."

"Might there have been a sleigh?"

"Don't see why not."

Burr sat back in his chair, crossing his legs, and slamming the floor with the heel of his well-polished shoe. "Yes or no," he called out.

Hardie's pen paused above his notebook.

Lispenard turned to Burr. "Yes."

Colden returned to the attorney's table, flipping through papers as if fully prepared to read the entire stack.

Burr clasped his hands together. "Anthony Lispenard, will you swear that Levi Weeks is the man you saw at the well?"

I studied Lispenard's wizened face. I wanted him to incriminate Levi, but I was suspicious of his motives.

His voice shook. "I cannot swear to it."

Midnight came and went. The boy who had fished the muff from the well was called. When asked if he could read, the boy admitted he could not, nor did he know the meaning of the word *oath*. Lansing glared impatiently at Colden, who summoned the boy's father.

"I went the next day and looked about," the farmer said. "There was a board off the top, which left it open, maybe twelve or thirteen inches."

"Twelve or thirteen inches?" Colden repeated. "Could you show the court precisely how wide?"

The farmer squinted as if only a fool, one who spent his days scouring books, would not understand the length of measurement. Shrugging, he held up his right arm, stretched out his fingertips, and chopped with his left hand slightly above his wrist.

Burr's dark eyes narrowed, and I understood why.

"The opening was too narrow," I told Hardie, watching as he took down my comment. "Elma could never have fit through, and who replaced the boards? This proves Levi pushed her and put the boards back to cover his crime."

Hardie stopped writing, tapping the end of his pen against his chin. "Why would Levi replace all but one board?"

"He probably put them all back," I said. The thought of Elma losing sight of the sky as she drowned in a dark and watery grave made the image of her death even more gruesome. It was a struggle to keep speaking. "The boy could have pulled a board off when he found the muff."

I turned back just in time to hear the farmer add that he had seen footprints around the open well.

"Footprints?" I wondered out loud. The farmer had mentioned a sleigh track, but he had never said anything about prints. Impatient to see the scene for ourselves, we had not given him a chance.

"I figured they belonged to the same man I had seen the week before," the farmer added..

Colden sounded almost breathless. "You had seen the man there before?"

"Yes," the farmer continued. "He was sounding the well with a pole. I went up and asked what he was about. He said he made the carpenter's work—"

"A carpenter!" someone shouted. "Levi Weeks is a carpenter."

The farmer scratched his chin and nodded. "I went up to him and asked what he was doing. He said he wanted to know the depth of the water."

"What!" I practically shouted. I was sure the jury would now pronounce Levi's guilt and the hangman would finalize his fate, but others disagreed.

Burr did not bother standing. "Three days had passed since the worst snowstorm in recent memory. More than a foot of snow had fallen and the wind was blustery, yet the footprints you saw–*three* days after the deceased vanished–were fresh." It was more statement then question and the farmer looked toward the judge as if he was unsure whether to respond. The clock struck one, the haunting clang heightening the moment.

There was a ragged noise, and I turned to see a man behind me snoring. The more I looked, the more exhausted the audience appeared. And it was not only them. An elderly juror's head bobbed toward his chest, then shot upright as he shook himself awake. Another man drummed his finger on the rail in front of him. Judge Lansing studied the jurors and announced an adjournment. Levi was led away. The jury was sequestered. They could only walk on the rooftop for air. And they would sleep in the courthouse's portrait gallery under the dignified likeness of General Washington.

The moon was full and bright as Elias and I walked home. I could not shake the notion that it was mocking me, demonstrating the illuminative powers that had failed us on the dark night Elma vanished.

—20—

I woke with a start. The bedsheets were twisted, the sky still dark. Elias was gone. Exhausted, I could not recall if he had spent the night in our bed. Aware of the grueling day ahead, I tried to close my eyes, but each time I did I heard Elma scream, *Lord have mercy on me, Lord help me.* Her cries echoed down a bottomless pit, hitting jagged stones and drowning in never-ending cold.

I wandered into the parlor. There was an empty drinking glass in front of Elias's chair; it from the same set as the glass that had broken the morning after Elma arrived. Elma had taken the blame for what I now knew was Elias's fault. I shuddered to think what else I had overlooked. I had imagined that single year in the city made me sophisticated or wise. I thought Levi was too worldly for Elma, but I was the one who was naïve.

In anger, I took the glass and smashed it to the floor, then collapsed beside the broken bits. A sharp sliver dug into the soft skin under my thumbnail, and crimson drops of blood splattered onto my dress.

"It's a ghostly 'our to be awake," Croucher said. His eyes darted anxiously around the dark room.

"Stop sneaking around!" I said, startled by his sudden appearance as well as my venomous response.

Croucher took a handkerchief from his pocket and wrapped my finger, applying pressure. "Not many 'ave kind words for me, but you, Mrs. Ring, 'ave always been above that."

I avoided his gaze, certain I was not as magnanimous as he seemed to believe.

"And unlike others," he said, releasing his hold, "I've no reason to lie to you."

There was a pathetic longing in Croucher's voice, and I had the impression he was on the verge of divulging something significant. He spoke with his usual bluster, but there was a note of sincerity I had never heard from him before.

"What is it?" I asked, aware that the truth might be more painful than anything I dared imagine.

Croucher jerked himself up off the floor. "I came to tell you the truth, and I want you to listen carefully," he said, pausing until I signaled my consent. He lowered his chin until his eyes met mine. "Weeks did it."

My curiosity turned to annoyance. "Yes, of course, but where is the proof?" I asked.

"Those fancy barristers want me to swing for 'is crime. 'e's paying 'em"—Croucher nodded toward my splattered dress—"blood money to lay the blame on me. Do you understand what I'm telling you? 'e trapped Elma, and now 'e's after me. Night and day someone's watching. I'm being followed."

I gazed out the dark window but saw nothing but my own tired reflection peering back.

"Mrs. Ring," he said, "you must believe me. Lord knows what I'm risking by coming to you. I'm just an old English bulldog, not pretty to look at and a bit of a brute. I may 'ave paid 'er too much attention, but I'm no killer."

"Then go to the sheriff, or anyone else." I could not understand why he was appealing to me, adding to my burdens. "Stop scaring people in the dead of night."

"I'd go, but—" He ran his hand over a bald patch on his head, which seemed to have grown in the short time I'd known him. "My past is a bit checkered. I've done some things I'm not proud of and racked up a bit of debt. I don't want to call any more attention to myself. Besides, the sheriff would never listen to the likes of me."

Croucher's disclosure was hardly a surprise. I had always had the impression he had fled England under a dark cloud.

"Is there no one who will listen?" I asked. The question I posed to Croucher was the same one I had been asking myself. Over and over, I saw myself storming the sheriff's office or approaching Judge Lansing, but as many times as I imagined the scene, their response was always the same: *Where is the proof?*

"Those lawyers are trying to smash me to pieces."

"Elias knows that Levi is guilty; perhaps together—"

"Elias?" He shook his head, then chuckled in a mocking way. "'e's the last one who'd come to my aid."

The white handkerchief was turning stiff with drying blood. "Why?" I asked. "What's passed between thee?"

Croucher shook his head. "I've never spoken ill of your 'usband, Mrs. Ring, and I'm not one to judge, but somewhere between your former 'ome and this city, 'e lost his way. Did you know that Ezra paid 'im a tidy sum on the condition that 'e'd keep an eye on that cad Levi?" "Ezra Weeks has eyes of his own," I said. "Besides, Levi's a grown man. Why should anyone watch over him?"

"Levi fathered a child back in New England and 'ad to flee after the girl's father put a pistol to 'is 'ead. Ezra didn't want 'im getting into the same kind of trouble. Course, this isn't anything like that. Adonis can't run now."

Wanting to believe but wary of Croucher and his gossip, I went to the fireplace, took the broom, and began to sweep the broken glass.

"What I'm saying," Croucher continued, "is, like it or not, Elias is indebted to Weeks and 'e's focused on playing his 'and."

I took a deep breath. "I may not know much, but I am confident that Elias does not see Elma's murder as a game. What's more, he was here with me the night she disappeared. Where were thee? Did thou pass the Manhattan Well that night?" I asked, fingers tightening on the broom handle.

"The meadow; not the well."

"Lispenard's Meadows?" The name made me shudder.

Croucher noticed. "'ere's the man they should be watching," he said. "'is wife heard Elma fighting for 'er life, but 'e 'eard *nothing*? 'e saw a stranger prowling 'is land and did *nothing?* Mark my words, all 'is *nothings* add up to something."

It was all I could do to make out Croucher's garbled speech, yet his lack of pretense, the notion that his guard was down, made him all the more believable. Whether from exhaustion or the prospect of a sympathetic ear, I had a sudden desire to speak frankly. "I saw Lispenard arguing with Ezra Weeks at the courthouse, and when I approached him, he said they were quarreling about money."

"Is that so?"

"Lispenard said he was owed stock in the Manhattan Company and, to buy his silence, Ezra Weeks found him a government post, with a political board of some sort—the Electoral College?"

Croucher rubbed his chin. "Important job. It means Lispenard will be one of only twelve men casting a ballot in New York for the next president. The outcome 'ere determines whether it's Adams or Jefferson."

"Lispenard is working with Burr. I saw him handing out flyers."

"Politicians reward their supporters. That's common enough."

"But that's just it. Lispenard complained that Ezra Weeks was telling him how to vote."

"Maybe 'e 'ad a change of 'eart and decided not to vote for Jefferson. That would be enough to infuriate Weeks."

"Ezra was the one criticizing Jefferson. He said Jefferson didn't understand New York."

Croucher chuckled. "Well, that's true. Still, Ezra's a staunch Republican. 'e and Burr are thick. Do you 'ear the way Burr defends Levi? You'd think 'e was 'is own flesh and blood."

"Lispenard made a deal with the devil," I said. "He looked the other way while Levi murdered Elma on his land, and he was rewarded with a prestigious job. But the pressure of the trial and his own guilt is eating away at him, and Ezra is anxious."

Croucher stepped uncomfortably close. "A curious theory. 'ave you told anyone else?"

"Elias. He promised to speak with the sheriff."

"Did 'e?"

Unable to answer, I looked down at the shattered glass. The shards twinkled in the light, like my own wavering doubts.

Elias was already seated when I returned to the courtroom. I smelled whiskey on his breath. He shook his head and mumbled when Ezra Weeks walked past, and when Hardie took out his notebook, he leaned forward and glared. He was a stranger to me.

Burr had donned a fresh suit for the second day of testimony. Hamilton was elegant as well, in a bloused shirt with white cuffs that gathered at the end of his jacket sleeves. I looked down at my own gray flannel dress, the same one that I had worn the day before.

Necks craned as Levi was led to the prisoner's dock. His jacket was freshly pressed, his hair neatly tied, but he shuffled while he walked, though his legs were free of shackles. The jurors too seemed worse for wear. I was sure Federal Hall's marble floor was not nearly as impressive when it served as a bed.

As Colden stood, Judge Lansing interjected, urging him to get straight to business. It was past ten. Everyone seemed braced for another long day of emotional and physical hardship, but the audience came to life when James Lent, our neighbor who had helped recover Elma's body, took the stand.

"The victim's hair hung over her head. In lifting her up, I found her head fell forward, and when we lifted her a little it fell back again, which caused me to suppose her neck was broke."

People let out a collective gasp, but I preferred to think that Elma's neck was broken. It meant she had not suffered long. But I still did not understand why the details mattered. Elma was dead. She had been found at the bottom of a well. Levi put her there.

The procession of witnesses melted into one another. Colden called a man who had been hired to drive the distance from our house to the Manhattan Well and back to Ezra Weeks's house. Though the roads were bad, he said, he had performed the trip in fifteen minutes.

Another man testified that Elma's left collarbone was broken and dislocated, but beyond that "she was a very lifelike corpse. The victim," he said, "looked as if she were asleep."

Colden scratched his head, making the short hairs stand on end. "Had you seen her alive?" His voice had a slight hitch, as if he were reluctantly approaching this new line of inquiry.

"Once."

I sat forward, suddenly recognizing the doctor who had examined Elma when she was sick with fever.

"The case stands out," he continued. "Miss Sands was in no grave danger, but she wanted medication. She specifically asked for laudanum. I was inclined not to give it to her, but she seemed desperate. I thought it might ease her conscience and, ultimately, improve her health."

I was on my feet before I realized it. "That's ridiculous," I shouted. "He knows Levi. The pair of them forced that vial on us!"

Hamilton leapt to his feet. "Objection!"

"Sit down!" Elias hissed.

Hardie gazed up at me with something like sympathy; it may have been pity.

"Mrs. Ring," Judge Lansing said, "if you were to be recalled, could you testify that the victim never asked for laudanum?"

It was tempting to lie, but my principles were all I had left. I collapsed back onto the bench, recalling how the doctor had sent me out of the room. Minutes had transpired while I went for water. Who could say what had really happened?

Colden's final witness was a physician who had had a "superficial" view of Elma's body when it "was exposed to the view of thousands." The doctor confirmed the scratches on Elma's hands and feet and described the "reddish-black" spots on her neck.

"Suppose, Doctor, that a person had been strangled by hand—would it not have left such an appearance on the body?" Colden asked.

"Yes, it would."

"In your opinion, could any person have committed such an act of violence on themselves?"

The doctor leaned forward. "I don't think it could be done."

Colden closed his case on a high note, but even that could not hide the lack of solid evidence. Stagnant air and the press of warm buddies lulled the crowd into inertia as he read from a fat legal text.

"Circumstantial evidence is all that can be expected and indeed all that is necessary to substantiate a charge." He paused, and his gaze traveled across the two rows of jurors as if he were individually appealing to each man.

Despite his impressive legal jargon, Colden was ultimately confirming the very same question that had been tormenting me: *Where is the proof?*

—21—

B urr's mouth curved slyly as he strode to the center of the courtroom. "Gentlemen, the patience with which you have listened to
this lengthy and tedious testimony is honorable to your characters."

Jurors and some members of the audience chuckled, and I could
not deny that the prosecution's case had been long-winded. Colonel
Burr allowed the laughter to die down before striking a more somber
note.

"Have the witnesses spoken with candor or have they spoken from
temper, hatred, and revenge?"

I couldn't help but feel that he was talking directly to me.

"Notwithstanding the intimacy between the prisoner and the deceased, it did not amount to courtship. Nothing like a real courtship
passed between them." Burr stood absolutely still, seeming to measure the intensity of his listeners' involvement. He lowered his voice
and, as if they were aboard a lurching ship, every member of the audience tipped forward. "It will be seen that the deceased manifested
equal partiality for other persons as for Mr. Weeks."

Elias sat up so forcefully that our bench wobbled. Only the horror of Burr's accusations kept me glued in place. Colden stood but
did not, or could not, object. Necks stretched, jaws dropped, and the
audience began to murmur.

Burr raised his voice above the din. "We shall show you that, if suspicions may be attached anywhere, there are those on whom they may be
fastened with more appearance of truth than on the prisoner at the bar."

Burr's penetrating eyes searched the audience, Elias's leg tensed
against mine, and, in that instant, all my doubts and suspicions turned
to dread.

Burr's features softened as he addressed the jury. "Certainly, you are not in this place to condemn others, yet it will relieve your minds of a burden."

"In other words," Hardie said, scribbling notes as he spoke, "free my client and you won't have to accuse anyone."

"We will show that the deceased sometimes appeared melancholy. She was dependent upon—"

Burr's eyes searched the audience and found mine. My fingertips clasped the edge of our bench, certain that he was going to say that Elma was dependent on laudanum. But it was not mentioned, not yet.

"She was dependent upon Mr. and Mrs. Ring and that gloomy sense of her situation might have led her to destroy herself."

"Woe," a man behind me said. He sounded as if he were trying to slow a runaway horse. "Which is it? Did someone do her in or did she do it herself?"

"Why should he say?" Hardie answered, "as long as Levi Weeks is set free."

Led by Hamilton, the defense called a string of witnesses. Unlike Burr, whose gestures were slow and deliberate, Hamilton moved with a flurry of activity.

Ezra Weeks's stable boy swore he had not noticed anything unusual about Ezra's horse the morning after Elma went missing. Our boarder, Isaac Hatfield, gave a damning account of what he called "Elma's melancholy temperament," seemingly pleased to impart every vice she ever possessed. Perhaps he was offended because Elma never returned his attention, but it didn't quite explain the intensity of his criticism.

"I saw her once take out a vial," he said. "This was after Elias Ring yelled at her about something. She held up a small glass bottle full of reddish-brown liquid—"

"Laudanum?"

"I suppose. I did not recognize what it was, but Levi was there. He snatched it away and said it would kill her."

The audience began to stir. Hamilton spoke above the fray.

"Though Elias Ring was excused from the oath, he testified that he had never threatened the prisoner—or at least he said *he could not recall doing so.* Is that your recollection?"

Hatfield shook his head. "The day Elma was found, after they brought her back to the house, I heard Ring say that if he ever met Levi in the dark, he would put a loaded pistol to his head."

My heart pounded as I remembered Elias's threats. Sadness seeped into me. I was drowning in it.

Condensation collected on the windowpanes as Ezra Weeks defended his brother. He spent the better part of two hours rambling on about Levi's efficiency, even producing notes of the business discussion he and Levi had the day Elma vanished. According to Ezra, Levi arrived at his home "just as we drank tea and were yet sitting at the table before we lit candles" and "tarried till about eight o'clock."

Spectators began to calculate time. One woman considered the lethal act as if listing chores. "Levi Weeks would have had to take off the harness bells, tack the horse, drive to the Ring's house, get Elma, go to the well, get back, unhitch the horse, and retie the bells. That's a lot to do in an hour."

"And he had to kill her," someone else said. "Don't forget that."

As the dreadful day ebbed into an equally dismal evening, the defense called the doctor who had examined Elma's body in our home.

"I was called upon by the sheriff on the third of January to serve as coroner to the body of Elma Sands," Dr. Prince said, implying that, unlike Colden's medical experts, he had made a full and authorized exam. "I was asked specifically by the sheriff to examine and see if Miss Sands was pregnant."

Clamor broke out in the courtroom. "I knew it," a woman cried. Though I did not turn to look, I was sure she was the same woman who had camped outside our home. Elias squeezed my hand, cautioning me.

"And what did you determine?" Hamilton asked.

I braced myself.

"I concluded that Elma Sands was not pregnant."

Elias's hand relaxed, while the room erupted.

"Impossible," said Elma's staunch supporter. I agreed. But everyone else seemed to take the doctor at his word.

"If she wasn't carrying his child," one man said, "he had no reason to kill her."

Though Dr. Prince looked perfectly composed, I could not understand his assurance. There were many variables, none of which he addressed. Could Elma have miscarried during the violent struggle? Would eleven days at the bottom of a well minimize signs of a pregnancy?

Hamilton drew a deep breath. "Is it your opinion, Dr. Prince, from all you saw, that the death was caused by drowning?"

Distinguished creases surfaced around the doctor's eyes as he closed them and nodded. "I saw no marks of violence," he said. "No appearance but what might be accounted for by supposing she drowned herself."

My knuckles were white against the bench. *Beating, kicking, pushing, choking, suffocating, and drowning:* The indictment's agonizing refrain ran through my thoughts. I was certain it would be lodged in my head forever.

Beside me, Hardie was flipping through his notes. "'Murdered by some person or persons,'" he read. "That was the verdict after he examined her."

Undeterred, Dr. Prince addressed the court. "At first I believed she was murdered, but after giving the matter considerable thought, my opinion changed."

"Why was that?" Colden asked.

"I've seen a number of drowned people at the almshouse and have seen livid spots upon the skin, much as I saw on Miss Sands. What I initially thought to be marks of violence were merely the result of suffocation."

"Would suffocation produce a row of spots around the neck?" Colden asked, grasping his collar.

"If the body was gangrened, it might."

The din died down. I marveled at how easily people were willing to accept the opinion of these supposed experts and wondered if I had once been the same way.

The courtroom stirred as the public came and went, but the jury was not offered any relief.

Joseph Watkins was called to the stand. He did not acknowledge Elias or me as he walked up. He repeated the oath with the somberness of a eulogy.

Burr was equally grave. "Was there anything in the conduct of Elias Ring that led you to suspect an improper intimacy between him and Elma?" he asked.

Thinking I had misunderstood, I looked around to gauge the reaction of others. The audience looked as shocked as I felt. I heard a soft moan, and though I recognized that it came from my lips, I was outside myself, past denial and beyond shame.

"Elias Ring seduced Elma?" rang through the room. The crowd was shouting, fists raised, feet stomping.

"Upon my soul! I knew it!" the crazed woman exclaimed.

Burr stood in the midst of the turmoil like a commander in the field, while I was as helpless as a felled soldier.

Next to me, Hardie crouched and shifted as he took notes, his back turned away, his expression hidden.

"Elias?" I pleaded. I wanted to ask what Burr was talking about, but asking outright would mean acknowledging the accusation.

"Lies," he muttered. His voice was angry and weak. "Burr's spewing lies at our expense. Caty." It was the first time he had addressed me by name since the trial began. "It's a tactic. He's trying to confuse the issues."

The defense had suggested many alternatives to the prosecution's argument. One moment Burr proposed that someone other than Levi had murdered Elma. The next he posited that Elma had killed herself. Was this just another attempt to muddle the facts?

Watkins's gaze settled above the audience as if he were focusing on the distant horizon. "When in the time of sickness Catherine Ring was in the country, I imagined one night I heard the shaking of a bed in the third story, where Elma's bed stood within four inches of the partition. I heard a man's voice. I am positive that it was not Levi's." Watkins shook his head, managing to look both regretful and outraged. "I told my wife, 'That girl will be ruined.'" "Dear Lord," I gasped, feeling short of breath. Watkins was correct about Elma's bed. I looked over to Levi. He had his head in his hands, but his fingers were splayed so that his expression was hidden.

"Did you recognize the man's voice?" Burr asked.

"Yes. I said to my wife, 'It's Elias Ring's voice.'"

Elias was staring at Watkins, slowly shaking his head with melancholy exhaustion. People turned and looked. Some pointed.

"Did you ever hear the shaking of the bed or voices after Mrs. Ring returned from the country?"

"No. I never did."

Elias set a clammy hand on mine, but the gesture seemed intended to stifle, not soothe.

Colden was on his feet. I held my breath, praying for him to discredit Watkins. "When was the last time you saw the room in which Elma slept?" he asked.

Watkins shrugged. "I don't know."

"Were you not there on the afternoon the deceased's body was brought home?"

"Yes," Watkins nodded. "I was there then."

Colden shook his head as if marveling at Watkins's selective memory. "Before that day, when was the last time you saw the room and the placement of the bed?"

"I can't say when."

"Were you there any time last fall?"

"I don't know that I was."

"Before the afternoon that you brought Elma's body back to the

Ring's house, had you ever seen Elma's bed?" The question was directed at Watkins, but Colden faced the jury.

"I don't know that I had," Watkins said.

"But you said the bed was next to your room. In fact," Colden consulted his notes, "you said it was situated 'within four inches of the partition.' How did you know that?"

Watkins leaned forward, looking past Colden to Burr. "I've seen the bed placed so," he answered.

"*After* her death," Colden clarified.

Watkins shook his head. "No. Before."

Colden held up his hands.

"See," Elias said loudly. "Watkins has no idea what he's saying."

The jurors looked puzzled. Even Judge Lansing frowned at Watkins's unfounded accusations. "No one believes him," I muttered. But I felt angry hives spring up on my neck, and I sat on my hands to keep from scratching.

Burr tried to reestablish Watkins's credibility. "Did you ever speak to anyone else of this noise that you and your wife heard?"

"I don't know." Watkins gazed out into the audience. His focus settled at the back of the room. "I once told Croucher that I believed he had a hand in it."

"You told Richard Croucher that you thought Elias Ring had a hand in Elma's death?"

"No. It was Croucher I suspected. I asked him where he was that night."

Burr returned to the attorneys' table, put on his glasses, and flipped through his notes. It was the first time he seemed ill prepared, and the audience began to murmur. The instant Burr wavered, Hamilton leapt to his feet. He patted Burr on the shoulder, patronizing and firm, as if pushing him down into the chair. Burr shot him a furious glance, but Hamilton smiled amicably and approached the witness.

"You say you asked Richard Croucher where he was on the night of December twenty-second." He made Croucher's surname sound like a curse.

On the stand, Watkins was nodding. "That's right. I wanted to know if Croucher had seen Elma the night she disappeared."

"And what was Richard Croucher's response?"

Watkins wrinkled his brow. "He went off on a tirade, accusing Weeks of murder. He seemed bent on seeing Weeks hang."

I turned to Levi, expecting him to recoil. Instead, he was standing at the front of the prisoner's box, looking more alert than he had during the course of the trial.

Hamilton was equally attentive. "Have you heard Richard Croucher say he was by the Manhattan Well on the night of the murder?"

"Sure, I have. He said it several times, once right after Elma's body was brought home."

Colonel Burr flipped his glasses to the top of his head and stood. "Judge Lansing, may I request a moment with my colleague?"

Lansing looked out the window. The sky was completely dark and there was nothing to see but flickering candlelight reflected in the glass panes. "Time is of the essence," he warned.

Burr bowed, "Of course." He looked sternly at Hamilton and the two walked to the far corner, away from the jurors.

"There's a sight," Hardie said, craning to see.

Burr spoke while Hamilton tapped the toe of his shoe on the marble floor as if it were all he could do to keep from interrupting. When Burr finished, Hamilton waved his arms with a flourish accentuated by his lacy sleeves. Burr glared and color rose in his cheeks, but Hamilton kept speaking, poking his finger in the air as if to mark each point. Finally, Burr held up both hands in surrender. He returned to his seat and Hamilton resumed his questions.

"Richard Croucher said he had gone by the Manhattan Well that night," Hamilton repeated, enunciating each syllable. "Did he say anything about visiting Ann Brown's house that same evening?"

Watkins fidgeted. He had been on the stand for well over an hour and seemed to be regretting his testimony. "He mentioned dining at someone's house. I can't recall the name."

"How about Ann Ashmore?" Hamilton asked. "Does that name sound more familiar?"

Watkins looked longingly at the courtroom doors. "That's right. He said he'd had supper at Ann Ashmore's home and that she could vouch for his whereabouts."

Heads turned as a mature woman with russet hair and a tight corset, which did little to contain her fleshy figure, took the witness stand.

"Pray, ma'am," Hamilton said, "tell the court your name."

"Ann Ashmore." Her throaty voice conveyed a weary wisdom.

"Do you not also go by the name of Ann Brown?"

"At times." She leaned forward, exposing her chest far beyond the point of subtlety.

Hamilton stood several feet away, as if reluctant to approach such a tawdry woman. "Pray, madam, why use two names?"

"Brown was my late husband's name. Ashmore is my family name."

"Why use them both interchangeably?"

"I use both names," Ann Ashmore said. She had not answered the question, but it didn't matter. Her credibility was already gone.

"Ah, like Miss Sands," Burr murmured, pleased to remind the court of Elma's illegitimacy. "Is Ashmore your mother's name?"

Ann Ashmore brushed a sleeve of her dress as if she had been dirtied. "Certainly not."

"Pray tell what happened on the night of December twenty-second," Hamilton said.

"It being my little boy's birthday, I invited some friends to come sup with me, and among the rest was Mr. Croucher. Between four and five o'clock in the evening, he came and remained there till four or five minutes after eleven."

"Could he have been absent at all during that time?"

"No. He wasn't."

"He remained at your house from four or five in the evening until, as you say quite specifically, four or five minutes after eleven without a single absence?"

"Yes."

Hamilton called four others who had been guests at Ann Ashmore's that night: lisping, pockmarked, lazy-eyed—the dregs of New York City. Each witness said they had had supper with Ann Ashmore on her son's birthday. All agreed it was a Sunday evening. Not a single one could recall the exact date.

Jurors began openly shaking their heads and snorting, as more witnesses came forward to cast suspicion on Richard Croucher.

"I had been acquainted with Mr. Croucher for some time, but I never liked his looks," said a barber who had a shop on Greenwich Street. "On the second of January, the day when the body was found, he was extremely busy among the crowd, spreading improper insinuations and prejudices against the prisoner. I told him I thought it was wrong that he should persecute Weeks in such a manner."

Someone cracked open a window and a draft blew through the room while a cobbler testified.

"One afternoon, a man—I don't know his name—came into my store and said, 'Good day, gentlemen; Levi Weeks has been taken by the sheriff for murder.' He seemed quite pleased with himself and happy to cast blame."

Hamilton snatched a candle from the attorneys' table. Wax dripped down the sides and the candle fluttered as he strode out into the courtroom. "Is this the man?" he demanded, thrusting the candle into Croucher's stricken face.

The cobbler did not hesitate. "It is."

Hamilton held the candle under Croucher's trembling chin. "The jury will mark every muscle of his face and every motion of his eyes."

Croucher reeled as though he had been struck. The defense rested its case.

$\sim$**22**$\sim$

I t was two-thirty in the morning. The candles had burned down and their wicks were smoking. The courtroom was sedate. Burr kept his closing argument brief.

"It's better that five guilty persons should escape unpunished," he warned with ecclesiastic authority, "than one innocent man should die." His somber words hung over the audience. The stale air added a religious austerity. A man's life was at stake. The entire room seemed to contemplate the gravity of the jurors' decision.

Colden alone was immune. In a hoarse voice, he asked for an adjournment, arguing that it was essential for the jury to hear his comments on the defense testimony but that he was too exhausted to deliver them at such a late hour. "I've been awake for forty-four hours," he complained, gesturing at the jurors, Levi, even at himself, as if trying to signal sentiments he was too tired to vocalize.

The jury grumbled, unhappy at the prospect of bedding down for a second night at Federal Hall.

Hamilton rose. He looked remarkably well and curiously unencumbered. The candlelight flattered his sharp features, erasing any sign of fatigue. The case, he said, required no "labored elucidation." Several jurors nodded appreciatively.

Only Colden objected again. The audience groaned. Judge Lansing frowned. Finally sensing the tide was against him, Colden began to waver. He conceded that unless the court was willing to grant an adjournment, he would have to accept the desire of the defense to submit the case now.

Judge Lansing turned to the jurors.

"It has unexpectedly become my duty to charge you without the assistance of the argument of counsel, which they have waived on account of the late hour. Your path of duty is clearly and distinctly traced: to find the prisoner, Levi Weeks, guilty, if in your consciences you believe him so, or to acquit, if you think him innocent."

I could hardly keep my eyes open and would have been as happy as anyone to lie down in my bed, but the simplicity of Lansing's explanation was madness. The case was as complex as the wants, desires, and passions that had led us to this courtroom.

Lansing continued, "It is not pretended that positive proof of murder is attainable, but the prosecution has attempted to prove the prisoner's guilt by circumstantial evidence. If it can be established by a number of connected circumstances that Levi Weeks was the perpetrator of the crime, it will be your duty to find him guilty, as much as if proof were made by direct testimony."

More satisfied, I sat back in my seat, but Lansing had not finished.

"There are points in which the circumstances were not so satisfactorily connected as to enable you to pronounce the prisoner guilty," he said.

His words flooded my ears. His mouth continued to move, but I could only make out bits and pieces.

"It is doubtful that Gulielma Sands left the house of Elias Ring in the company of the prisoner. It is doubtful the prisoner's brother's sleigh was removed from his yard."

I pressed Elma's comb into my palm, feeling each tooth dig into me, as Lansing performed the defense's final work for them. "The prisoner appears to be a young man with a mild disposition and fair character, and it is difficult to discover what could have motivated him to commit the crime."

In the back of the courtroom, the crazed woman who was Elma's greatest advocate began to sob. I envied her extravagant display.

Lansing continued, "The witnesses produced on the part of the prisoner have accounted for the manner in which he spent the evening. It is very doubtful that Gulielma Sands was exposed to any other violence than that occasioned by drowning."

Elias wrapped his arm around me, and I became aware that I was gasping. I heard Croucher cough. I heard Elma scream.

Lansing concluded, "The court is unanimously of opinion that the proof is insufficient to warrant a verdict against the prisoner. With this general charge, we commit the prisoner's case to your consideration."

"He's already considered it for them," I nearly shouted. Other members of the audience echoed the same concern. Elias lowered his head into his hands. My chest constricted and my vision narrowed.

"What's happening?" one man asked.

"The judge says there's no proof," someone said.

"What about the dead girl?" a woman yelled.

The clerk led the jury out of the courtroom. Some shuffled; others gazed over their shoulder at the judge or the courtroom; all looked confused.

"Are they being dismissed?" I asked, unable to hide my mounting panic.

"They're going to deliberate," Hardie explained.

Levi watched the jurors file out. There were dark circles under his eyes. His hair was spiky, as he ran his fingers through it constantly. One moment he appeared innocent, the next he looked like a monster, incapable of emotion.

Judge Lansing ordered Levi back to his brother's house to await his fate. The attorneys began to collect their belongings. The crowd debated whether to wait for the verdict or return home. As officers led Levi away, a group of men in the back of the room began to shout: "Weeks is a villain!" "Hang him!"

Relief washed over me. The public was incensed; perhaps the jurors were as well. Judge Lansing might believe that the evidence was insufficient, but the final decision rested with the jury. I crossed and uncrossed my legs, unable to still my anxiety. I had imagined that the trial would prove Levi's certain guilt, but I had more doubts than ever.

Elias put his hand on my forearm, and I shivered at his touch.

"Come," he said, leading me to a dark corner. He looked around to make sure we would not be overheard. "You can't possibly believe that smut."

He had used "you" instead of "thou," but it hardly mattered. We had nothing left. Elias seemed furious, but I had no words to respond. Words were useless. I had just sat through a trial filled with nothing but futile words.

Elias swore under his breath. "Watkins is a vicious liar."

"Why would he lie—under oath?" Joseph Watkins had helped us search for Elma. He was a kind man. Elias said so himself.

"He was sitting within arm's reach of Ezra Weeks, within reach of Ezra's pocketbook, I should say.'"

"Not everything is about money," I said. "Not everyone can be bought."

"Watkins's story changed with every question. No one believed him."

I nodded. Colden had created quite a bit of doubt over Watkins's accusations. Judge Lansing had hardly acknowledged his testimony. Even the defense attorneys had quickly moved on to their next point. The problem was that Watkins's words rang true with me. Somehow Elias had laid the trap that had snared Elma.

"But . . ." I recalled Levi's warning, uttered in the dark room the afternoon Elma's body was found. "Richard Croucher saw *you*—with Elma."

Elias exploded. "Richard Croucher!" People turned and he lowered his voice. "He was after that girl from the moment he laid eyes on her."

Croucher was obnoxious and crude, but there was something in him that was plain and authentic. Our early-morning talk had only added to my confusion. "Elma would never have had anything to do with him," I said.

"That doesn't mean he didn't lust after her. It doesn't mean he didn't kill her." Elias pointed at the attorney's table. "Hamilton practically accused him of murder."

"Because he's an easy target. Croucher said they would try to pin this on him."

Elias looked bewildered. "You're defending Richard Croucher?"

"He had an alibi, Elias. Perhaps not one as respectable as Levi's, but that woman, Ann Ashmore, said he had supper with her."

"That wench? She could not swear to her own name."

I started to tremble. "There were others."

"A bunch of misfits. They were there to celebrate her son's birthday but no one knew the date? They hardly know Ann Ashmore, and I'd say they don't know Croucher. The man's lived under my roof for nearly a year and I don't know a thing about him."

"He's misunderstood."

"His excuses make no sense. One minute he's bragging that he was by the well that night; the next he says he took another route or can't remember. He's accused Levi from the moment Elma disappeared, because he was trying to draw attention away from himself. And he hated Levi from the moment they met."

"Hating Levi does not make him a murderer."

"Printing handbills and spreading rumors doesn't make him innocent. The morning after she disappeared, he was racing around town spewing ghost tales."

"Ghosts?" I saw bricks stacked higher than my head and a tangle of black hair slowly rising from the loamy pit. "Elma's ghost?"

"He claims her spirit rises from the Manhattan Well at midnight, condemning Weeks."

"Croucher wrote those things?" I asked. Croucher enjoyed spreading speculation and he had always disliked Levi, but printing handbills required money and forethought, an effort that went well beyond hate. It was not that I found it objectionable, in all honesty, but I was shocked by his vehemence.

I scratched my neck, unable to understand why Elias was being so forthright now, when it was too late. "If thou are so certain of Croucher's guilt, then why was Levi charged? Why didn't Croucher stand trial?"

"Ask yourself," Elias snarled. "You put Levi on trial while the real culprit walks free."

I leaned against the wall behind me, urging my knees not to buckle.

Elias glared. "I warned you to be careful, not to blindly accuse, but you wouldn't listen. Never did."

"No," I said, although there was truth behind Elias's words. "Levi left our house with Elma. He said so."

"There's no proof he killed her." Elias waved at the witness stand. "Two days of testimony and not a shred of proof."

"Levi is not innocent!"

Elias shook his head. "He soiled Elma and treated our home like a brothel, yes, but she was ripe for the taking—just like her mother. She may not have thrown herself down a well, but she paraded around in her nightgown, she remained alone in a house full of men, and she encouraged him and flaunted herself in front of all of us—"

"Elias," I asked. "Did thou speak with the sheriff about Anthony Lispenard?"

Commotion broke out as Judge Lansing returned. As if in a trance, I followed Elias back to our bench. Levi was led to the prisoner's stand. He looked as hopelessly lost as I felt.

The jurors returned but remained standing. A deep hush settled over the court as the clerk called their names.

Judge Lansing spoke. "Gentlemen of the jury, look upon the prisoner. Prisoner, look upon the jury. Have you reached a verdict?"

The juror at the end of the first bench responded, "We have."

"How say you, gentlemen? Do you find the prisoner Levi Weeks guilty or not guilty?"

A thin slip of paper trembled in the foreman's hand. His voice was weak as he pronounced, "Not guilty."

"Good God!" a woman screamed. Others burst into tears. Men hissed and stamped their feet in protest.

In the time it took for the clerk to repeat the jury's verdict, Levi was freed and had collapsed in his brother's embrace. His face was hidden, but his body heaved with sobs.

I fought my way out of our row and to the front of the room. Elias called after me, but I pretended not to hear. Levi remained in his brother's arms, but Ezra Weeks kept an eye trained on the angry crowd. I could see him quietly urge Levi to retreat to safety. Colden was shaking the judge's hand. Hamilton and Burr patted each other on the back, offering hearty congratulations on their success.

While the details were still hazy, intentionally obscured and blurred by the gentlemen before me, I had no doubt that these men had destroyed my family. They had belittled Elma's life and defiled her grave. I approached them, fist held high, shaking so hard my teeth chattered. Ever watchful and intuitive, Hamilton turned first, not a glimmer of remorse in his clear blue eyes. Following Hamilton's lead, Burr spun around. My lungs filled with air and I swore, "If thee dies a natural death, there is no justice in heaven." Then I fled.

—23—

Elias shouted after me, but I didn't stop. I would never listen to him again. It was three in the morning, but the mob outside the courthouse was growing louder and more excited by the moment, demanding Levi's immediate hanging, determined to take matters into their own hands if necessary. I wondered if he would escape unharmed. I knew I never would.

A block north of Wall Street, the crowd abruptly dispersed. Oil lamps cast yellow shadows on the lonely streets. A mangy dog searched the gutter for scraps. I was neither afraid nor concerned with propriety. I marched up Broadway in my own solitary funeral procession.

Elma's life had been exterminated, her reputation ruined. Burr and Hamilton had used the trial as a stage for their political games, defiling her as surely as her killer had. Their renowned oratory skills were more famous than ever. One of them—I did not care which—would capture the presidency for his party. Elma's grave had served as their stepping-stone.

As I turned the corner onto Greenwich Street, my stride became more purposeful, and anger replaced sorrow.

I pounded on the Watkinses' door for several moments before I saw the flicker of a candle within.

"Who's there?" called a sleepy voice.

"It's Caty—Catherine Sands." I was dull with grief, but even that could not explain why I used my maiden name.

A long moment passed before the door inched open. Elizabeth rubbed her eyes. Her hair was tousled, and she had a blanket wrapped around her shoulders. "Is it over?" she asked.

I pushed past her into the house. The children were asleep on a makeshift bed in the parlor. A quilt was tangled around Charles's legs, and he held Patience in the crook of his arm like a doll. I knelt beside them and, as I watched their narrow chests rise and fall, my own breath began to slow.

"What's happened?" Elizabeth whispered.

I stroked Patience's hair. I couldn't imagine saying the words out loud.

Elizabeth blinked, and her drowsy eyes became alert with worry. "Let me warm something up," she offered.

I shook my head. The motion freed my tongue. "The jury found Levi innocent. He's free." The room blurred and I sat back on the floor.

Elizabeth gathered the blanket around her, looking ashamed but not surprised.

Resentment rose within me. "Did thou know?"

She set the candle on the mantel but took a seat in the room's darkest corner. "I . . ." She covered her mouth with both hands.

"Thy husband testified in court." My breathing became shallow, and I had to look at the children to remain calm. "Joseph said he heard Elias with Elma. He said he heard them together in her bed." My voice began to rise. "He said Elias had his way with her."

Elizabeth's eyes darted from the children to me. "Caty, I beg you. It's not my place."

"Did thou know?" I repeated.

Fat tears began to roll down her cheeks. "Joseph said it was them."

"And thou? What did thou hear?"

She gulped. "I heard voices. A man and a woman, and the squeak of a bed, but I cannot say for sure. I did not see anything with my own eyes."

"Was it Elias's voice?"

"Joseph said it was."

"And Elma's?"

She opened her mouth but remained mute.

"Why not come to me?" I said, rising to my feet. But as I watched Elizabeth tremble, I realized she was merely another victim caught in this whirlwind of violence and lies. There was nothing she could have said or done. I never would have believed her. My fury began to subside, replaced by regret. "Why?" I asked. "Why did he do it?"

Elizabeth sighed. "Who can say what comes over men? Even the best can be weak. The worst can be cruel."

I shook my head. Elias had deceived me and set the path for Elma's downfall. But Elma had kept secrets as well. "Why didn't she say something?" I wondered out loud. "Why didn't she tell me?"

Elizabeth wrung her hands. "She was a young girl. Perhaps she was ashamed."

"Yes." Elma had spent her life trying to overcome the shame of her birth. It was easy to understand how she could have been convinced of her guilt.

Charles stirred, hugging his sister close. The gesture awakened my dull senses. For the first time in a very long while, I was aware of a strong, firm voice within me. I could not follow Elma and withdraw from the living. The world was filled with darkness but also with infinite light. I needed to recapture that light, to reclaim it for my children and myself.

Elias was waiting just inside the door when I arrived home, standing guard like a sentry.

"Where were thee?" he asked, deftly reverting back to plain speech like the chameleon he was.

I did not remove my bonnet. "I plan to take the children to Cornwall," I said. "The sooner the better." I could not predict what the future held, but I would never live under the same roof as him again.

Elias stepped in front of me. "I won't allow it."

"We'll leave on the noon boat."

"I won't stand by while you take my children."

I shook my head, ashamed that I had been too blind to see the truth but also no longer afraid. Elias was a coward and a bully. But I would not be as easy a target as Elma.

"I will no longer live as thy wife," I said.

"That girl was a minx, just like her mother. 'The righteous shall never be removed: but the wicked shall not inhabit the earth.'"

My hand was up before I could stop it. I felt the slap vibrate up my arm, and Elias stepped backward, holding his cheek. "Elma is dead!" I said. It was the first time I had uttered the words aloud. Fresh pain seared through me along with the awful acceptance of its truth. Patience would never know Elma, and Charles, who had loved her dearly, was only a child. In time, his agony would recede. It was right and normal, but the idea that she would be forgotten made my heart ache.

"Caty . . ." Elias's voice wavered, though it was unclear whether he was challenging me or preparing his own defense. "I had nothing to do with that. You saw me here that night. I didn't kill her."

"Thou defiled her as surely as the murderer who threw her down that well."

"According to Joseph Watkins, that rambling fool."

"And his wife. I've every reason to believe them and none whatsoever to listen to thee."

"Catherine." Elias grabbed my arm. "Please. I've been punished enough. Don't destroy our family."

"Thou destroyed our home," I said, turning away. Elias was pathetic.

"Caty, I'm begging—"

"Elias," I said softly, in need of full command of the facts before I could fully rest. "Did thou father Elma's baby?"

His chest fell. "That doctor said she wasn't with child."

I had seen enough to know that, in a court of law, a solemn oath by a man in thrall to an even more powerful man meant nothing. "I can't explain why he said what he did, but I know that Elma was expecting. Who was the father?"

He covered his eyes. "I don't know, Caty, I swear it. Please, believe me."

"But it might have been thee."

Elias turned toward the fireplace. I thought that I heard him sob but did not stay to listen.

The sun was rising as I neared Lispenard's Meadows. It was a mild morning. The ground was soft and moist. The air was heavy with mist and sweet fragrance, as if winter had turned to spring over the two days we sat captive in court. I picked my way through spiky brush. The hem of my skirt dragged through swampy puddles, and my heels sank into the mud.

The well looked less menacing now, free of its cover of snow and ice. Splintered boards, broken buckets, and abandoned jugs were tossed aside. A rooster crowed. In the distance, smoke curled from the chimney of Lispenard's farmhouse. The field boasted green sprouts and a handful of purple buds. I saw no trace of the violence that had occurred here.

I sat on the well's edge and leaned as far over the opening as I dared. Then I felt a soft, almost caressing hand on my shoulder. It was a gentle pressure, but I gripped the rough bricks, sure it would send me toppling into the dark waters.

I spun around, expecting to find Elias, here to lead me to Elma's fate so I would not live to expose him.

"Caty?" Tall and dark in the early-morning light, Levi appeared gaunt but handsome as always. Perhaps I should have been frightened. At the very least, I should have been surprised. But I wasn't. Levi's presence was as natural as the breeze.

"I hoped I would find you here," he said.

"Did thou follow me?"

"I knew you would be here. This place," he took a deep breath of loamy air, "this place holds Elma's spirit."

I was too exhausted to bother shaking my head. "I don't believe in ghosts."

"Nor do I, but Elma's spirit exists. She's here with us now."

It was impossible to disagree. The wind filled with the scent of lavender, and while, logically, I knew that the flower did not bloom in early spring, I did not doubt its perfume. The sense that Elma was nearby was so powerful that I looked for her. My eyes scanned the desolate field, then came to rest back on Levi's haunted face.

"Thou are a free man," I said. "Why bother with me?"

Levi gazed anxiously over his shoulder. "That mob wants me to hang. I'm leaving the city. But I couldn't go without telling you the truth."

"Thou had every opportunity to tell the truth."

Levi ran his fingers through his hair. "Please understand. I was desperate and scared. I thought I was protecting myself."

I had little sympathy for his sorrow. "What about Elma? Who was protecting her?"

Levi shook his head so violently that I wondered at his sanity. "Elma was already lost."

In a sickening instant, I understood. From the start, I had been convinced that Levi killed Elma, but as I listened to his feeble muttering, I realized my grief had obscured the truth. Out of all those who mourned Elma, only Levi shared my devastation.

"Levi, who killed Elma?"

Levi kicked the boards by his feet. "Caty, I beg you to forgive me. I've already caused you so much pain, but it is important that you know that Joseph Watkins was telling the truth. Elias took advantage of her." His eyes grew moist with the tender expression I had seen on his face the night I saw them together. "She was carrying his child."

I watched a robin pick through the wet ground until it flew away with a worm dangling from its beak. "Yes," I said.

Levi looked startled. "You knew?" When I did not respond, he continued. "Elma turned to laudanum. She thought she might lose the child that way, but I confronted her. I told her she would destroy herself."

"So now thou are her savior?"

Levi looked desperately into my eyes. "You don't know. You weren't there."

"Yes," I said quietly. "There is enough blame to go around. I will regret that for the rest of my days."

"I took the vial from her but poured the contents out. And I kept it as a reminder to both of us."

"A reminder of what?"

"That life is precious." Levi's gaze, which had always seemed so arrogant, was entirely changed. It was clear he had also been permanently scathed.

"Caty," he said, "you're a mother; you understand. I told Elma that no matter how her baby came to be, it was a miracle. I explained how my mother had died while giving birth to me, and Elma told me how much her mother loved her despite her disgrace."

I remembered the evenings Levi and Elma had spent locked away in her bedroom and the assumptions I had made. In my eight years with Elias, it had never occurred to me that love and friendship could coexist.

"Elma was a loving person," Levi said, echoing my thoughts. "I knew she would be a wonderful mother."

I recognized the tenor of his voice. I had heard it when he stood over Elma's sickbed, when he addressed her, and when he defended her. But it was the first time I understood how desperately Levi wanted to be loved, as did Elma. And they had found each other.

"I wanted to help her," he said, "but it was more than that. I loved her, and I wanted to be a father to her child. Our baby would enjoy the happy home she and I had never experienced. We would be a family, but instead . . ."

My former self might have accepted Levi's tearful confession and left it at that. But I was singularly focused on the truth, the only possible succor to my pain. "Elias will suffer for his sins, but he was with me the night Elma died. He could not have killed her. Tell me who did."

"She's dead. Does it matter how?"

"Yes." I looked down. My shoes were muddy. My hemline was in tatters. I had not eaten in days, and I had deserted my children to visit this wretched hole in the ground one final time. Elma deserved the truth, and so did I.

A blue jay squawked and a woodpecker tapped, but Levi was

oblivious to all but his own sorrow. "She's dead and buried," he moaned. "Let her rest in peace."

It occurred to me that Levi was weak. He was handsome. He may even have loved Elma. But he was no match for wills and wits stronger than his own. "I am tired, Levi," I said. "Please, do not delay me further. Thou came here to tell me the truth; now out with it."

Levi's dark-blue eyes darted back down the road.

"Elma is dead, yes," I continued, seeing his resolve wavering, "but the truth will set her spirit free. It's all we can do for her now."

Levi gazed helplessly around the swampy meadow. "It was snowing when we left the house. My brother drove up in his sleigh . . ."

I remembered Croucher's predawn confession: *Weeks did it.* He had been trying to tell me the truth. "Ezra?"

Levi continued as if he had not heard me. "It was a dark night and he startled us both. You see," his voice trembled, "the sleigh had no bells."

My throat grew dry. It was the hundredth time I had heard Levi deny his involvement in Elma's murder, but it was the first time I had truly listened. "What then?" I asked, because Levi had stopped speaking. He was wringing his hands as if trying to stanch some physical pain.

"He swore at me and called Elma all manner of despicable names. She ran off." He began to sob. "I never saw her alive again."

My fingers clutched the well's jagged rim. Elma's body had been battered and bruised. Her knuckles were scraped: proof that she had fought to save herself. What was it like to feel one's feet leave the ground? To have reached for something solid to grasp—and slipped? How had it felt to fall headfirst into darkness? I heard a splash. I heard Elma scream, *Lord have mercy on me, Lord help me.*

"Elma may have been with child, but she didn't—" I looked into the well, a bottomless pit leading to hell. "I know she did not kill herself."

"No," he admitted. "She did not."

"Lorena Forrest saw Ezra's sleigh racing up Greenwich Street with Elma in it."

Levi's features froze.

"Lorena saw two men in the sleigh that night."

Levi nodded. It was clear that, like me, he had thought of little else since the day Elma disappeared. "That foul creature."

"Lispenard," I said, furnishing his words.

Levi looked up, jolted out of his remorse. "Who?"

"Anthony Lispenard. Elma was found here on his land. He admitted it was no coincidence. He said it was a warning."

"It was. My brother had been threatening that man all winter. When that wasn't enough—" Levi wiped his brow. "Ezra swore he would deliver the same fate to Lispenard if he didn't do as he commanded."

"What does Ezra want?"

"To make Aaron Burr president."

"Vice president."

Levi shook his head. "President."

"Jefferson is the Republican candidate for president," I said, aware that I was repeating Lispenard's words.

"That's not so. The man with the most votes will be president. And the way the states are split, it will take very little to tip the scale. New York is key. All Lispenard has to do is vote for Burr—twice."

"It can't be that simple."

"All brilliant plans are simple. Whoever controls New York will be the next president. If that happens, Ezra will receive a government appointment, maybe a cabinet post. He's pressuring Lispenard to demand a secret ballot, one in which he can cast both his votes for Burr. Lispenard refused. Ezra tried to scare some sense into him."

"By murdering an innocent girl?"

"Ezra didn't see her that way. My brother can be very cruel. Even Hamilton and Burr are afraid of him, I think. They didn't charge him for their services in my defense."

"But why Elma? She was only twenty-two years old, with no family or wealth. Why harm her?"

Levi followed my gaze into the well. "Elma was my friend. I

confided in her. I told her about the Manhattan Company fraud and she blurted it out, to Ezra of all people. The day of the snowstorm, I went to my brother's house. I told him Elma was carrying *my* child and that we planned to marry that night. I thought he would be pleased to have an heir. I thought—" Levi shook his head. "Ezra called her a whore and accused me of spilling family secrets. No matter how much I denied it, he refused to listen. I had had enough of Ezra and his crooked schemes. I only wanted to be with Elma and our baby. Out of spite, or Lord knows what else, I told Ezra he was right. I said Elma knew all about his plan to fix the election and if he did not let us marry in peace, we would expose him. I thought I was ensuring her safety. I thought if she was a threat to him, he would leave us alone." Tears streamed down his face.

I shuddered, back with Levi on that miserable night. Stars had dotted the sky, but the moon refused to shine. "Then what?" I asked.

"I never could have predicted Ezra's reaction. He's capable of many things, but . . . He must have followed me back to Greenwich Street." Levi tugged at the roots of his hair. "I may as well have killed her myself."

"This is no time for self-pity," I said. "Ezra must be punished."

"He's my brother. He raised me—"

"Coward!"

"Elma's dead. We can no longer help her."

"So thou will stand by while her reputation is ruined and her murderer walks free?"

"I'll never speak to my brother again, but I can't turn him in. I won't."

"He let thee suffer for his crime."

Levi let out a low, chilling laugh. "Ezra is guided by his own principles. He would never have let me hang, but he wasn't opposed to seeing me suffer."

"Lorena saw two men in the sleigh that night. If Lispenard wasn't the second man, who was?"

"Croucher had a hand in it, of that I am sure." Levi winced. "Elma was so petite and fragile, Ezra could have—there was no need to involve anyone else. Ezra used him as a foil."

"Someone to pin the blame on?"

"Pointing the finger at him made me look innocent. Croucher was a ready scapegoat."

"But this is no petty crime or gossip—it's murder. Why would Croucher involve himself in such ugly business?"

"Who can understand that wretched being? Ezra pays him well, but it is more than that. Croucher's depraved."

"Then how could thou allow him to walk free?" Though I shouted the question out loud, I was really asking myself. My desire for revenge had destroyed my judgment.

"I told my attorneys," Levi said. "Hamilton was eager to question him, but Burr refused."

I remembered Hamilton and Burr quarreling in the dark corner. I saw Hamilton's smug expression and Burr's simmering rage. "Why would Burr protect a man like Croucher?"

"Burr did not want to gamble on what a man like Croucher would or would not say when cornered. It was enough to raise suspicion; there was no need to incriminate him."

"Burr knew who killed Elma?"

"It's impossible to say, but I know my brother well enough to say he would have warned him."

"And Burr intentionally overlooked Croucher?"

"Voting for the election begins this month," Levi said, as if I was not grasping the magnitude of the prize. "If Croucher had implicated Ezra, it could have been connected to Burr. Burr bought Croucher's silence by letting him go free."

My head ached and my heart pounded. "What about Hamilton? Why didn't he expose them?"

"He's not finished. There's nothing to tie Croucher to Elma's murder. And there's certainly not enough to taint Burr, which is Hamilton's true aim. But they both understand that Hamilton knows, and, when he has the most to gain, heads will roll."

"And what of justice?" The word echoed down the well shaft like a muted splash. I would not sink into despair. Elma had not drowned so that evil men could prosper. I looked across the sodden field to Lispenard's farmhouse. While I could never bring Elma back, I could make life unbearable for those who had caused her death. Burr would not become our next president if I exposed his scheme.

I was leaving Manhattan forever, but before I did I would pay a visit to the reporter Hardie. I could never find a punishment harsh enough, but the damage to Burr's reputation would make his life a living hell. Without Burr's patronage, Ezra Weeks would never achieve the prestige he so desperately sought. And I had little doubt that, when it all started to crumble, he would throw Croucher to the wolves. Most important, I knew my premonition was real. It was only a matter of time before Alexander Hamilton and Aaron Burr destroyed each other.

As rays of sunlight filtered through the morning fog, Levi stepped closer, resting his hand again on my shoulder. I unfolded my palm, exposing the ivory comb. A ghost of a smile flitted across Levi's face, and a silent pledge passed between us. I leaned over the well and my reflection rippled in the gray water below. A cool draft wafted upward, turning my fair hair dark and flowing. I had little doubt Elma had suffered, but as the breeze engulfed me, my hatred drained, replaced by resolve. My grief would never abate, but it could be channeled into wisdom and strength that I could pass along to my children and grandchildren. Levi was right when he said life was precious. There was profound sadness, but there was also immense joy.

In a single swift gesture, I pressed the ivory comb to my lips, stretched out my arm, and opened my hand. The comb lingered weightlessly before falling and I knew, in that brief instant, that Elma's spirit had taken flight.

Author's Note

In the same way that this book found itself in your hands, Elma's story found me. I was reading Ron Chernow's biography of Alexander Hamilton when I came across the "Manhattan Well Tragedy." Only four pages were devoted to the Levi Weeks trial, and most of those focused on Hamilton's oratory skill and his rivalry with Burr, but I was riveted. An Internet search led me to *The Trial of Levi Weeks*, Estelle Fox Kleiger's historical account of the case. When I sought out the Manhattan Well, I discovered that the structure in which Elma drowned still existed in the basement of a New York City restaurant. What's more, twenty years earlier, I had lived on Spring Street, steps away from the well. At the time I was unaware of Elma's story, but I was twenty-two years old, the same age as Elma Sands when she was murdered. Two hundred years had passed since Elma's death. The rustic farmhouses of Lispenard's Meadows had morphed into trendy Soho boutiques, but Elma's story resonated with me. Young women, including myself at the time, are in search of excitement, recognition, perhaps love. Many succeed; an unfortunate few make mistakes; some pay dearly. Elma's death was a cautionary tale with modern-day relevance.

Two nineteenth-century novels based on Levi Weeks's case contributed to my understanding of Elma's story. The first, *Norman Leslie*, written in 1835 by Theodore S. Fay, is about a man wrongly accused of murder. The second, *Guilty or Not Guilty: The True Story of the Manhattan Well*, written in 1870, is unsigned. In her book on the Weeks trial, historian Estelle Fox Kleiger attributes the work to Keturah Connah, Catherine Ring's granddaughter, and reprints the dedication:

To thee, my venerated GRANDMOTHER, I dedicate this, my feeble attempt at authorship. The truths which it contains I gathered in childhood from thy own lips, and though thou has been resting for many a year, and thy name and age stand registered upon imperishable marble, I see thee vividly as in years gone by, when thou didst sit, the center of an admiring throng, and tell to us the sad history of Cousin Elma.

To establish a link to Catherine Ring and her loved ones, I have chosen to open the novel with an adaptation of Connah's poetic description of the Hudson River's western horizon and the distant hills. I have also taken my description of Levi Weeks (his long, fashionably tied hair; dark-blue eyes; and restless expression) directly from Connah's work and have revived Elma's barnyard stories about the red calf and white colt, because of their authenticity. . Most significant, I have built upon Connah's theory that Ezra Weeks was intent on seeing his brother marry up.

The theory that Ezra Weeks had Elma killed to protect his family's reputation is plausible. But the more I delved into the facts, the more fascinated I became by the connection between Elma's murder and Aaron Burr's Manhattan Company. Elma had drowned in the Manhattan Well, one of the company's fraudulent wells, and I could not shake the notion that it was a clue to the true motive behind her murder. Establishing a link was not difficult. Ezra Weeks had laid the pipes for the Manhattan Company, Levi worked with his brother, and Elma was Levi's lover. It was logical that Ezra and Levi Weeks would know about Burr's scam. And it made sense that Levi might have shared his misgivings with Elma (the proverbial pillow talk). Ezra Weeks and even Burr may have had cause to worry about what Elma might know or what she might say. Neither could afford to have rumors or speculation sully their names months before the upcoming presidential election.

The details were as murky as the city's water supply. While the Manhattan Company scheme was a closely guarded secret, the New

York State Legislature approved the company charter at the tail end of its 1799 session, months before Elma was killed. Her knowledge of the plot would not have been sufficient motivation for murder. Still, the idea that an innocent girl had become snared in a political conspiracy continued to haunt me. Burr had successfully manipulated the Manhattan Water Company into the Manhattan Bank, but the election was still up for grabs.

By all accounts, the election of 1800, sometimes called the "Revolution of 1800" because it was so hotly contested, was too important to lose. It was the first time in United States history that two parties were vying for the presidency. New York was a swing state between the emerging parties. Aaron Burr was chosen as Jefferson's running mate because he had promised to deliver New York's twelve electoral votes. Researching the election, I learned that one member of New York State's electoral college, Anthony Lispenard, insisted he be permitted to cast his ballot in secret, apparently so he could switch his vote from Thomas Jefferson to Jefferson's running mate, Burr, without anyone's knowledge. Lispenard's name was a startling discovery, because the Manhattan Well in which Elma had drowned was located in Lispenard's Meadows. If Levi had told Elma about the Manhattan Company scheme, it was plausible he had told her about the electoral plot. Was her insider knowledge the motivation behind her murder?

It is important to note that CITY OF LIARS AND THIEVES is historical fiction. Testimony from Levi Weeks's trial has been adapted and simplified, well-known historical figures have been fictionalized, and their dialogue and actions are, for the most part, products of my imagination. Speculation as to the motive behind Elma's murder are my own and are not based on factual evidence, and all modifications required to turn fact into fiction are my responsibility. Most significantly, while the Manhattan Well was located in Lispenard's Meadows, Anthony Lispenard is not historically linked to Elma's story. Trial testimony attributed to Lispenard (and his wife) was actually spoken by Lawrence and Arnetta Van Norden whose farmhouse was located in close proximity to the Manhattan Well.

Though CITY OF LIARS AND THIEVES is fiction, I have relied on many sources. Thomas Fleming's book *Duel: Alexander Hamilton, Aaron Burr, and the Future of America* offered an unbiased account of the intricacies of Hamilton's and Burr's complicated rivalry as well as the nuances of the *code duello*. Two biographies on Aaron Burr, one by Milton Lomask, the other by Nancy Isenberg, gave me a better understanding of this elusive figure. But my favorite resource was Gore Vidal's brilliant novel *Burr*. In the opening chapter, Vidal creates a scene in Trinity Church cemetery and writes, "In the half-light of the cemetery, Burr did resemble the devil—assuming that the devil is no more than five foot six . . . slender, with tiny feet (hooves?), high forehead (in the fading light I imagine vestigial horns), bald in front with hair piled high on his head, powdered absently in the old style, and held in place with a shell comb." Because the description so succinctly captures Burr, I used the phrase "resemble the devil" to describe him. Vidal's novel also references Elma Sands's murder. The story's narrator and Washington Irving are riding past Lispenard's Meadows, when Irving becomes agitated and says, "That's it! There! Look. See that well?" He then recounts the story of Elma's involvement with Levi Weeks, her death, and Burr's eloquent courtroom defense, saying that Burr convinced "the jury and the judge—and no doubt the devil himself . . . that Elma Sands was a woman of no virtue while Levi Weeks was a young Galahad."

The history of New York City and its role as a stage for the tragic rivalry between Hamilton and Burr, two of the city's most prominent citizens, is truly fascinating. Historians dispute whether Catherine Ring did indeed spew a curse following the dramatic conclusion of Levi Weeks's trial, but no one denies the tragedies that would soon befall each man.

One month following Levi Weeks's trial, New York's Electoral College members cast ballots for the nation's third president. The Republican candidate, Thomas Jefferson, defeated Federalist incumbent John Adams by a margin of seventy-three to sixty-five Electoral College votes. But the race was not over. One member of New York

State's Electoral College, Anthony Lispenard, had asked to cast a secret ballot, rather than the public one the state law required. In an era when ballots did not distinguish between votes for president and votes for vice president, Lispenard's dissenting vote would have been enough to make Burr president. Ultimately, Lispenard's duplicity was discovered. When the votes were tallied, Burr and Jefferson had tied each other with seventy-three votes each. Although Burr had actively campaigned for the vice presidential spot and had acknowledged Jefferson as the presidential candidate, he refused to concede. For seven days, the country was sent into a tailspin while the House of Representatives voted on the electoral outcome thirty-six times, until Jefferson emerged victorious. Some say it was Hamilton's under-the-table maneuvering that led to Burr's defeat. Jefferson and his Republican cohorts branded Burr a traitor for trying to steal the election. In 1803, congress ratified the Twelfth Amendment to the Constitution. The amendment requires votes be cast separately for president and vice president, ensuring the mishap would never happen again. In 1804, as retribution for his treachery, Jefferson dropped Burr from the Republican ticket.

After losing his vice presidential seat, Burr decided to run for the governorship of New York. Hamilton is said to have insulted Burr while discussing the election at a dinner party. His words became public knowledge when a letter, written by another dinner guest, was printed in the *New York Evening Post* (the newspaper founded by Hamilton in 1801 and edited by William Coleman, Hamilton's protégé, who served as court reporter during the Weeks trial). Hamilton denied that he had spoken disparagingly of Burr, but rumors persisted. And the news-mongering dinner guest made matters worse when he said he could tell of "a still more despicable opinion which Hamilton has expressed of Colonel Burr." No one is entirely sure what to make of the statement "a still more despicable opinion," but Colonel Burr, who blamed each loss on Hamilton's political and personal machinations, took great offense and challenged Hamilton to a duel.

The encounter took place on July 11, 1804, at a secluded spot on the banks of the Hudson River in Weehawken, New Jersey, due west of Manhattan's present-day 42nd Street. Hamilton fired first, into the air, although it is not clear whether he intentionally threw his shot away. Burr returned fire and hit Hamilton in the lower right hip. The bullet then passed through his liver and lodged in his spine. Hamilton died the next day, leaving behind his wife and six children. Hamilton is buried at Trinity Church, half a block away from Federal Hall, where the Weeks trial took place. The monument is a dull marble square about the size of a desk. Four urns decorate the corners and there's a pyramid in the center, the top of which has been lopped off. It stands feet from the sidewalk and oncoming traffic. An inscription reads:

> The PATRIOT of incorruptible
> INTEGRITY.
>
> The SOLDIER of approved
> VALOUR.
>
> The STATESMAN of consummate
> WISDOM:
>
> Whose TALENTS and VIRTUES will
> be admired
>
> Long after this MARBLE shall have
> mouldered into
> *DUST.*

A glance in one's wallet will reveal the enduring influence Hamilton has had on our nation. If someone had asked me before I began this project if I knew who was on the ten-dollar bill, I might not have been able to answer. Hamilton is one of two non-presidents featured on

U.S. currency. (The other is Benjamin Franklin, on the hundred-dollar bill.) The portrait of Hamilton on the bill was painted by John Trumbull in 1805. It belongs to the New York City Hall portrait collection. Hamilton is depicted with wavy hair that flows back from a broad forehead, a square chin, and strong cheekbones. The image is grainy and has a green hue, but there's no mistaking Hamilton's striking good looks.

Aaron Burr survived the duel, but his reputation was shattered. Dueling was illegal in New York, and he fled south to evade arrest. During this time, Burr (perhaps modeling himself after his contemporary Napoleon Bonaparte) organized an army, solicited aid from England and Spain, and devised a plot to steal the Louisiana Territory away from the United States and crown himself king. The plot was foiled when a ciphered letter to a co-conspirator was intercepted. Burr was captured and brought to trial. Few doubt Burr's intentions, but it was impossible to prove that he had committed an overt act of war. He was acquitted and fled, incognito, to Europe.

After four years in exile, Burr returned to New York. During his absence, his Richmond Hill estate had sold for a fifth of its value. (An ex fur trader named John Jacob Astor bought the estate, on the western edge of Soho, around 1807. Astor would divide the property into four hundred parcels and make a fortune.) Arriving home, Burr learned of the death of his cherished grandson and only heir, Aaron Burr Alston (affectionately known as "Gampy," because the child referred to himself and his grandfather by that name). In her book *Fallen Founder*, Nancy Isenberg cites a letter Burr wrote to his daughter, Theodosia, which illustrates his devotion to his family. (By coincidence, the letter is dated January 4, 1799, two days after Elma's body was discovered in the Manhattan Well.) Burr wrote, "The happiness of my life depends on your exertions, for what else, for whom else do I live?" Following Gampy's death, Theodosia Burr Alston made plans to travel to New York for a reunion with her father, but her ship was lost off the Carolina coast. Debris washed ashore, but no bodies were ever recovered. Some believe Theodosia Burr Alston perished in a storm, while others contend that pirates overtook the ship. In 1834, at the age of seventy-eight, Burr suffered a debilitating stroke. Two years later he died, impoverished, disgraced, and alone. He is buried in Princeton Cemetery near the graves of his father and grandfather.

If Catherine Ring did utter a curse, then Judge John Lansing also fell under its spell, with a fate that was as tragic and strange as that of Hamilton and Burr: In December 1829, he left the City Hotel to catch a night boat for Albany and was never seen again.

Others involved in the case fared better. Cadwallader David Colden was assistant attorney general when he tried Levi's case, but ten years later he became mayor of New York and, later, a U. S. congressman.

James Hardie, the reporter seated next to Caty in the novel, recorded one of three trial transcripts (the others were written by David Longworth and William Coleman). Levi Weeks's trial is the first fully recorded murder trial in U.S. history. The testimony in the novel is based on "The Defense of Levi Weeks" in the American Bar Association Journal as well as the version recorded in Estelle Fox Kleiger's book. During the trial, sixty-five witnesses testified in two days. The novel has condensed and edited testimony, melded several real-life figures into a single character, and changed the order in which witnesses testified.

Little is known about the story's less famous characters.

The Lispenard family has a somewhat crooked two-block street named in their honor; it runs from Sixth Avenue east to Broadway. In 2012, a portion of the Collect owned by the New York City Parks and Recreation Department was renamed "Collect Pond Park." The park, located steps away from New York Criminal Courthouse, includes a bean-shaped pond that is supposed to evoke the original topography.Levi Weeks moved to the remote frontier town of Natchez, Mississippi, and became a successful architect. Auburn, a home he designed, still stands. Levi married a seventeen-year-old girl named Ann Greenleaf, and together they had four children. He died in 1819 at the age of forty-three.

Ezra Weeks's fate is less certain, but landmarks historians have cited his work on Hamilton's estate, the Grange, as evidence that Weeks may have built Gracie Mansion, New York City's mayoral residence. Hamilton's Grange is now a national memorial, located on West 141st Street in Manhattan.

On July 8, 1800, seven months following Elma's disappearance and death, Richard Croucher was tried in a New York City court for molesting a thirteen-year-old girl. According to Estelle Fox Kleiger, he was sentenced to life in prison, but he was pardoned and fled south to Virginia. There he was arrested for fraud. He escaped to England, where he was hanged for committing a "heinous crime." Recently published, Paul Collins's nonfiction account of the Weeks's trial, *Duel with the Devil: The True Story of How Alexander Hamilton and Aaron Burr Teamed Up to Take on America's First Sensational Murder Mystery*, concludes that Richard Croucher murdered Elma Sands. In his book, Collins reprints a wonderful poem by Philip Freneau entitled "The Reward of Innocence."

> *Could beauty, virtue, innocence,*
> * and love*
> *Some spirits soften, or some*
> * bosoms move.*
> *If native worth, with every charm*
> * combined,*
> *Had power to melt the savage in*
> * mind,*
> *Thou, injured ELMA, had not*
> * fallen a prey*
> *To fierce revenge, that seized thy*
> * life away;*
> *Not through the glooms of*
> * conscious night*
> *Been led*

To find a funeral for a nuptial
bed,
When by the power of midnight
fiends you
Fell,
Plunged in the abyss of
Manhattan-well . . .

In the interest of plot, I have altered several details. Elma had been living in New York City for three years before her death. Others, including women, most notably Caty's sister lived in the Ring boarding-house at 208 Greenwich Street. Finally, Catherine Ring did not leave Elias following the Weeks trial. The two remained married and had ten children together. Society of Friends records show that Elias Ring remained a Quaker for sixteen years after the trial but was disowned in 1816 for the "continued intemperate use of intoxicating spirits." Elias is thought to have died in 1823 of yellow fever.

Yellow fever, which was not fully understood until the twentieth century, is an acute infectious viral disease that attacks the liver cells. It is spread by the bite of female mosquitoes. The disease most likely originated in Africa and was brought to America through the slave trade. Eighteenth-century New York City, with its stagnant swamps, filthy rivers, and lack of sewers, was an ideal breeding ground.

After Elias's death, Caty returned to Cornwall, where she lived with her aged mother until her death in 1855. She ran a boarding-house known as Rose Cottage. The house still exists today on a grassy knoll leading down to the Hudson River. A small plaque out front reads SANDS RING HOMESTEAD, CIRCA 1760.

The Manhattan Company did construct a reservoir on the north side of Chambers Street between Broadway and Elk Street, completed in 1801. Despite its elaborate façade, embellished with four Doric columns and a statue of the god Oceanus (the company symbol), it was woefully inadequate. The reservoir supplied only four hundred homes, though the city's population at the time was upward of sixty thousand people. (If there were an average of eight people per home, the reservoir would have served only thirty-two hundred people—literally a drop in the bucket.) Water came from wells sunk on Reade and Centre Streets, near the base of the polluted "Fresh Water Pond." Many residents were forced to resort to cisterns to collect rainwater. It was not until 1842 that an aqueduct was completed that carried clean water from the Croton River north of Manhattan to two newly constructed reservoirs. The first was located on Fifth Avenue and 42nd Street (now the site of the main branch of the New York Public Library), the second in Central Park at 86th Street (which still exists but is no longer in use). Today, the city's eight million residents receive water from Westchester and Putnam Counties, the Catskill Mountains, and the Delaware River. It is said to be some of the best quality in the world. Because these watersheds are so essential, portions of them are under federal protection, yet freshwater supplies are threatened by overpopulation, toxic waste, and large-scale demands for agriculture and energy. Water is our most essential finite resource. As W. H. Auden famously wrote, "Thousands have lived without love, not one without water."

Aaron Burr's Manhattan Company may never have provided the city with clean water, but the bank thrived. In 1955, the Manhattan Bank merged with Chase National Bank and became the Chase Manhattan Bank. In 2000, Chase Manhattan merged with J. P. Morgan & Co. to become J. P. Morgan Chase & Co. In 2006, mega-bank J. P. Morgan Chase acquired the retail division of the Bank of New York, uniting the two-hundred-year-old rivals and, no doubt, causing Hamilton and Burr to spin in their graves. In 1930, the dueling pistols used in Hamilton and Burr's fatal encounter were sold to the Manhattan Bank. J. P. Morgan Chase still owns the original pistols, displayed in a conference room, but replicas can be seen at the New York Historical Society. What's more, the Chase octagonal company logo is said to represent a cross section of the wooden pipes once used to transport water for Burr's Manhattan Water Company—pipes supplied by Ezra Weeks for the well in which Elma Sands drowned.

And last but not least, the Manhattan Well survives in the dank, dark recesses of a Spring Street restaurant, the "tavern" Caty envisioned in her dream.

On a rainy November night in 2009, I returned to my former neighborhood and sought out what I had come to think of as Elma's well. Though I must have passed the place a thousand times, I approached it now with trepidation. As depicted in Caty's dream, 129 Spring Street was wedged in the middle of the block, its upstairs windows dark and grimy. Dormers rested on the roof like sleepy eyelids. The four-story building was made of weathered red bricks. Built in 1817, it had once served as a carpenter's shop (which seemed both just and ironic, given Levi's profession). For the past fifty years, it had housed a French bistro.

I climbed the stoop and entered.

The inside was dimly lit. There was a long bar up front and a more formal dining area with white tablecloths in back. Both were empty. The walls were decorated with shadowy murals. The one in front featured patrons at a two-dimensional bar. A rotund woman saunters across the scene in a revealing red dress and matching pumps. Behind her, a man sits hunched over his drink.

Street development and time had raised ground level so that the well was now located in the building's basement. The owner only learned about its existence from locals who told stories of a ghostly female figure whose face was "not quite human." In 1980, while a wine cellar was being dug, the well was unearthed.

Descending, I smelled the dampness and was reminded that the river inspiring Spring Street's name continued to flow beneath my feet. The lower level was narrow and tiled like a bathhouse. There were two doors leading to the restrooms and a metal fire door with a sign that read EMPLOYEES ONLY. DO NOT ENTER.

I took the knob in hand. It refused to turn, but I was able to push the door open. I peeked inside, then looked over my shoulder before closing—without completely shutting—it behind me. Bare bulbs illuminated a narrow corridor that led left and right. The walls were made of slender bricks, bound with crumbling mortar. Five paces away, the bricks jutted outward and in, forming a small alcove. Framed in the cobwebbed recess was Elma's well.

I had imagined that the well would be damp, but the bricks were dry, more tan than red. They were narrow and small, but the well itself rose several feet above my head. The bricks on top were broken and rough. I gazed at my feet, wondering how far the hole descended, then looked straight ahead, knowing that Elma fought for her last breath inches from where I stood. I reached out, touching where Elma died and Caty mourned. It was a remarkable feeling, satisfying, yet sad.

AFTERWORD

In August of 2014, more than six years after I first learned of the Manhattan Well, and a handful of days before I was to return this manuscript to my publisher for the final time, I paid one last visit to the site where Elma died. The bistro that sat above the well was gone.129 Spring Street was nearly invisible behind scaffolding and, while the façade seemed to be intact, the building was gutted. The ground-floor plywood was stamped with white block letters that read "post no bills," but someone had spray-painted "The Love Child" in hot-pink script on either side of the makeshift door. The reference makes me wonder for the umpteenth time if Elma was pregnant when she died. A pair of black-and-white signs read "Danger: Do Not Trespass," which also seemed strangely appropriate. Fifteen feet below, in the dark recesses of the basement, Elma's well awaits the future.

Acknowledgements

I am grateful to my inspirational editor, Nina Shield, who helped me bring Caty and Elma back to life. To my husband, Dave, who accompanied me on field trips to abandoned wells and cemeteries. To my friend and witness Liz Rosebaum. To Carolyn Foley for her expertise and friendship, and to all the others who have lent their ears and support: Peggy Weiss, Linda Clark, Elizabeth Laytin, Shelley Lichtenstein, Christine Knapp, and my agent, Stephany Evans.

ABOUT THE AUTHOR

EVE KARLIN lives in East Hampton, New York, with her husband and their triplets. *City of Liars and Thieves* is her first book.

Made in the USA
Middletown, DE
23 December 2019

81880732R10156